# Forbidden King

Laura Pavlov is the *USA Today* bestselling author of sweet and sexy contemporary romances that will make you both laugh and cry. She is happily married to her college sweetheart, mom to two amazing kids who are now adulting, and dog-whisperer to one temperamental yorkie and one wild bernedoodle. Laura resides in Las Vegas where she is living her own happily ever after.

## *Also by Laura Pavlov and Published by HQ*

*The Magnolia Falls Series*

Loving Romeo
Wild River
Forbidden King
Beating Heart
Finding Hayes

# Forbidden King

LAURA PAVLOV

ONE PLACE. MANY STORIES

This novel is entirely a work of fiction. The names, characters and incidents portrayed in it are the work of the author's imagination. Any resemblance to actual persons, living or dead, events or localities is entirely coincidental.

HQ
An imprint of HarperCollins*Publishers* Ltd
1 London Bridge Street
London SE1 9GF

www.harpercollins.co.uk

HarperCollins*Publishers*
Macken House, 39/40 Mayor Street Upper,
Dublin 1, D01 C9W8, Ireland

This edition 2024

1
First published in Great Britain by
HQ, an imprint of HarperCollins*Publishers* Ltd 2024


A catalogue record for this book is available from the British Library.

ISBN: 9780008719609

This book contains FSC™ certified paper and other controlled sources to ensure responsible forest management.

For more information visit: www.harpercollins.co.uk/green

Typeset in Sabon Lt Pro by HarperCollins*Publishers* India

Printed and bound in the UK using 100% Renewable Electricity at CPI Group (UK) Ltd

*Never be afraid to hold tight to your dreams. Big or small, they are yours and yours alone. Find yourself a dandelion and make a wish . . .*

*And never stop believing.*

*'Where some see a weed, others see a wish.'*

# Prologue

## Kingston

*Ten Years Ago*

I couldn't sleep. Thinking about River and Romeo being locked up in a juvenile detention center haunted me. Wondering how my brother and our best friend were surviving was something that I couldn't shake. They'd both put on brave faces, and I'd done the same, but I knew they had to be scared as hell.

Add in the fact that Hayes and his sister, Saylor, had been taken from their home as well, and this shit show just kept getting better.

"Mom! No!" Saylor's terrorized voice had me jumping to my feet and hurrying to the room across the hall. I pushed the door open, and she flailed around on the bed like she was fighting for her life.

Lately, it felt like we all were.

"Saylor. Saylor, hey." I moved to sit on the edge of her bed and placed a hand on her forearm. "You're okay. It's King. I'm here."

Her hands moved over her face to protect herself, and my chest squeezed.

She was fucking scared, and that shit pissed me off.

"Hey, hey. Look at me. I'm not going to let anyone hurt you again, okay?" I whispered, as her wild eyes locked with mine. She blinked several times, her breathing frantic, and I could see a layer of sweat covering her forehead from the sliver of moonlight shining through the window in River's bedroom.

"King?" She said my name as a question, and I heard the fear in her voice.

"Yeah. I'm here. You're okay. You were having a nightmare."

She used the back of her hand to swipe at the tear that broke free from her eyes, and she looked away. She'd always been a little shy—too sweet for her own good. She was my best friend Hayes's little sister, so she was family.

End of story.

She cleared her throat. "I'm sorry I woke you up. I'm fine."

I reached for her chin and turned her face so that she was looking at me. "You don't have to be fine. This is a lot to take. Do you want to tell me about it?"

Her blonde hair was in a long braid that hung over her shoulder, and her blue eyes locked with mine. "I just—I can't believe all that's happened over the last few weeks, you know? And now I'm here. I feel bad about your grandparents taking me in, and I'm worried about River and Romeo. I'm worried about my mom and brother."

Her bottom lip trembled, and I stroked the loose strand of hair that had broken free away from her pretty face. "Everyone is going to be okay. I promise." I gave her a reassuring smile. That was sort of my shtick. I could find something good in the shittiest of situations. It had always helped me when things went down, and I wanted to help her right now. "And my grandparents are devastated about River being sent to that hellhole. So having you here gives them a little bit of needed sunshine."

She nodded, and her teeth sank into her bottom lip as tears started streaming down her cheeks, catching me off guard. I pulled her into my arms as sobs left her body. And I just held her there. I didn't have a lot of experience with girls that were crying, because the girls I hung out with were usually trying to get in my pants, or vice versa. It was all laughter and flirtation, nothing deep.

That's how I liked it.

*What can I say? I'm a fifteen-year-old horny dude. Well, technically, I'll be sixteen in a few months.*

My hands stroked her back, and I breathed in all that goodness. Saylor Woodson was good to her core.

Smart and pretty and sweet.

And she was Hayes's little sister. The most important person in my life.

We had a pact, the five of us. River, Romeo, Hayes, Nash, and me.

*Ride or Die.*

We were all brothers in our own way. So I'd promised Hayes I'd protect his sister while she stayed with us. My grandparents couldn't afford to take both her and Hayes in. Nash lived alone with his dad, and his father wasn't willing to take in a teenage girl, so they'd been split up temporarily.

We all had, in a way.

But this was better than the alternative, them being split up and living with strangers.

"I shouldn't have called the police that night. None of this would have happened. But I was scared because Hayes wasn't home to break up the fight this time," she whimpered. "I thought Barry was going to hurt my mom. I thought I was doing the right thing."

"You did the right thing, Saylor. Hayes is so fucking proud

of you." I continued stroking her head as I held her against my chest.

"I guess I should be glad the police got there right after Hayes got home, because he probably would have killed Barry, and then he'd be sent away like River and Romeo." She spoke through her tears, her voice soft, and I could hear the sadness. The fear. We knew something had gone down, but Hayes hadn't given much detail. Saylor had somehow been struck by Barry just as Hayes arrived home and flew into a murderous rage. Thankfully, the police got there shortly after. They were both removed from the house and would have been placed into the system, but as soon as he called me and Nash, we got our families involved. They'd spent two days in a foster home before Saylor had come here and Hayes had gone to stay with Nash.

"Is that what your nightmare was about?" I asked, as she pulled back and let out a few long breaths.

"I see Barry in my nightmares. The crazed look in his eyes. The way he turned to me when I tried to pull him off my mom. I was so scared," she said. "I can't sleep without seeing his face, King. I haven't slept in days, and I'm so tired."

"I know you are. What if I stay with you tonight? I can sleep in here so you know you're safe."

"This is so embarrassing. I'll be fourteen years old next week. I shouldn't be afraid of the dark." She shook her head, shoulders pushing back as if she were trying to prove she was okay.

To me.

To herself.

I wasn't sure. But it didn't matter.

Because Saylor Woodson didn't need to be okay on my behalf.

I'd walk through fire to make sure she was safe.

I glanced over at the pile of green stems on the nightstand, and she followed my gaze to see what caught my eye.

"Those are dandelion puffballs that you can make wishes on. I figure if you make enough wishes, someday it'll work, right?"

"Of course it will. Come on. Lie down. I've got you. No one will ever know about this. It'll be our secret, okay?" I slipped in beside her, and we both rolled onto our sides, facing one another.

"Thanks, King. I'll be fine tomorrow. I know I will. I'm just worried right now. About everyone and everything."

"Yeah. Me, too," I said. "You're actually helping me because I couldn't sleep either."

"You're worried, too, aren't you?"

"Yeah. I get to go visit next week. It's been the longest two weeks of my life since they were sent away. I haven't slept much at all. And then I was worried about you and Hayes being pulled into the system. I'm a lot happier now that you're here and Hayes is with Nash."

"Me, too. I wish we could get River and Romeo out of there, too."

"Yeah. I can't believe all the shit that has happened."

"Hayes told me that they didn't do it. They were set up by Slade Crawford, right?" she whispered.

"Yep. And his family has more money than they know what to do with, so who do you think they're going to believe?" I hissed. I was still so fucking pissed off about the whole thing. The rich asshole robs the Daily Market, pushes a man down and hurts him, and then runs out of there and lets two innocent dudes serve his time in juvie hall?

It was bullshit.

"It's not right," she said, and I could hear the exhaustion.

"It's not. But we need to keep it together for them. You and me going without sleep is not going to bring anyone back, or get you home any sooner."

She shifted closer to me. "I don't know where home is

anymore. I'd be scared to go back there. But I don't like being separated from Hayes. And I need to know that my mom is okay. But all I see is Barry when I close my eyes."

I found her hand and pulled it between us. "I've got you, Saylor. I'm not going to let anyone hurt you. I promise."

She squeezed my hand, and I held her close.

And I kept my fingers wrapped around hers until the sound of her breathing slowed.

Her chest rose and fell against mine, and it soothed me in a way.

I'd been a little lost these last few weeks, and if I were being honest, right now, with Saylor, was the most content I'd felt since everything had gone down.

Maybe protecting my best friend's little sister was just what I needed.

She needed me, and maybe, in a weird way, I needed her, too.

# 1

# Saylor

*Present Day*

"Okay, I'm going to take these teas over and meet Nash and King," I said, unable to hide my excitement.

"I can't believe you're finally starting renovations on the bookstore." Demi beamed.

I'd been working at Magnolia Beans coffee shop, which Demi owned, for months now. I'd had to jump through all sorts of hoops to get a business license and a bank loan to open my bookstore, as well as save up as much money as I could for living expenses. And today was finally the day.

"You look like a total lady boss," Peyton said. She worked at Magnolia Beans as well, while she was taking courses online to get her master's in education. She'd be graduating soon, and Demi would need to hire all new people, as I'd be working next door, and Peyton would go back to the classroom.

I glanced down to see my white tank top and the denim overalls that I was wearing. "This is lady boss attire?" I asked over my laughter.

"Tell her, Rubes. It's not about the clothing; it's about the woman beneath," Peyton said.

Ruby chuckled. The four of us had become the best of friends over the last few months, and I'd been happy about my decision to return home to Magnolia Falls. I had friends here, real friends. My brother was here. I was opening a business.

My mother was also here, which had been a big part of the reason that I'd wanted to come back to start pursuing my dreams. Unfortunately, I didn't see much of her as she'd gotten back together with Barry, my stepfather, which shouldn't surprise me, yet it always did.

And as long as Barry was in her life, I had to put up boundaries.

"Correct. You are channeling your inner lady boss. You rock those overalls like a badass bitch." Ruby smirked, grabbing her tea from Demi, who was laughing hysterically now.

"I'll do my best. Are you sleeping at River's tonight?" I asked. She and I were roommates, but she spent a lot of time over at her boyfriend's house. We were all close, and I loved seeing that she and River were so happy.

I loved it for both of them.

"Probably. But I'll come by the bookstore after work because I want to see how much they get done on the first day of renovations," she said.

"This is so exciting, Say. You had a goal, a dream," Demi shook her head as if she were trying to hold back the emotions, "and you made it happen."

"Oh, my gawwwwdd. You are such a sap lately." Peyton laughed hysterically. "I swear it's all the wedding planning. It makes you such a weepy mess."

Demi and her fiancé, Romeo, had gotten engaged a few months ago, and I was thrilled for them.

Demi shrugged and had a big smile on her face as if she couldn't help herself.

"Hey, I'm the one opening a romance bookstore. I'm all about being in your feels, you know?" I said.

"Speaking of being in your feels . . . how did your date go with Coach Hotty? Damn, that man is one fine specimen," Peyton asked as she loaded the pastries she'd brought out from the kitchen into the display case.

"Why do we call him *coach* if he's a trainer?" Ruby raised a brow.

"I asked him that, and he said that he considers himself more of a coach than a trainer. He works on the mental and the physical aspects with his clients," I said, trying to hide my smile because he really was hot as hell. He'd just moved to town and was working over at Romeo's gym, which was now somewhat famous after Romeo had put his name on the map when he won his big fight last year.

"What about his dick? Does he work on that? Because that's what our girl needs," Peyton said, and Ruby's and Demi's heads fell back in a fit of laughter.

"You are so crude," Demi said, shaking her head at Peyton before turning to me. "Ignore her. She's just a horny one these days."

"It's all these damn romance books you have me reading. Everyone is six foot four with big, magical dicks. So, I've *raised* my expectations," Peyton said over her laughter.

"Pun intended." Ruby winked. "How did it go? Do you like him?"

"Coach Hotty or his dick?" Peyton asked.

"Shhh . . . we're talking about Coach Hotty. The morning rush is about to start, and I want to know what happened." Demi shot Peyton a warning look.

"He's funny and really nice. I don't know. It was fine. Good, maybe? We'll see if he calls me today."

"You sell yourself short, girl. Of course, he'll call you. You're such a catch. I mean, who looks this good in freaking farmer pants?" Ruby kissed my cheek. "I've got to run. Good luck today. I'll see you tonight."

"You're not working today at all?" Peyton looked at me, pushing out her bottom lip. "It's going to be so boring without you."

"Hey! I can hear you." Demi laughed as she bumped her bestie in the shoulder. "She'll be back tomorrow. This is a big day. Let her enjoy it."

"I'll pop in during the day and see if you guys need help. I'm just next door. But I want to make sure everything goes smoothly today." I gave them each a hug. "Love you. I'll see you later."

I grabbed the drink carrier and made my way to the kitchen, pulling open the door that led to Love Ever After. That was the name I'd chosen for the bookstore. It connected to Demi's shop from the inside, but each space had its own exterior entrance for customers, as well.

It couldn't be in a better location, next door to Demi. I set the tray down on the table beside the drawings for the design and layout we were using. Kingston and Nash didn't think this would take more than a few weeks.

I couldn't wait.

I was grateful to have friends who owned a construction company and were willing to do this job for a very fair price.

It was nice to have something to look forward to. I'd been dreaming about this for a long time, and it was all finally happening.

I flipped on the lights and pushed open the front door, waving as I saw Kingston and Nash getting out of their truck. My phone vibrated in my hand, and I looked down to see a text from my brother.

HAYES

Big day today. Congrats. Proud of you for pushing hard to make this happen. I'll stop by after my shift to see how it's going.

Thanks. Be safe. Love you.

Hayes was a firefighter, and I always worried about him, but I tried not to let him know that every time he went to work—unlike my brother, who was a barbarian when it came to being protective of me.

"*Say* it isn't so," Kingston sang out, because he loved making Saylor jokes every chance he got. He leaned over and kissed my cheek. "Big day today, wouldn't you *say*?"

I laughed because he was always on, always making me laugh. The guy had more charm in his pinky finger than most people had in their entire bodies.

*No wonder the women in Magnolia Falls are feral for the man.*

"Are you seriously going to be doing this the whole time?" Nash rolled his eyes as they both stepped inside.

"What? She's got a good name for it, wouldn't you *say*?"

"Speaking of good names . . . I was ordered to give you this." Nash reached into his back pocket and handed me a folded piece of paper. "Cutler made this for you."

I opened it and found he'd drawn all the places downtown that were important to him. The firehouse where Hayes worked. River's law office was on there. Whiskey Falls bar, which was owned by Ruby's dad, Lionel. RoD Construction, also known as Ride or Die Construction, owned by both Kingston and Nash, Magnolia Beans, and then Love Ever After was right in the center of the picture.

Kingston leaned over my shoulder, and the smell of sage and mint flooded my senses.

"*Congrats to my girl, Saylor.*" Kingston read the handwriting on the top of the page. "Damn, Beefcake has more game than most of the dudes in Magnolia Falls."

Beefcake was the name Cutler had asked us all to call him, as he no longer liked his real name.

"Yeah. I told you, his teacher said we need to start calling him Cutler. She said it's wrong to let him change his name." Then nodded to the drawing. "He spent a lot of time on that. Really tested my patience by making me spell everything over and over because he needed it to be perfect."

"Hold up, now. Are you seriously telling me you're going to listen to that lady? She's got the worst case of resting asshole face I've ever seen. Kind of fits with her name being *Ms. Heathen.*"

My head fell back in laughter. "I thought his teacher was Ms. McKeathen?"

Kingston was right. She was one of the scariest teachers I'd ever had. She'd been my first-grade teacher when I was a kid, and I was terrified of her back then.

"It is." Nash rolled his eyes. "He just insists on calling her Ms. Heathen. And it's *resting bitch face*. Not asshole face. Get your insults straight."

"Listen, she gave him the tuna casserole for lunch last week when you'd ordered him the pizza. She's an asshole. And so is her face." Kingston folded his arms over his chest.

Nash pinched the bridge of his nose, and Kingston winked at me.

*He's always the brightest light in every room.*

"Okay. Can we focus, please?" Nash turned his attention to me. "We've got a crew coming over to start building the bookshelves, and King is going to build the checkout counter for you. He'll be the one working at this site most of the time. I've got to be out at Brighton Ranch because that renovation has been a real shit show."

"You've got this. Just be careful. Mrs. Brighton is such a horndog. Nash will tell you, Saylor, the woman purposely grazed my junk with her hand when she was talking to us last week. She just helped herself to the goods, like she was entitled to them." Kingston shivered dramatically, and I laughed harder.

Nash shook his head and tried to hide his smile. "Yeah. She wasn't even smooth about it. So now this one doesn't want to be over there at all."

"Listen, I don't need Mrs. Brighton, aka Mrs. Robinson, grabbing my dick and getting her crazy-ass husband jealous. The man has a room just for his guns. I'll work much better over here. It's all about love at the bookstore. Plus, I'm the better woodworker, and we have a lot of bookshelves to build, as well as getting this register station put together."

"Fine, you big baby." Nash glanced around the space and paused to look at the architect drawings on the table, as I handed them each their iced tea.

"Thanks," they said at the same time.

"Magnolia Beans's finest." I stared down at the design with them.

"You've already ordered the couches that you're bringing in, right?" Kingston asked, and I swear his gaze zeroed in on my mouth when I pulled my drink away, before it snapped back up.

"Yes. They're already here. I've got them in my garage. I figured you'd want to wait until the floors are in and the shelves are built."

"Yep, that's the plan," Nash said, as he glanced down at his phone when it vibrated. "For fuck's sake. Mrs. Brighton wants to know where we are. I'm going to head out with a few of the guys. I'll stop by later today."

"Good luck. We've got this." Kingston took a long pull from his iced tea, just as his team showed up, and they parked in the large alley behind the building.

He stepped out to help them unload the palettes of wood and supplies, and everyone got to work.

I'd purposely taken today off because I wanted to watch and learn, because who knows? Maybe I'd expand my business someday. Learning how to take an empty space and turn it into something magical was a skill. And Kingston Pierce was a very talented woodworker. He had his saw set up on a table in the back lot as he directed everyone to specific tasks. His team was working on the bookshelves inside, while he was framing out the checkout station that I'd sketched for him. I wanted it to look like a piece of vintage furniture and match the aesthetic of the place.

"You sure you don't want to have the guys paint this when they paint the bookshelves? It's going to be a big piece, and it'll be a beast to paint yourself." He ran his large hand over the piece of wood that he'd just cut for the base.

"Nope. I've watched a ton of YouTube videos now, and I am determined to put my stamp on this particular piece. It'll be a real focal point for the bookstore."

He nodded. "All right. I can help if you need me to."

"I'll be fine. I like getting my hands dirty." I shrugged, and the look in his eyes after I'd said that had me squeezing my thighs together. Kingston was a flirt by nature, so I knew not to take it seriously. He and I had always shared a bond, one not everyone even knew about. I trusted him immensely, and he'd been a really good friend to me. But he was also sexy as sin, and sometimes I had to remind myself to stop staring. "I just mean I want to help where I can."

"Yeah? All right, how about I teach you how to use this table saw? You've already got the eyewear on, so we'll just be careful."

"Really?" I moved beside him, where he was cutting the next piece. "I'd love that."

"Come here," he said, stepping back and making room for

me to stand in front of him. "It's all about taking your time and guiding the piece carefully where you want it."

His arms came around me, and his hands moved on top of mine. They were calloused and covered in sawdust, and they engulfed my much smaller hands. He turned on the saw and moved our fingers along the wood, with his chest pressed against my back. He spoke in my ear. "Follow the line and keep it steady."

I focused on the wood and leaned forward before I realized my butt was pressed against his groin.

"You need to stop wiggling your ass, Saylor. I can't concentrate when you do that." His voice was gruff, and I startled when I realized that something was poking me in the ass. I was fairly certain it was Kingston's erection, unless he had a large flashlight tucked in his groin. I stayed perfectly still until the wood was cut, and he leaned forward and turned off the saw.

"Sorry about that," I said, trying to hide my smile when he pulled back. "I didn't realize that was, er, you know."

"My dick?"

"I thought it was a flashlight at first," I said over a fit of laughter before turning around to look at him.

"I'll take that as a compliment." He ran his hand over his jaw. "I'm assuming you're referencing a very *large* flashlight?"

I smacked his shoulder. "Stop. You're ridiculous. You better not tell Nash that I grazed your junk like Mrs. Brighton did."

His gaze moved to my mouth. "Trust me. Those are two very different things. And there isn't a man on the planet that wouldn't react to your ass rubbing against him."

My cheeks burned, and I tried to play it off. "Okay. So what do we do with the wood?" He raised a brow, and I realized how that had sounded and threw my hands in the air. "You know what I meant."

He laughed. "Come on, let's take this inside and get the base built."

When we walked back into the bookstore, my eyes widened at the sight of Coach Hotty holding a bouquet of flowers and smiling at me.

This day just kept getting better.

# 2

# Kingston

I set the panels down, took the moldings out of Saylor's hands, and followed her gaze to the douchedick standing there gaping at her.

"Jalen, hey, what are you doing here?" Saylor's voice was all light and flirtatious.

The girl was like sunshine on a cloudy day. Always had been.

I set the wood down on the floor, but listened intently, because I was a nosy dude, especially when it came to Saylor Woodson.

She was my best friend's little sister. It was my job to protect her.

"I knew today was a big day for you, so I thought I'd stop by and give you these flowers and let you know that I had a great time last night," he said.

I glanced over my shoulder to see him hand her the bouquet, and my eyes widened when I took in his baby blue shorts that were far too short to be worn by a man. Sure, he was all chiseled muscle, but the dude should consider wearing shorts that were made for men. *Am I right?*

I turned around and brushed my hands back and forth loud enough to make a clapping sound, which startled Saylor and had her turning in my direction.

"Oh. I'm so sorry. Do you two know each other? I assumed you would because Jalen just started working at Knockout Gym with Romeo a few days ago."

"Yep. We've met." I raised a brow and crossed my arms over my chest. "You two went out last night, huh?"

"Yeah, mate. We had a great time."

Mate? He wasn't from down fucking under. Romeo had told us that the dude was from New Jersey.

"Nice." It was all I could say. I didn't know she had gone out with him, not that she told me everything, but we were close. She had been on a few dates since she'd moved back to Magnolia Falls, but she'd yet to meet anyone she wanted to go out with again.

And I'd be lying if I didn't say I liked that.

Saylor was special. Different. I cared about her. She deserved the best, and I was fairly certain this dude was not that.

He was too tan. And his wavy blond hair was a little too perfect.

"It was so sweet of you to bring me these. They're gorgeous," Saylor said, shooting me a confused look because I was normally a friendly guy.

I turned around and got back to building the frame for the counter. Normally, we would do most of this at the shop, but with the space being more like a warehouse inside and having access to the large parking lot behind the building, we could work here, and we wouldn't need to transport all the pieces once they were built. I tried to focus on the project at hand while I turned my head just enough to hear everything they were saying.

"Beautiful flowers for a beautiful girl," he said, and I rolled my eyes before pulling out my nail gun and shooting it into the wood more times than necessary.

Saylor chuckled at the dude, and I couldn't believe she was buying this bullshit.

"Hey, Saylor, can you give me a hand with this piece?" I said, glancing over my shoulder.

Did I need her help? No.

Did I have six guys here that were working a few feet away that could help me? Absolutely.

But I couldn't stop myself. I didn't like the way he was looking at her.

"Oh, yeah, of course."

"I need to get to the gym anyway. I've got a client meeting me in five minutes. I wanted to see if you'd want to watch that movie tonight? The one I told you about?"

"Oh, yes, about the Australian surfer?" she asked, as she moved in my direction and set the flowers on the table, before her hand rested on the piece of wood that I was holding up just fine on my own.

"Yes. I could grab takeout, and we could watch the movie over at my place if you'd like."

"That sounds great. I'd love to."

Really? An Australian movie? This guy was pouring it on thick.

And she was going out with him two nights in a row? Did she actually like this dude?

And should she be going to his house already? We barely knew him.

"Great. I'll text you later." He kissed her cheek, and my hand gripped the wood a little harder as he turned his attention to me. "Catch you later, mate."

*Yeah, how about you pack your shit and go on over to the Outback and order yourself some shrimp on the barbie, you fake Australian motherfucker.*

"Yep. If you're lucky," I said, with a forced smile.

He waved and walked out the door.

"What was that?" Saylor asked, eyes wide as she held up the wood that was already attached and didn't require any support whatsoever.

"Exactly. What was that?" I repeated her words back to her.

"I'm talking about you." She barked out a laugh. "Why were you so rude to him?"

"What? I wasn't rude. I'm never rude."

"Once again, that's my point. You're never rude, and you were definitely not friendly. Do you even know him?"

I pounded the nail gun in about four times too many and really secured the piece. This counter could survive a category ten natural disaster at this point.

"I didn't know you went out with him last night," I said, as I pushed to my feet and assessed my work.

"Well, we didn't talk last night because you told me you were going to Whiskey Falls, which means you probably ended up taking home the latest flavor of the week, so I didn't know you'd want to do pillow talk with me." She tried to hide her smile because she was pleased with herself.

"Hey now, you know pillow talk with you is my favorite thing." That's what she used to call it all those years ago when I'd climb into her bed to keep her nightmares away. We fell asleep every single night for over six months the same way. My grandparents had no idea, as we'd each go to our own rooms after saying goodnight, and then I'd sneak across the hall after the house was quiet.

We would tell one another about our days and share all our worries and dreams before she'd fall asleep in my arms.

We were young. Nothing physical ever happened. I'd never cross that line.

But I'd be lying if I said pillow talk with Saylor Woodson wasn't the best part of my day back then.

"I don't know why you're being so weird. Yes, we went out, and he's a good guy. I like him." She reached for her tea and took a sip. "How about you? Who'd you take home last night?"

I scratched the back of my neck and looked into those pretty blue eyes that had always been my favorite. "For your information, I didn't take anyone home. But thank you for thinking the worst of me."

"What is with you today? Why are you being so weird about this? I'd never think the worst of you." She set her drink down and moved right in front of me. "But you like to keep things casual. That's kind of your shtick, right?"

I sighed. "Yes, Saylor. I love women, and I enjoy sex. But I don't take a different woman home every night of the week. I'm not a sex addict, for God's sake. I have quite a few returning customers, by the way. So, it's not quite as dirty as the picture you're painting."

Why was I being so defensive? I made no secret about who I was. I always treated women with respect. I just got bored easily. But I never lied. I never played games. I was a straight shooter.

"I don't think you're dirty, King." She laughed, placing her hands on her hips as she studied me. "I think anyone who gets to spend time with you is lucky. You know you're my favorite."

And just like that, she walked into my arms, and I hugged her.

The way I adored this girl was unexplainable.

Saylor Woodson was my girl.

Not in a sexual or inappropriate way, but in an *I'd-walk-through-fire-and-kill-for-you* kind of way.

If that were a thing.

"You're my favorite, too," I said, as she stepped back, and I moved around her to grab the last piece that needed to be attached to the frame. "So, tell me about Jason."

"His name is Jalen. The girls call him Coach Hotty." She chuckled. "He is hot. There's no denying it."

"Really? Those shorts don't bother you?" I nailed the next piece into place.

"His shorts? Um, no. They don't bother me. What's your problem with his shorts?"

"The color and the length." I pushed to my feet and brushed off my hands.

"You are seriously ridiculous. He's a trainer. That's what they wear." She ran her fingers along the edge of the wood and whistled. "This is going to be gorgeous."

"Hey, can you grab me a hammer out of my toolbox over there?" I said, as I bent down to check the corners.

Saylor walked a few feet away to where the metal toolbox I'd brought in with me sat beneath the table. When she lifted the top, I knew she'd see what I'd left in there for her.

She walked back over with a hammer in one hand and a dandelion in the other.

"Very creative, King. I'm going to have to up my game." She handed me the hammer, put her nose to the flower, and closed her eyes.

It was our thing. We'd started it all those years ago when she was going through a really hard time. I'd shocked her a few months ago when she'd moved back to town, and I'd started hiding them for her again. She'd jumped right in and done the same for me.

Like no time had passed.

"What can I say? It's a big day for you. The start of something new."

"Do you know that I used to wish for this? Everything that's happening right now," she said.

"For the bookstore?"

"Well, it wasn't for a bookstore in particular. But it was for this . . . this feeling that I have."

"Tell me," I said, as I turned to look at the bookshelves the guys were building on the other side of the room. They were following the blueprint I'd given them, and I'd add all the molding and detail to them after they got the base built.

"That I'd have something of my own. A life, I guess. That I'd go home and feel safe and comfortable and not be bracing myself for what I'd walk into. That I'd know I was building a future for myself. One I could be proud of."

*And this is why she's my girl.*

"I'm so fucking proud of you," I said, as I wrapped her up in a hug.

"Thanks, King." She pulled back and smiled up at me. The deepest blue eyes that resembled my favorite place on the lake, where the water was this bright turquoise blue when the sun shone down on it. Those eyes always took me to a peaceful place. "I'm so glad you're helping me with this."

"Yeah, me too. Now let's get this beast of a counter finished."

"Okay. I need to go put these flowers in some water, and I'll be right back to help." She grabbed her bouquet off the table, along with her single dandelion, and made her way next door to Magnolia Beans.

I got back to work, because making her dreams come true was just as good as making my own dreams come true.

Maybe even better.

The rest of the day went by in a blur. I'd jumped into my truck to head home for a quick shower, before I met the guys for a bite at Whiskey Falls. Once I pulled up in my driveway, I made my way to the front door. Spring was in full bloom, and I welcomed the warm weather. When I walked toward the front door, I chuckled when I saw something taped there. It was a dandelion at the end stages of its life, and what Saylor called a fluffball because the golden pedals were gone, and it was all white. I peeled it off the door along with the little note that read: *Thanks for helping to make my dreams come true. Now it's your turn to make a wish. Xo S.*

I stared down at it for a moment, but I didn't have a wish, per se.

Life was good. I was happy.

Happy enough, at least.

I'd use my wishes for the people that I loved. I'd always wished for River to be happy, and for the first time in our lives, I felt like my brother was genuinely happy.

That made me happy.

And seeing Saylor get what she always wanted.

That made me happy.

Romeo winning his fight and his girl.

That made me happy.

Beefcake was giving baseball a shot, and our little man was the happiest kid I'd ever met.

That made me fucking happy.

Nash and Hayes were happy enough, so my crew was good, and that was enough for me. My grandmother was in a nice place over at Magnolia Haven, and I couldn't ask for more.

But I squeezed my eyes closed and made a wish, just like I always did.

*Let the people I love the most have everything their hearts desire.*

It's what I always wished for.

I blew hard and watched as the white fluffballs moved around me. I sent Saylor a quick text and a screenshot of the petal-less stem.

Done.

DANDELION

You better not be doing that same ole wish. Wish for something for YOU.

You getting your bookstore is as good a wish as any. Happy for you, Dandelion.

It's what I'd always called her in private, when no one was around. In the dark, when I'd held her in my arms, when we were just teenagers. None of the guys knew about it, or they would have given me shit. They would have thought something was going on between us, but it wasn't like that.

DANDELION

I want you to find a wish of your own.

I have everything I want already. So, you get today's wish.

DANDELION

What am I going to do with you?

Have fun tonight. I'm heading to meet the guys for dinner. Be safe. Text me when you get home.

DANDELION

You do know I can take care of myself. But I'll text you later to make sure YOU ARE SAFE. ❤

I showered quickly and made my way to Whiskey Falls to meet the guys.

We ordered food, and Lionel, Ruby's father and the owner of this fine establishment, came over and chatted with us for a bit, before he got called away by someone in the kitchen.

"I stopped by the bookstore on my way here and peeked in the windows. It looks like you got a lot done for the first day," Hayes said.

"Yeah, we want to get her up and going as quickly as we can, so she can start making money." Nash popped a tater tot into his mouth before flicking his thumb in my direction. "And this guy likes to build, so he put in a long day."

"It's going to look good. We'll get it done as quickly as possible. Couple of weeks should be plenty of time." I took a long pull from my beer. "Did you know Saylor was going out with that coach dude, Jeremy?"

"Jalen? The guy who's working at Romeo's gym?" Hayes asked.

"Jalen's a good guy. You don't have anything to worry about." Romeo shot me a confused look, probably wondering why I was bringing it up in front of Hayes. Saylor was a grown woman, and she didn't like her brother being in her business. We all knew that. They'd had many arguments in front of us about it.

"I don't like him." I shrugged, and River raised a brow, most likely also wondering why I was doing this. But we were straight shooters, and I wouldn't hold back. These were my brothers.

Nash smirked because he enjoyed it when I did this kind of shit.

"You don't even know him. He had great references, and he's a good guy. What is your issue with him?" Romeo crossed his arms over his chest and stared at me.

"First off, his shorts are too fucking short. He calls me *mate*. His hair is too shiny. Shall I go on?"

River barked out a laugh. "He called me mate, too. Is he Australian?"

"No. He's from Jersey," I hissed.

"Who gives a shit? Mate is a universal term. And his shorts are fine. That's what dudes are wearing these days in the gym. As for his hair, I think your hair is just as shiny," Romeo said over his laughter.

"I get it. He's new in town, and you're looking out for Saylor. It's what we do. But if Romeo thinks he's a good dude, I think we can trust that," Nash said, reaching for his steak sandwich. "It's a date. She's not marrying the dude."

*Is everyone losing their fucking minds?*

We knew nothing about this guy.

"I appreciate you looking out for her. She didn't mention anything to me about going out with him, but I know she doesn't want me getting involved in her business. I'm trying to back off." Hayes took a long pull from his beer and then turned his attention to Romeo. "You think he's fine?"

"Yes. And they went to dinner one time. I don't think there's anything to worry about." Romeo shrugged like it was no big deal.

"Actually, they are on date number two tonight. *Movie night*. So I'll be watching that dude like a fucking hawk," I said, not hiding my irritation.

River's gaze met mine, and it spoke volumes without saying a word.

*What the fuck is going on with you?*

Ride or die, brother.

This is what we do.

# 3

## Saylor

Spring in Magnolia Falls was my favorite. I was meeting the girls at The Golden Goose for lunch, and we had lots to catch up on.

Midge Longhorn, who owned the place, greeted me with her usual straight-faced nod and led me to the table.

Ruby, Peyton, and Demi were already there, sitting in our favorite booth. This had become a ritual for us. Saturdays were for grilled cheese, tomato soup, and girl talk.

"Hey, sorry I'm late. I was at the bookstore all morning. They got one wall of bookshelves installed today. It's really coming together."

"I cannot wait to have the bookstore open for business. Romeo said that King has been putting in long hours over there this last week."

We were two weeks into renovations, and we were definitely ahead of schedule.

"Yeah. He knows how badly I want to get the doors open, so he's been pushing hard." I paused when Letty came over to take our orders.

"I'm so excited for you. We all need to relax this weekend. River wants to have everyone over tomorrow for a barbecue.

He insists King take a day off, so we can all hang out on the lake if it's warm enough. We'll be cooking up a lot of food, so come hungry."

"Yay. Can I bring Bobby?" Peyton asked. "I'm dying to see him with his shirt off. He's such a freaking gentleman; he hasn't made a move on me yet."

Bobby worked for Nash and Kingston, and he was helping with the bookstore renovations. They'd gone out a few times over the last two weeks.

"Yes. The more the merrier," Ruby said. "Why don't you make the first move?"

"I don't know. I usually wouldn't hesitate, but it's kind of hot that he's taking his time, you know?" Peyton reached for her drink. "How's it going with Coach Hotty? You've been out several times, right?"

"Yeah. He's nice. We're taking it slow, too, I guess. But I like him. He took me out on his boat two days ago, and we had a picnic out on the water, so that was fun."

"I love that. Very romantic. You should invite him to the barbecue tomorrow," Demi said. "Romeo told me that he's a really good guy, and Slade really likes him, too." Demi's brother had moved back to town and was working at the gym for Romeo now, as well.

"Yeah, he mentioned that he's training Slade on the side. That's great," I said.

"Well, apparently, not everyone is happy with Coach. Romeo said that King has a problem with him." Demi shrugged.

My head fell back in laughter, just as our food was set in front of us. "King doesn't like his shorts. Or his hair. Or the fact that he calls him mate. I think he's just being protective, but it's a little ridiculous. I'm used to this kind of madness from Hayes, but not from King."

"Damn. A protective King is freaking hot. That guy is so damn good-looking and charming in that *I-will-give-you-*

*all-the-orgasms* kind of way, and then you add in him being protective—it's almost too much." Peyton fanned her face.

"You guys have always been close, huh?" Ruby asked as she turned to look at me.

"Yep. No one really talks about it, but I lived with the Pierce family for several months when I was a teenager. So we're more like family, you know?"

"It was when Romeo and River were sent away, right?" Demi winced, and I knew the topic was still painful for her to talk about. They'd been pulled from their homes and sent to Fresh Start, where Ruby now worked, for a crime they hadn't committed but that Demi's brother, Slade, had. But everyone had moved on and put it behind them.

"Yeah. King really helped me through a hard time. I was a mess. Separated from my brother, terrified of my stepfather, worried for my mother, and the Pierces opened their door to me."

"Where did Hayes go?" Peyton asked, not knowing any of this had gone down.

"He stayed with Nash and his dad."

It had been a horrible time in my life. The darkest to date. And I was still healing from the fact that my own father wouldn't help me and Hayes during that time. But once he left us, he never looked back. Otherwise, if he had even given us a little bit of interest, we wouldn't have had to deal with Barry. It was a lot to take all at once. But King had gotten me through it.

"That had to be so hard," Peyton said, before a wicked grin spread across her face. "*Speaking of hard*, you were living with a teenage Kingston. Come on, something must have gone down. All those months in the same house with raging teenage hormones and the hottest guy in town across the hall from you?"

"Oh my gosh. Never. First of all, I was just surviving back then. I was really struggling emotionally, and that was the last thing on my mind. Not that King would have ever done anything either. He doesn't look at me like that, and we all know that Hayes would have lost his shit on him if anything had ever happened."

I groaned as I took a bite of the best grilled cheese sandwich in town.

"You never tiptoed over to one another's beds in the middle of the night?" Peyton pressed, and Demi and Ruby both laughed hysterically.

"Girl's got a one-track mind," Ruby said, shaking her head and thrusting her thumb at Peyton.

I chuckled. I wasn't going to tell them that he'd slept in my bed every single night for six months.

No one would ever believe that nothing had happened if they knew about it.

But Kingston Pierce had just been there to comfort me.

To scare all the bad guys away.

"Nope. Nothing. I told you that I was a late bloomer in that department. I think with my home life being so up in the air, I was just—a nervous kid, I guess. I never dated or went to dances or any of that stuff back then. I didn't have my first real boyfriend until college. So, I can assure you, nothing ever happened with King."

"Well, you sure had all the guys beating your door down in college, didn't you?" Demi said as she bumped her shoulder into mine. We'd become close friends once we'd gone away to the same school, and I couldn't imagine my life without her now.

"Well, damn. You had Kingston Pierce under the same roof as you back then. Every girl in town has tried to reel that boy in over the years." Peyton waggled her brows.

"Well, I'm pretty sure he's talking to Selena George right now. He said he took her out for drinks and dancing last week, and they had dinner together two nights ago," I said after I finished chewing. "I think he's trying to prove a point to me, because a few weeks ago, I'd teased him about having different women in his bed every night."

"He's the easiest-going guy on the planet, but he can get defensive when he's passionate about something." Demi chuckled, and we all nodded in agreement.

"Yes. If I hear one more time how sensitive his nipples are, I'm going to pierce them in his sleep," Ruby said with a straight face as we all laughed. "He saw a bee the other day and literally freaked out and ran into the house. But that's what we love about him, right?"

"He's adorably charming," Demi said, with a big smile on her face.

"Yeah, I used to tease him about how irrational he was about bees." I laughed hard at the memory. "He's this bigger-than-life, confident guy, but a bee buzzes by, and the fear is real. But then I found out that he was stung as a child and had a bad reaction, so I think it stems from that."

"River loves it. He taunts him and buzzes in his ear all the time." Ruby rolled her eyes. "I told him to stop being evil. It's clearly a genuine fear."

"That man is so sexy I'd be willing to suck the venom right out of him, if he got stung in front of me," Peyton said, and the table erupted in laughter.

"Let's hope he doesn't get stung. I don't think he'd handle that well." I reached for my drink just as the door was pulled open, and Jalen walked inside with Demi's brother, Slade, beside him.

"Ohhhh, Coach Hotty is here. And I've got to say, the small shorts work for him," Peyton whispered, and I tried hard not to laugh. "And can we talk about how hot Slade is these days?"

"We cannot. The last thing I want to hear is you talk about how hot my brother is. Save that for a time I'm not around," Demi said over her laughter.

"I get that, and I hate to take King's side on this one, but I'm not sure how I feel about those little shorts." Ruby raised a brow. "But if you like him, I can live with them."

"It shows off his thick, muscled thighs," Peyton said.

"Stop. He's going to hear you." I cleared my throat, trying to hide my words as they approached the table.

"Well, aren't we lucky to run into these beautiful ladies today," Jalen said, his eyes locking with mine.

I liked him enough to keep saying yes to more dates. But it felt more like a friendship, if I was being honest. We'd made out a couple of times, and it was fine. Not horrible. Not magical.

Not a romance book-worthy kiss, but I also knew that I couldn't compare everyone I dated to the heroes in the books that I read.

My expectations were probably way too high.

Slade chuckled and snagged a few fries off Demi's plate. "Hey, I forgot Saturday was your girls' lunch."

"Always the fry thief, aren't you?" she teased.

"Did you both hear that River and Ruby are throwing a barbecue tomorrow? We'd love for you to come." Peyton clasped her hands together and rested them on the table as Ruby shot her a look.

"Yeah, Romeo told me about it this morning. I'll try to stop by for sure," Slade said.

"Are you going to be there, Saylor?" Jalen asked.

"Yeah. I just heard about it, too. I'll definitely be going."

"Well, then, so will I." He winked, and I waited for the flutters to come, but they never did.

He was perfect on paper.

Good-looking, nice, reliable, thoughtful . . . The list went on and on.

That's why I was still giving him a chance.

Maybe the flutters would come.

"All right, we better get to our table. I told Romeo we'd

be back at the gym in an hour." Slade rapped his knuckles on the table twice.

They walked away, and Jalen held up his hand, his gaze never leaving mine.

"Damn. He's got it bad, girl," Ruby whispered as she studied me. "If he's taking it slow, it's because he can tell that's what you want. I think that guy would jump your bones right here if you'd let him."

Demi fell forward in laughter. "Well, that's one way to put it. But I do agree. He's definitely into you."

"I say go for it. He's hot. Let him rock your world. Maybe that's how you'll figure out if you really like him. You're young and beautiful. This is your time to explore." Peyton shrugged.

"Explore?" I said, over a fit of laughter.

"Yeah. It's your *dick era*. Go get it, girl."

"What is wrong with you? Not everyone wants to be in their *dick era*," Demi said, shaking her head with a huge smile spread across her face.

"Agreed. No pressure. If you want the dick, go get it. If you don't, run like hell, Saylor." Ruby smirked, and the table erupted in laughter again.

"Sounds like a party over here," Kingston said, as he and Cutler approached the table. I startled because I hadn't seen them walk in, and I hoped like hell that little Cutler's ears hadn't heard that conversation.

"Why does my girl, Saylor, need to run? Are you in trouble?" Cutler asked, concern causing his eyebrows to pinch together.

"Oh, my," Demi whispered, a horrified look on her face.

"Um, no. I, er, they were joking. I'm fine." I looked from Cutler to Kingston, and he couldn't wipe the wicked grin from his face.

"This guy was talking a mile a minute. He didn't hear what you were saying aside from you needing to run for your life apparently," Kingston said, reaching for the brim of his baseball cap and turning it around slowly.

And there were the flutters that I was hoping would come from Jalen. They were in full force now. It came with the territory. Kingston was probably the best-looking guy I'd ever seen, so obviously he had this effect on women. I wasn't immune to that just because we were friends or because he was my brother's best friend.

Tall. Lean. Broad shoulders. Dark eyes that felt like they could see into my soul. He had plump lips and a chiseled jaw, peppered with day-old scruff.

*I mean, who wouldn't swoon over this guy?*

"You're all right?" Cutler reached for my hand. "Because Uncle King will beat up all the bad guys for you."

"You got that right, buddy. Saylor's our girl." He winked at me, and damn if my lady bits weren't blazing now.

*Maybe I do need to enter my dick era.*

My hormones were clearly raging. It had been a while. And obviously, they were ready to come out and play.

"I'm fine, but thank you both."

"All right, we're going to grab some burgers, and then we're heading over to visit Grammie."

"I was there last night. We played cards and swapped books." I smiled. I loved Pearl Pierce more than life itself. That woman had saved me, just like her grandson had.

"Yeah, she told me you were there. She loves your visits."

"There's a wait for a table, King. So if you want to keep this one, you need to follow me over now and get your order in, or I'm giving it away," Midge hissed, walking up out of nowhere.

"Calm your horses, Midge. We're going there now," he said, and Cutler waved and followed Midge toward their table, but Kingston paused as he watched them step away.

He leaned down and whispered in my ear, his lips grazing my skin and causing goose bumps to spread down my arms. "Don't be afraid of the dick, Dandelion. It's my favorite piece of equipment."

He pulled a golden dandelion out of the pocket of his tee, like it was nothing out of the ordinary to have it there, and he placed it behind my ear like some sort of freaking magician.

A sexy, hot magician.

This guy could take his show on the road.

I'd buy tickets every time.

Every. Single. Time.

I just stared up at him, and he chuckled before walking away.

*What the hell was that?*

Ruby pushed my soda toward me and raised a brow. "You look a little parched."

I let out a breath that I hadn't even realized I'd been holding.

"What did he say?" Demi asked with wide eyes.

"Nothing. Just a little inside joke about the renovation." I sure as hell wasn't about to tell them what he'd said. That would just make everyone think there was more going on than there was.

Demi and Peyton nodded, but Ruby didn't look like she was buying it. She studied me for a few seconds before reaching for her sandwich.

"Well, I'm here to say that Kingston Pierce would make any girl enter her dick era. Because I'm guessing that boy is packing a punch in those pants." Peyton crossed her arms over her chest.

Demi spewed soda all over the table. Ruby rolled her eyes and shook her head with disgust. And I tried desperately to hide my smile.

Because I had a flashback to a few weeks ago when he'd been pressed up against my backside, and I got a front-row seat to what he was packing.

And Kingston Pierce was definitely packing a punch.

# 4

## Kingston

"What's going on with you and Selena?" River asked, as we looked out at the water from the dock. There were several chairs on the wood structure, and he and I had just gotten out of the water.

"Nothing, really. It's casual. She heard you were having a barbecue and asked if she could come." I shrugged, my eyes moving to where Saylor and Coach Assmunch were sharing a raft. They were awfully cozy lately. The guy just rubbed me wrong. I didn't know why Hayes wasn't asking more questions about this guy.

*Must I be the one to do everything?*

"You've been out with her a couple of times, huh?" my brother pressed.

"What is this? An episode of *The Bachelor*?" I barked out a laugh. "Yeah, dude. I do take women out now and then. I'm not a barbarian."

"She seems really . . . invested. I was just checking in to see if you felt the same. Because from where I'm sitting, you seem to be watching Saylor a lot more than the woman you brought here today."

"For fuck's sake. Of course, I am. Do none of you see that this guy is a total player? He's putting on this fake Australian bullshit charm, and he's wearing a goddamn Speedo for a bathing suit. Am I the only person who sees how crazy this is? I can't believe Hayes isn't concerned."

"I guess Speedos are back in style. Maybe it's an Australian thing," he said with a sarcastic chuckle.

"That motherfucker is from Jersey. This is outrageous."

River raised a brow. "You seem pretty worked up, King. You sure there isn't something more going on? You've been a little edgy lately, and for most people, it wouldn't be noticeable. But when fucking happy-go-lucky Kingston seems moody, it's noticeable."

I rolled my eyes, my gaze moving from Selena back to Saylor. I couldn't see her dipshit boyfriend's hands, as they were hidden in the water, and I was two seconds from diving off this dock and finding out what he was up to.

"Let's see . . . I've got two huge renovations going on, we're trying to get the bookstore open for Saylor so she can start making money, it's fucking bee season, so I'm constantly on the lookout, and my brother won't stop harassing me about being edgy."

He raised a brow and studied me. "Dude. You were stung by a bee when you were a toddler. Are you seriously going to do this every spring for the rest of your life?"

"Hmmm . . . I nearly died. I wonder why I overreact to bee season?" I tried to hide my smile because I knew my fear of bees was irrational. But those little black-and-yellow fuckers had me on edge.

And now this muscle man in a Speedo made me want to go all caveman. It made no sense.

"I was there, remember? Your lips swelled, and you got a rash on your face. You did not almost die."

"Well, Grammie said it was bad. And they rushed me to the

hospital, where an actual doctor told her the next time could be worse. Second-time allergies can be deadly. And I don't remember your law degree coming with a medical license."

"Then get a fucking EpiPen and stop whining."

"That is a very insensitive attitude, River." I tried to act annoyed, but the whole thing did sound slightly comical. "You better check yourself before you think about making a baby with Ruby. You can't be a dick and a father. It doesn't work."

"I'll work on it," he said, as everyone started climbing out of the water and onto the dock.

"We're getting hungry," Ruby said, as she wrapped a towel around herself and dropped to sit on my brother's lap.

Selena was next, and she did the same. I never minded a beautiful woman sitting on my lap, but for whatever reason, I just wasn't feeling it romantically with her. I liked her enough. I wrapped my arms around her when she shivered, and I kissed her cheek. We hadn't done more than make out, and I knew she wanted more. But something was holding me back. I'd found excuses to cut our nights short every time we went out, usually blaming work.

"Come on, lover boy. You can help me cook the burgers and dogs," my brother said, as he pushed to his feet, and I helped Selena stand.

"Can I help, too?" Cutler shouted, running toward me as I caught him on a whoosh.

"You know it, Beefcake. And I'm a master on the barbecue, so I'll teach you my skills," I said, following River through the yard.

I set Cutler down when we got to the house and used the towel to dry off his hair, and he followed me into the kitchen.

This little dude was basically all of ours. We'd all been in his life since the day he came into the world, and I loved him in a way I didn't even know was possible.

Ruby followed us into the kitchen and helped River pull

out the platters of meat and started making a salad. I grabbed a beer before reaching for the milk and chocolate syrup to make my little dude his drink of choice. We all kept chocolate syrup at our homes for him, because chocolate milk was his favorite.

"I think I want to get a swimsuit like Coach has."

My head spun around, and I gaped at him. "Abso-freaking-lutely not. Beefcake! You do not want to rock a Speedo."

Ruby and River's loud laughter filled the room. But I didn't find this funny at all. It was our job to mold the little guy, and short-shorts and Speedos were not a good fashion choice.

"Why? I think it looks cool."

"Well, if you want to wear colorful underpants that don't leave anything to the imagination, I guess it's a choice," I grumped as I poured the milk into the glass and stirred in the chocolate.

"Maybe he's got nothing to hide," River said, knowing exactly how to provoke me.

"Listen, it's not about having something to hide. I don't like the look, that's all I'm saying. You want to leave a lady guessing, Beefcake. Let your personality do the talking."

"Uncle River says that you have a colorful personality, Uncle King. I want to have a colorful personality, just like you."

I handed him his glass of milk and clinked my beer bottle to his. "You've got it in spades, buddy."

"I do like my trunks a lot. And I don't know if they make those small suits like Coach has with little dinosaurs on them."

"We can look into it if it's something you want to try out," River said, a wicked grin on his face.

"I'd just need to make sure my sea monster fits inside that kind of suit, right, Uncle King?"

"Correct. You need to keep your sea monster real safe."

"Seriously? You called it a sea monster?" Ruby whispered so only I'd hear. Cutler had moved on to asking my brother questions about the meat he was going to cook.

"What? That's what I called it when I was young."

She shook her head and glanced over to make sure River was deep in conversation with Cutler. "So, Selena's nice."

"Yeah. She's really nice. Great girl."

She raised a brow before turning back and chopping cucumbers like she was a damn sous chef. "What's your deal with Coach?"

"I told you. I'm not a fan. I don't trust him."

"That's not like you, King. Do you know something that we don't?" There was concern in her voice now, and I knew she and Saylor were close. Of course, she'd want to protect her friend.

"That's the surprising thing. You all see what I see, yet none of you have a problem with him?"

She shook her head and smiled before leaning in again and whispering. "You sure you aren't just jealous?"

I gasped dramatically, because theatrics were kind of my thing. "I don't get jealous. But I am protective, and I trust my gut."

"All right. Just don't be so hard on the guy. He likes her, and she seems to like him. She deserves that, you know?"

My chest squeezed. Was I being a total dick? Had I misread the guy?

*Am I fucking jealous?*

"I'll try harder. How about that?"

"That would be nice. At least give him a chance. It's not all that serious, but I think she's enjoying things right now."

I took a long pull from my bottle and glanced out the window. Saylor was wearing a pink bikini, her golden skin impossible not to stare at. Her perky tits, which would fit perfectly in the palms of my hands, had my mouth watering.

My gaze moved down to her flat stomach and toned, lean legs, settling at the apex of her thighs.

*Good Christ. I am losing it.*

I quickly shifted to look at Selena. My date. She was gorgeous. Why the fuck wasn't I scanning her body? She was curvy and voluptuous and sexy as hell.

Why couldn't I keep my attention there?

Right where it belonged.

It was probably my history with Saylor that made things so complicated. Our connection.

And, of course, I was attracted to her. That was completely normal. She was hot. It didn't mean anything.

"You all right?" Ruby studied me as she tossed the veggies into the bowl.

"Of course. I'm great." I kissed her cheek and followed my brother and Cutler out to the grill, and we got to work.

Country music played in the background, and I took it all in. The sun was still shining, and the lake glistened in the distance. Romeo, Nash, Hayes, Slade, Bobby, Coach Junk-on-display, Demi, Saylor, Selena, and Peyton were all playing football out in the yard. They called Cutler over, and I high-fived him before he jogged over to the group.

River and I moved the cooked meat to the platter just as they finished the game. Everyone helped Ruby carry the food out to the big table that I'd built for my brother as a housewarming gift years ago when he'd purchased this place. The two matching benches made it so we could all sit together.

"Where did you find a table this large, mate?" Coach asked my brother, and I made a conscious effort not to show my irritation.

"King made it for me when I bought the place," River said.

"It's a nice table." Coach glanced over at me.

Maybe I was being a dick. I needed to try. Everyone else liked the dude.

"Thanks. I appreciate it." My gaze moved to Saylor, who smiled in response.

I could do this.

Hayes didn't seem bothered by the guy, though I knew he'd have a comment about the Speedo later.

Coach's hand moved to caress Saylor's shoulder, and he kissed her cheek. There was that anger again.

*Yep. I definitely still don't like the guy.*

*Or his stupid fucking Speedo.*

"Are you sensitive to the sun? I noticed you put your shirt on as soon as you got out of the water," Selena said, looking up at me from where she sat beside me.

"You checking me out?" I teased, and I looked up to see Saylor watching us before she quickly looked away.

"Always."

Yeah, I'd made a point to keep my back turned away from Saylor while my shirt had been off. And I'd covered up as soon as I got out of the water. Normally, I liked being shirtless and showing off the goods, but I had my reasons for not doing that today.

"Well, I think it's harder for bees to sting you through your clothing," I said, my voice light.

"I have a nephew who's allergic to peanuts, and my sister has to carry an EpiPen with her. I get it. It's scary when your body has a reaction to something like that."

"Thank you. My brother's a real cocksucker about it, and the guys always razz me. But this time of year has me a little on edge when I'm outside." I shrugged.

"That makes sense. I hate bees, too." She batted her lashes.

I didn't hate bees. I feared bees.

"When do I get to get my Ride or Die tattoo, Pops?" Cutler asked, just like he had many times before.

"We've talked about this, buddy. You can't get a tattoo until you're old enough to make a decision like that."

"But I want to match you and all my uncles."

"You all have the same exact tattoo?" Peyton asked, setting her corn on the cob down on her plate.

"Give or take," River said. "We each chose different fonts and styles. And of course, King went and threw a flower on his."

*Fucking River. The guy never has much to say but manages to say exactly what he shouldn't.*

"I saw that on your shoulder before you pulled your shirt back on. It's a yellow flower, right?" Selena asked.

"It's a weed," Nash said over his laughter.

I rolled my eyes and reached for my beer. "Says the guy who knows nothing about flowers."

"It's a dandelion," Cutler said proudly. "Uncle King told me so."

Keeping something under wraps in this group was next to impossible. When I got the fucking tattoo, Saylor didn't live here, and no one was the wiser. It was my thing.

Just for me.

Maybe a little for her.

I looked up, and my gaze locked with hers briefly, just as Ruby led Cutler from the table and turned the sprinklers on for him. He was running around the yard in the water as we sat there sipping our drinks, and I wanted to change the subject.

"Anywho, it's bee season, and we should all be aware," I said.

"I think it's very manly to be honest about your fears," Selena said, and I internally groaned because that was like leading a horse to water. She lined that up perfectly for the guys.

"Are we talking about King's fears?" Hayes said with a cocky grin. "He's got three fears, and we all know what they are."

"That doesn't make you a genius, you dicksicle. I've been

telling you what they are since we were kids." I rolled my eyes but found it hard not to laugh.

"Well, not all of us know them. What are they?" Bobby asked, and he seemed a little too excited about hearing what they were, and I shot him a glare.

The guys were all laughing now because they loved to give me shit.

"There's no shame in being fearful of things. I think we all are," Saylor said in my defense.

*Atta girl.*

This girl always had my back, and I'd always have hers.

"Agreed. But King's fears are not what you'd expect," River said over his laughter.

"Bees are clearly number one." Nash nodded confidently. "And I don't fuck with bees either, so I get it."

"And clowns, which is fair. They used to freak me out, too," Romeo admitted.

"Dude. Have you seen that movie where the serial killer is a clown, and he's worn the makeup for so long that it never washes off his face? It's stained to look like a fucking killer clown for the rest of his life." I shivered, and everyone laughed some more.

"I like clowns," Coach said.

*Of course, you do. You also like Speedos, so we aren't going to trust your judgment.*

"Good for you. I hope you don't find yourself in a dark alley with a serial killer clown and invite him in for a beer." I raised a brow.

"I'll keep that in mind, mate. What's the last one?"

I never hid who I was. I was the life of the party. A perpetual good time. I'd also throw down and fight for the people I loved. I'd fought dudes much larger than I was and walked away without a scratch. I worked hard to build my business, and I put in long hours.

But I didn't hide the fact that there were three fucking things in this world that I did not care for.

Bees.

Clowns.

And . . .

"White vans. Our boy can spot a white van from a mile away," River said.

"I drive a white van," Coach said. "I haven't used it much because I can walk everywhere in Magnolia Falls. Why don't you like white vans?"

*Boom.*

*There you go.*

*My work here is done.*

If I had a mic, I'd be dropping it onstage right about now.

*This fucker likes clowns and drives a white van.*

Saylor's head fell back in hysterical laughter, and everyone followed suit. It must have been the knowing look on my face.

*Coach is clearly a serial killer.*

"Are you going to tell me you have a part-time job as a beekeeper, and you have a clown suit hidden in your white van?"

"You're hilarious, mate." Coach chuckled.

I wasn't fucking kidding. And he wasn't fucking Australian.

"Uncle King, come and chase me!" Cutler called out from a few feet away, and I was on my feet and jogging toward him.

I ran into the water with him and scooped him up, bringing us both to the ground to wrestle. He was giggling, and he pushed me over so he was kneeling beside me and started tickling me.

I rolled onto my stomach and laughed, just as a sharp pain poked me in the groin.

It only took seconds to register what had happened.

*I'd been stung by a motherfucking bee.*

Hell hath no fury like a man under attack.

# 5

## Saylor

It was like something straight out of a movie. Kingston let out a scream, and Cutler shouted at us.

"Uncle King got stung by a bee!" The concern in Cutler's voice was impossible to miss.

"No fucking way," River hissed and jumped to his feet.

Nash moved quickly as well, and ran to grab Cutler to calm him down. Demi and Peyton were consoling him, as the rest of us followed a crazed Kingston into the house, screaming about needing someone to grab a credit card.

River pulled a credit card from his wallet, as a frantic Kingston dropped to sit on the toilet.

"They release venom after they sting you. Get the fucking stinger out of me." He yanked his shirt off, chucking it onto the floor before pulling the waistband on his trunks down low enough to expose the stinger. My eyes widened as I took in his impressive six-pack before moving down to the deep V, leading to a large red circle with a white center that was already starting to swell.

"Dude. You need to relax. I can't get the stinger out if you're acting like a fucking lunatic," River hissed, and I heard laughter from behind me and turned to see Romeo and Hayes, and I shot them a warning look.

This could be serious.

Before I could process what was happening, Kingston slapped the credit card right out of River's hand, and it went flying through the air before landing at my feet.

"Holy shit," Ruby said against my ear. "He's losing it."

"Don't fucking touch me, River!" Kingston was frantic, and it felt like I was in the midst of a rom-com gone bad.

I picked up the credit card, and his gaze locked with mine. "Let Saylor do it. Everyone needs to get the fuck out. Now!"

"Good luck," River said, as he slipped past me, and I stepped forward.

Someone must have pulled the door closed because we were suddenly alone. He sat on the toilet, dark eyes blazing. "Do you see it?"

I dropped to my knees, moving between his thick thighs, and handed him my phone after turning on the flashlight so I could get a better look.

"Keep the light right there. I can see the stinger," I said, as my fingers grazed over the little patch of dark hair leading down to his . . . bee sting.

He sucked in a breath as I moved closer. My heart raced, and it sure as hell wasn't because I was worried about getting the stinger out. I placed a hand on his muscular thigh before realizing I was dangerously close to his penis, which was now straining against his swim shorts. My eyes shot up to his.

"Fuck, Saylor. I can't help it. Just get the damn stinger out."

I nodded as I positioned the hard plastic just above the base of the stinger. I didn't want to drag it out because I knew he was freaking out. I pressed the credit card beneath the point of the stinger and lifted. The stinger came out on the first try. "Got it."

"Oh my God. It's swelling. And it fucking hurts. What if the venom goes to my dick, and I have to get it amputated?" His voice was part tease, but I heard the fear that he was trying to cover.

"I wouldn't worry about that. It seems to be working just fine." I glanced over at him as I dropped the stinger onto a piece of tissue. I reached for my phone and stood beside him. "Let me google it and see what we need to do."

"How bad is it?" he asked, his head falling back and eyes squeezing shut.

"It's definitely swelling," I said, as I looked in the cabinets and found a washcloth and some hand soap and turned on the water. "The first most important step is removing the stinger, which we did. You were correct. The venom pumps into you until you remove the stinger. Did you know that only female bees can sting you?"

"Well, that makes sense. Typical woman. She had her eye on my dick," he said, his voice quiet as he sat completely still, waiting for me to tell him what we should do next. "I think River keeps Benadryl here for me. Can you look in the medicine cabinet?"

I searched through the cabinet until I found the bottle of Benadryl.

"Okay, found it." I handed him two pills and filled the little cup beside the sink with water, and he popped them into his mouth and took a sip.

"Thank you," he said.

"I need to clean the area with some soap and water." I grabbed a washcloth and turned on the water before moving back between his thighs. I gently dabbed at the swollen area as his head fell back, and he closed his eyes again. I blew lightly across his skin to try to soothe him, and his head shot forward, eyes open now.

"Jesus, Saylor. You can't do that."

"Oh." I startled, noticing something else swelling beneath his trunks once again. My God. This thing had a mind of its own. "I'm so sorry."

He leaned back again, staying completely still as I set the washcloth on the counter and dropped to sit on my butt. I leaned my back against the wall, putting some distance between us.

"Sorry about that," he said with a chuckle. "He clearly likes you. Don't tell Hayes about this because he'd probably cut it off before the doctors amputate it."

It was my turn to laugh now, as I continued reading on my phone. "That's a little dramatic. Nothing is getting amputated. We just need to watch for a bit to see if you have any other symptoms."

"Such as?"

"Shortness of breath is the big one. You've got some swelling, and I should probably go get some ice for that."

"No. Please don't go. And I don't want everyone coming in here and giving me shit right now. I know I'm ridiculous about bees, but I'm not in the mood to be razzed at the moment."

I nodded, even though he wasn't looking at me. "How about we just sit in here for a while and wait to see if anything happens? I'll text Ruby and ask her to bring a little bag of ice, and I'll tell her not to let anyone come in here right now. Would that work?"

"Yeah. Thanks." He was quiet, which worried me because Kingston was rarely quiet or at a loss for words. But his breathing was fine, and the swelling wasn't getting any worse, so I figured that was a good sign.

I sent the text to Ruby, and she said she'd be right over.

There was a light knock on the door. I opened it, and she peeked inside. "You okay, King?"

"Yeah. I'll be fine. Just don't bring that dickhead brother of mine in here right now. I need a minute, okay?"

"Absolutely. Can I tell everyone that you're okay? Cutler is pretty freaked out."

"Yeah, tell my little dude I'm fine. I'll be out in a little while."

She nodded and handed me the bag of ice and she mouthed the words *thank you*. I gave her River's credit card before she turned to leave.

She pulled the door closed, and I moved back over to kneel between his legs. I traced my fingers lightly over the skin around the raised area, wanting to soothe him any way that I could. I set the bag of ice on the swelling and continued tracing around the area with my free hand.

A light moan left his lips, and I sucked in a breath. "Is that bothering you?"

"No," was all he said, his voice gruff. "It feels good."

"Good, I want to help," I whispered.

Why was I breathing so heavy? Why was I touching him?

As if we both realized it at the same time, his head shot up, and his hand took the ice from me. "I've got it."

"Okay. Great." I pushed to my feet and moved to the sink, washing my hands, just because I needed a distraction.

*Pull yourself together.*

I dropped to sit against the wall again, leaving distance between us. I wanted to know why he had a dandelion tattoo, but it didn't seem like the right time to ask about it.

"Do you remember the first time you got stung? It must have freaked you out to make you this anxious all these years later."

"Yeah. It was maybe a year or two after my parents were killed. River and I were playing outside, and I'd climbed a tree and must have run into a hive or something. I don't fully remember. But I do remember them flying around me and surrounding me, and River yelled for me to jump down and run. I only got stung once, which I guess was lucky. But it was right on the rim of my eyelid."

"Oh my gosh. That's terrible," I said. "What did they do?"

"I don't remember much aside from my grandmother crying hysterically after they removed the stinger. They rushed me to the hospital because I'd swelled up. I just have this vivid memory of hearing her say over and over that she couldn't lose me, too."

I knew that Kingston and River had moved to Magnolia Falls and were raised by their grandparents after their parents died in a car accident.

"And you were okay?" I asked.

"Yeah. They kept me in overnight because my tongue and lips swelled, and they just monitored me. I'm probably being a big pussy. I've been in bar brawls that left me in a much worse condition than this," he said with a chuckle, lifting the ice pack and shaking his head.

"Hey, don't do that." I pushed up on my knees to inspect it.

"Do what?"

"Make less of what you went through. That's scary for a little kid. And allergies are no joke. I think it's best to be cautious."

A wide grin spread across his face, all the anxiety gone now. "Of course you do."

I found another clean washcloth and dabbed at the area, drying off the remnants from the melted ice. My eyes scanned up his ripped abdomen before I could stop them, and I cleared my throat and forced my gaze back to his. "It looks like the swelling isn't getting any worse."

"Yep. I think I'm going to live." He reached down and grabbed his tee and pulled it over his head. "I guess I've got to go out there and face the music. They're going to have a field day with me, aren't they?"

"Just ignore them. They just like to give you a hard time. But I saw the concern on River's face." I dropped the washcloth into the wicker hamper.

Kingston pushed to his feet and leaned down and kissed my cheek. "It's all good. Thanks for putting up with me."

I nodded, and he pulled the door open.

Everyone turned to look as we walked into the room.

"Do you still have all your parts?" River asked, his voice all tease.

"Yeah, thanks to Saylor, everything is still intact."

The room erupted in laughter, and everyone started hugging him and making their rounds. The party had come to an end, but they'd all waited to make sure Kingston was okay.

As much as they joked and teased one another, these friendships ran deep. I'd known these guys most of my life, and they were loyal to the core.

"I see medical skills are also one of your many talents," Jalen said, as he smiled down at me. He really was a beautiful man, aside from the horrific choice of swimwear. I'd been stunned speechless when he'd dropped his shorts and donned the bright red banana hammock. But he was clearly proud of his ripped body, and he liked showing it off.

"I don't know about that. I guess I'm good with credit cards." I chuckled.

"You want a ride home?" Hayes interrupted and moved to stand beside me.

"I brought her here, and I'd like to take her home, if that's all right with you, Saylor?" Jalen asked.

"Yeah. Of course. I'm ready when you are." I shot my brother a look to back off.

I hated that he treated me like a child. It would take time for him to adjust to me living back here and realizing I was a grown woman now.

The guilt I had regarding my brother was heavy. He'd been forced to grow up at an early age, and he'd stepped up for me. Over and over again. He'd taken on a parental role when we were young, and I think he'd found it difficult to accept that

I didn't need him to do that for me anymore. But as much as his being overly protective bothered me, it didn't compare to the fact that my brother had been robbed of a childhood in order to preserve mine.

So, at the end of the day, I could tolerate him being ridiculous at times, because he was the only family member I had who had showed up for me without fail, time and time again.

I ran my fingers over the dainty, gold evil eye necklace that he'd gotten me before I left for college. He'd said it would keep away all the bad guys when he wasn't around, which had made me laugh. But I'd worn it every day since, because I loved it, and I loved him.

We said our goodbyes, and everyone walked out together. I watched as Selena linked her fingers with Kingston's, and for whatever reason, my hands fisted at my sides. I was used to seeing him flirt with women, and I knew that he was not the settling-down type, but I didn't like seeing someone hold his hand, which was outrageous of me.

I had no claim over this boy.

This man.

I never had.

I never would.

# 6

# Kingston

I'd dropped off Selena at her house after she'd pushed hard to come over and spend the night. She'd said she wanted to take care of me. I was probably confusing the hell out of her. I was always upfront about what I had to offer.

But I sure as hell hadn't delivered on that this time.

We hadn't had sex, which was usually all I was offering. A fun night, which often meant dinner and drinks. A few laughs. And a good fuck.

I loved pleasing the lady I was with.

Hell, it was my calling.

My gift.

There was nothing hotter than getting your woman off. Making her feel good.

If there was a professional sport for that, I'd be the talk of the town.

They'd call me *The Orgasm MVP.*

It was a title I'd wear with pride.

But lately, I just wasn't feeling it. Tonight, I'd used the excuse of the bee sting when I'd taken her home. I'd said I just wanted to be by myself and thanked her for the offer.

I grabbed a beer and dropped to sit on my couch before taking a long pull. Thoughts of Saylor flooded my mind, because I was a needy bastard when it came to her. The way she'd pursed her lips and blown that warm breath right above my dick nearly had me coming in my pants like a fucking horny prepubescent teenager.

I wondered if she'd gone home with that douchebag in a Speedo.

I reached for my phone.

Thanks for pulling the stinger out of my groin. 🐝🍆

DANDELION

What can I say . . . I'm good under pressure. 😉

You should have been a surgeon. You missed your calling.

DANDELION

Very funny. Pulling the stinger out of your groin is hardly rocket science, but thank you. I hope Selena wasn't upset that you didn't have her do the honors.

Nah. She's got those long, pointy fingernails, so I don't think having her next to my junk with a sharp edge is a good idea.

DANDELION

Fair point. Feel free to call me for all surgical needs around your junk.

Oh, God. That didn't sound right. Sorry.

I chuckled. She was so damn cute.

*So damn off-limits.*

Are you still with Coach?

I shouldn't ask, because it was none of my business. But I was curious.

DANDELION

Yeah. He convinced me to come sit out on the water under the stars for a bit. He just ran to use the restroom inside. But I'll be heading home soon. I'm pretty tired.

Yeah, I hear you. I'm beat, too.

DANDELION

Hey, can I ask you a question?

Of course. Anything.

DANDELION

The dandelion tattoo. What's the story there?

Fuck. I knew this would come up. I was glad she didn't ask in the bathroom when I was under duress. I'd probably have confessed the whole sappy truth.

No story. It was supposed to be a rose but came out looking more like a weed, so I call it a dandelion.

DANDELION

Ohhh . . . that's why Nash called it a weed.

Well, you can't make a wish on a weed, so a dandelion sounds a lot cooler. 😉

DANDELION

That makes sense. And you're feeling okay?

You worried about me, Dandelion?

DANDELION

Always. Is Selena with you?

I sure as hell didn't want her pity. And I needed to keep these lines in the sand very clear. There was no room for gray area where Saylor Woodson was concerned.

Yeah. We're probably going to watch a movie. Have a good night.

DANDELION

You, too. I'll see you tomorrow.

Remember to keep an eye on your wound. If it swells or your breathing strains at all, tell Selena to take you straight to the hospital.

So goddamn sweet.

I turned off my phone and decided not to respond. I headed for the shower, needing to clear my mind.

Why the fuck couldn't I get the vision of Saylor on her knees, pressed between my thighs, out of my mind?

Aqua blue eyes. Plump lips.

Begging for my cock.

Good Christ.

I was a sick fucker.

I needed to get her out of my system. I turned on the shower and let my forehead fall against the wall as the hot water beat down on my back. I wrapped my hand around my dick, ever eager for a stroke. This was the only place I'd ever allowed myself to be inappropriate with Saylor.

It was my secret, and one I'd take to my grave.

Being attracted to my best friend's little sister wasn't a sin. Acting on it would be a different story.

But fantasizing about it alone in my shower? I could live with myself.

I gave a few quick strokes as I imagined her on her knees, between my thighs, teeth sinking into her plump bottom lip as her heated gaze locked with mine.

*I take her chin between my thumb and my pointer finger and lean down to cover her mouth with mine.*

*I kiss her as if my life depends on it.*

*Tasting and teasing, as her little breaths come hard and fast against my mouth.*

*She pulls back, her tongue swiping out slowly along her bottom lip.*

I stroked harder.

*"I want to taste you," she whispers.*

*"You want me to fuck that sweet little mouth of yours?" I ask.*

*She nods as her mouth covers my swollen cock, taking me all the way in. My head falls back as she moves up and down in perfect rhythm, knowing just what I want.*

*What I need.*

*My fingers tangle in her hair as she takes me deeper.*

*My hips buck in response, loving the feel of her lips sealed around me.*

*"Fuck," I grunt as I come hard.*

Grateful that I was in the shower, I continued pumping myself under the hot water, my head resting against the shower wall.

I made a silent promise to myself that I wouldn't fantasize about Saylor after today.

Having her back in town these last few months was complicating things.

I needed to get my head straight.

This was the last time I'd let my mind wander there.

It was happening too often, and it needed to stop.

* * *

The last two weeks had been a blur. I'd been putting in long hours at the bookstore, and I'd stayed true to my promise about not getting off to thoughts of Saylor Woodson. I'd gone out a few times, but I'd yet to take a woman home. I'd let Selena know that I thought we were better off as friends, and though she'd made it clear that she was disappointed, she appreciated my honesty.

I'd never had such a bad case of blue balls in my life. It didn't help that I couldn't even rub one out now, because my mind automatically went to Saylor.

So, I threw myself into work.

Once I finished this job, I would be able to put some distance there. This was a phase, and it would pass.

I met the guys over at Romeo's gym. We had lunch every week together, and it was our time to catch up on everything.

"I thought I was going to have to come pull you out of there," Nash said when I walked in.

Romeo tossed me my sandwich, and I dropped down to sit. "Nah. Just finished getting the molding on the last bookshelf. Things are really starting to come together."

"You've been putting in long hours, huh? I've barely seen you these last few weeks." River reached for his soda.

"Who's the clingy fucker now?" I teased as I unwrapped my turkey on wheat and took an oversized bite.

"Always you." He laughed.

"Thanks for pushing so hard to get the doors open for Saylor. Means a lot, brother," Hayes said.

"Of course. You know I'd do anything for her." It was the truth.

"Well, considering she pulled a stinger out of your dick, it's the least you could do," Nash said over a fit of laughter.

"Hey, now. Don't talk about my dick and bees in the same sentence. Anyway, that stinger was several inches from my package, but it was still scary as shit."

"Don't be having my little sister go anywhere near that filthy cock of yours," Hayes said, a wicked grin on his face.

"He sure as shit wasn't going to let me take the stinger out." River raised a brow.

"Dude. You threatened to stab me in the dick. You don't

get to take the stinger out when you use those kinds of fighting words."

Laughter simmered around the room.

"How's the wedding planning going?" I asked Romeo, because he and Demi were officially tying the knot in June.

"Things are coming along. She's doing all the hard work. I just smile and nod, because I really don't give a shit about a wedding. I just want to marry her, and if she's happy, I'm happy. So she can have whatever she wants, as far as I'm concerned."

"Spoken like a pussy-whipped motherfucker," River said, balling up his wrapper and tossing it into the trash.

"Says the dude who tattooed *Queenie* over his chest." Hayes reminded him.

"Hey. I'm a sucker for my girl." River smirked before turning to Hayes. "I saw you getting awfully cozy with Trish Windsor last week at Whiskey Falls. Something going on there?"

Trish Windsor was a woman who'd moved to town last year, and she was hot as hell. A few months back, she'd shown up at the firehouse when Hayes had been working, wearing a trench coat while completely naked beneath. She'd shot her shot, as they say, but it had not worked out the way she'd planned. Hayes didn't care for women that came on too strong, and he'd turned her down. We'd all given him shit for it, because she'd practically thrown herself at him.

He brushed the nonexistent crumbs from his hands and leaned back in his chair, turning to look at each of us slowly.

*This is going to be good.*

"How many times have I told you that I don't like when a woman gets pushy with me?"

"Too many to count," I said, leaning my elbows on my knees, because I couldn't wait to hear what he was going to share.

"Yeah. I should have trusted my fucking gut and not you cocksuckers." He reached for his drink. "You were relentless about it, and she was all over me at the bar two nights ago."

"And . . ." Nash threw his hands in the air.

"And . . . I agreed to go back to her place. I tried to take control because I'm a fucking man and I like to lead when it comes to that shit. But this woman—fuck me." He shook his head like he was still recovering.

"By the look on your face, I'm guessing she didn't fuck you?" River asked, trying to hold back his laughter.

"Nah. I called that shit off after she took me to her bedroom." He leaned forward, glancing around the space to make sure no one else could hear. "The room had blood-red velvet curtains and bedding, and there were handcuffs on the posts of the bed frame. It was freaky as shit."

"I like velvet," I said with a shrug.

"Yeah. Of course, you do. But she had a bunch of cameras set up around the room. I was trying to process what was going on, and she goes to the closet and comes out with all this . . . shit. Like clamps and whips. I was not down with it. She wanted to tie me to the bed and film me, and I got the hell out of there."

I shivered. "Damn. I don't think I'd be down with that either."

"Really? You don't like pain?" River laughed, and he didn't hide the sarcasm before turning his attention to me. "You got stung by a bee and lost your shit. I don't think you're going to let anyone electrocute your dick for kicks."

I flipped him the bird, even though he was right. "I like a passionate lover, but I don't do pain. Lick some dark chocolate off my body all day long, but you pull out a Taser, and I'm out the door."

"Well, let's just say, I've never run my ass home so fast." Hayes shrugged.

More laughter.

"How 'bout you? You've been blowing everyone off the last few weeks," Nash said, turning his attention to me because I hadn't been out in a while.

"Just not feeling it lately. I've been working long hours to get the bookstore open, and I don't know, I'm just beat at the end of the day." It was the truth.

River raised a brow. "Is this a sign of maturity, or the after-effect of nearly having a bee sting you on the dick?"

I flipped him the bird. "It's called hard work and long hours, brother."

"Well, we're all going out for country music night next week, so you better pull your shit together, or Demi will have your ass. She's looking forward to all of us having some fun."

"She texted me about it. You know I'll never disappoint Beans. Of course I'll be there," I said, calling her by the nickname we used and reaching for my soda.

"You're still okay with cutting out early and picking up Cutler from school today? I've got to oversee the beams that are going in later at the Brighton Ranch, so it'll be a late one for me," Nash said.

"Looking forward to spending time with my favorite little dude." I set my cup down. "And we've got his first baseball game coming up this weekend, right?"

"Fuck. It's a good thing I'm coaching the team," Nash said as he shook his head. "Cutler is a lot of things, but a baseball player is not one of them just yet. He can't seem to grasp the concept that you swing the bat before the ball makes contact with it. He waits till it passes, and then swings hard, and then celebrates the hell out of missing the ball, like that was the fucking goal."

Laughter erupted around the room.

"He'll figure it out. You weren't born a baseball star either." River raised a brow at him because Nash had been recruited to play college ball back in the day. "If memory serves, you were a tall, gangly, awkward kid. You didn't grow into that body until high school."

"That's true. It came later for you," Romeo said over his laughter. "Demi had shirts made for everyone to wear to the first game, so we'll meet at the house beforehand on Saturday, and we'll all head over together."

"Looking forward to seeing our boy shine," I said, and I meant it.

This was the shit that I lived for.

# 7

## Saylor

We all met at Romeo and Demi's house before the game, and Demi passed out the jerseys that she'd made for us all to wear. It was Cutler's first game playing for the Magnolia Falls Ducks, and we were all going to be there to support him.

"These are so cute," I said, as Kingston came around the corner wearing the white and light blue jersey that read *Beefcake Heart #3* on the back.

He had on a pair of dark jeans, slung low on his hips, and his broad shoulders filled out the jersey like he was made for it. The buttons weren't buttoned yet, and his golden-tanned abs were on full display. His gaze met mine as I was pulling the shirt on over my tank top, and he strode toward me.

"What's up, Dandelion?" He kept his voice low so no one else could hear. The nickname had always been our secret. Something that just stayed between the two of us.

"Not much. Just excited about the game." I sucked in a breath when he grabbed each side of my jersey and started buttoning the buttons for me.

I breathed him in. Mint and sandalwood flooded my senses.

We were so close that the back of my hand grazed his stomach, and I didn't pull away as quickly as I should have.

He'd been working long hours at the bookstore, and I'd always go over at the end of my workday at Magnolia Beans to check on the progress.

I'd noticed he'd not been going out much at night lately. He said he was tired from the hours he'd been putting in.

"Me, too. Looking forward to seeing our boy shine out there today." He finished buttoning my jersey but didn't let go of my shirt. "This looks good on you."

"Thank you," I said, just as Ruby cleared her throat, and I turned to see my brother walk through the front door.

Kingston glanced over his shoulder before turning back to wink at me, and then he stepped away and started buttoning his jersey.

There was this strange pull between us.

Maybe it was our history.

Maybe it was an attraction.

Or, what I feared was that this was just a one-sided pull.

Kingston saw me as a friend. Part of his family.

I needed to remember that.

"Let's go, Ducks!" Hayes shouted, and Demi tossed him his jersey.

"Okay, let's get going. I want to get the best seats," Ruby said.

"Baby. It's six-year-olds playing peewee ball. The stadium is not selling out. It's wooden bleachers at the park, and if we show up on time, we'll still get the best seats in the house."

"I'm with Ruby," I said. "We need to get there early. I promised Cutler I'd be in the front row."

"Agreed. I'm not willing to risk it. Grab your water bottles and let's go." Demi high-fived me and Ruby. Peyton showed up just in time to grab her jersey as we made our way out the door.

We walked the short distance to the ballpark, and I slipped my hand into the pocket of my jersey and smiled when I felt the little flower that Kingston must have slipped in there.

I'd been trying to be slyer about doing the same to him. I'd gone to his office when he was at the bookstore last week and placed one on his desk. I'd slipped one on the dashboard of his truck yesterday when he'd been eating at The Golden Goose, and I happened to walk by and see his truck. Lucky for me, the man never locked his doors.

It was becoming a game more than ever now.

And I'd be lying if I didn't admit it was the highlight of my day when I'd find them.

He'd been real sly and left one in my bathroom the other day when he and River had come by to play board games with me and Ruby. He hadn't said a word, because Jalen had been there as well, but I found it after everyone had left.

"Is Coach coming?" Peyton asked as she linked arms with me.

The sun was shining above, and I loved the way it heated my skin.

"I think so," I said, clearing my throat because I didn't quite know how to handle that anymore.

"You don't sound too excited. Is that why he didn't meet us at Demi and Romeo's?" she asked.

"No. He had to work this morning. Demi invited him, and I've got his jersey," I said, holding up the shirt in my hand for her. "I'm just feeling bad because it feels more like a friendship."

"You don't have to feel bad. I still think if you'd just sleep with him, your feelings would change. You haven't progressed from the make-out stage." She shrugged.

Unfortunately, I just wasn't attracted to him that way.

"Yeah, maybe," I said, even though I'd already made a

conscious decision to end things. It wasn't going anywhere, and I knew it.

"You don't need to force anything, Saylor Woodson." Kingston popped his head between us, and we both startled and let out a squeal.

"Damn, King. You came out of nowhere, you nosy little bastard," Peyton said over her laughter.

"It's my job to know what's going on." He pulled a handful of sunflower seeds from his pocket and popped them into his mouth.

"There's nothing going on," I said, because I sure as hell wasn't going to tell them I was ending it, before I told Jalen.

"It's the shorts, isn't it?" he whisper-shouted between us, and Peyton's laughter bellowed around us.

"No. There's nothing wrong. The shorts are fine." I didn't know what it was, because Jalen Holt was perfect on paper.

"The Speedo? Come on, it's got to be the Speedo."

"Nope. Unlike you, I don't judge people by their clothing, King," I said, feigning annoyance, even though I'd hated the Speedo. "He's great. We're great."

"Well, if you want my two cents . . ." My brother moved beside me and smirked. "The Speedo was a bit much."

"Why are we talking about this? He's a great guy," I said defensively.

"I didn't say he wasn't," Hayes said. "But you can't force something if it's not there."

"Wow. That's some sound advice, coming from you." I smiled at him as we walked toward the bleachers. "You don't think anyone is good enough for me."

"And he'd be right," Kingston said, popping a few more sunflower seeds into his mouth.

"See. We know best." Hayes and Kingston pounded their fists like they'd just said something brilliant.

"Jalen is probably intimidated by you guys being this way with Saylor," Peyton said.

"Tough shit," Hayes said. "If he isn't willing to put in the work, he can hit the fucking road."

"No one is hitting the road. Everything is good. I've got this handled. Can we please stop talking about it? Because there's nothing wrong." I shook my head.

"Well, if you can get past the Speedo, you're a better person than me," Kingston said over his laughter.

Peyton dropped her arm as we approached the bleachers, and Coach was sitting there waiting for us. She nodded toward where he sat and waggled her brows at me. "Yeah, look at him. That is one hot dude right there."

"He really is," I said as Jalen waved me over.

I walked toward him, and he pushed to his feet and wrapped me in a hug. "Good to see you, beautiful."

*Damn it. Why can't I be all in with this guy?*

"Thanks. It's good to see you, too." I handed him his jersey and turned to look out at the field, as Nash jogged toward us, while the kids all continued stretching in a circle.

He gave us all high-fives and thanked us for being here.

"How's our boy doing?" River asked.

"Well, he wanted to wear his leather jacket over his jersey, so that was a whole thing." Nash shook his head and turned to glare at Kingston. "And thank you for introducing him to sunflower seeds, you dickweasel. I've got shells all over my truck, and I'll probably have a hefty dental bill if he keeps chomping on them."

"It's a freaking rite of passage. Sunflower seeds and baseball. It's like country music and apple pie. They just go together." Kingston smirked before popping a few more into his mouth.

"Country music and apple pie? Do those even go together?" River looked at his brother like he had three heads.

"Sure they do. I always crave some apple pie after I get my dance on."

We all laughed at the same time, and everyone turned in our direction.

"All right, it's game time. I'll see you after." Nash jogged off, and we all took our seats.

Demi, Ruby, Peyton, and a few of the guys sat up on the second row, while I remained on the bottom row, because that's where Cutler had told me he wanted me to sit.

Jalen sat on my right, and Kingston decided to sit on the other side of me, chewing his sunflower seeds like he didn't have a care in the world.

"Do you want some sunflower seeds?" he asked me.

"I'm okay, but thank you."

"I'd love to try them. Are they an American thing, mate?" Jalen asked, holding his hand out, and I heard River bark out a laugh from behind us.

Kingston narrowed his gaze and stared at Jalen for a long moment before reaching into his bag and dropping three tiny seeds into Jalen's large palm. "Are you not from Jersey, dude?"

Jalen stared down at the small offering and smiled. "Sure. But I consider myself a man of the world. I've traveled quite a bit and ingrained myself in many cultures."

"Well, baseball and sunflower seeds are a thing. I don't know if they chew on them everywhere, because I'm clearly not as worldly as you."

What in the hell was he doing?

"Most are not. I've been fortunate enough to see the world at a young age. But there's nothing wrong with being a small-town guy," Jalen said, and his words made it clear that these two were in some kind of pissing match.

Obviously, there was no love there, but Jalen had never reacted like this before.

And for whatever reason, I felt defensive for Kingston.

"I haven't been to many places either, and I'm most definitely a small-town girl." I cleared my throat, my gaze locking with Jalen's.

"That's my favorite kind of girl," Kingston said from the other side of me. "It's game time. Beefcake is up."

Before I knew what was happening, we were all on our feet, screaming. Cutler wore his uniform, a pair of gold aviator sunglasses, and his Ducks baseball cap turned backward as he walked toward home plate. He turned to look at us all screaming and cheering, his very own fan club, and he lowered his glasses and waggled his brows.

Everyone sitting on the bleachers started laughing because the kid just radiated magic.

"Let's get after it!" River shouted.

"You've got this, Beefcake," Kingston and Romeo called out at the same time, and then they turned to high-five one another.

I glanced over at my brother, who had his hands clamped together while his jaw ticked, like he was nervously watching his own firstborn try something new.

"Hey," I said, leaning over Kingston to look at Hayes. "He's got this. It's just a baseball game."

Hayes nodded, his eyes moving back to the field as Cutler gripped his bat and tapped it against the dirt twice before holding it up over his shoulder.

The slowest pitch of all time was tossed to him, and he swung at it way too late, his bat not coming anywhere near the ball, and we all cheered.

It didn't matter if this kid never hit a ball.

We were proud as hell of everything he did.

We just loved him that hard.

Cutler turned and smiled at us, like he had zero concerns.

Kingston's hand found mine and squeezed hard as the next

pitch was tossed to Cutler, and he swung, missing it again. I didn't miss the way Jalen's gaze moved to where my hand was connected to Kingston's. I gave him a forced smile. He didn't understand the relationship that existed between me and King. Between all of us, really. Even my brother wouldn't find it odd for our hands to be locked at this moment.

"One more try, Beefcake!" Romeo and Slade both shouted.

"You've got this!" Demi followed.

"Come on. Come on. Give him the hit," Kingston said under his breath, and I turned to see the intensity in the way he was staring at the field. Kingston was a natural athlete. Always had been.

The pitch was thrown. Cutler's bat shifted, and by the grace of God, he made contact.

It was a foul ball.

It shot straight up in the air and somehow lodged into the linked fencing in front of us.

But he'd made contact.

And our group erupted like he'd just won the World Series. He dropped the bat and turned to face us as he broke out in one of his hilarious dances. Nash hurried over to tell him it was a foul ball, but he didn't care, and neither did we.

Kingston jumped up and climbed the fence like a freaking ninja warrior, knocking the ball free as it rolled toward home base.

Before I knew what was happening, Kingston had me off the ground and was spinning me around. Everyone was laughing as we all over-celebrated the foul ball.

Well, everyone but Jalen was having a good time.

And I knew it was time to end things for good.

# 8

# Kingston

I finished the last coat of paint and stepped back to take it in. The bookshelves were covered in a sage green color, and the counter I'd built was painted in two tones, the sage green with white trim that Saylor had been spending the last week painting. She'd sanded and antiqued it and really made it look like a vintage piece of furniture by the time she was finished.

Today we'd be bringing in all her furniture and getting the place set up as much as we could. She'd be unpacking all the books over the next few days, but at least we could get all the big pieces in.

HAYES

Are we still doing this this morning?

ROMEO

Yep. I'm on my way with Demi to Saylor's place to help you load everything.

NASH

Let me know if you need my truck. Otherwise, I'll meet you at the bookstore.

RIVER

Same. Ruby and I will meet you at the bookstore. Did you get any sleep, King?

Sleep is overrated. I'm here and ready to go.

ROMEO

Damn, dude. You're a fucking warrior.

HAYES

Appreciate you, brother.

NASH

I'm on my way. Do we need to get the crew back there to finish painting?

Nope. Got it done.

NASH

Did you pull a fucking all-nighter?

You know they're my favorite.

HAYES

I think your all-nighters usually have something to do with a beautiful woman, not a can of paint.

Potayto . . . potahto.

RIVER

I've never understood that ridiculous saying.

ROMEO

It means that it's one and the same.

RIVER

I know what it means, asshole. I just think the saying is stupid.

NASH

You think most things are stupid. On another note, Cutler can't stop fucking talking about Easter. You sure you're up for hosting after pulling an all-nighter, King?

You know Easter is my favorite. Marshmallow-covered chicks and egg hunts and baskets full of treats. Damn straight, brother. I'm on it.

RIVER

Ruby said she's going to get there early to set up.

Of course, she is. That's my girl.

NASH

Careful, River. He's moving in. You better put a ring on it.

RIVER

Trust me. I'm trying.

That made me happy. Seeing my brother and Ruby building this life together. It's everything I wanted for River.

ROMEO

Demi said you went for a ride with her, Ruby, Saylor, and Cutler the other day, King. How are you feeling? She said you were walking funny after.

RIVER

It was more than walking funny. He made me stop by the Daily Market and find some sort of ointment for cows' tits.

NASH

I believe those are called udders, dickhead.

Dude. I had to work, and I could barely walk. It had been a while since I'd been on a horse, and I thought I'd be cool by skipping the saddle.

HAYES

I'm not following. What was the cow tit ointment for? Your nipples were sensitive from riding a horse?

RIVER

It wasn't for his nipples. 

You are such a cockfucker. You don't know what you're talking about. It wasn't for my dick.

ROMEO

I like cockfucker. It just hits different.

HAYES

Agreed. I like it.

RIVER

So tell us . . . where did you put the ointment?

It was for the devil's driveway. It hurt like a bitch. We rode for miles.

HAYES

What the fuck is the devil's driveway?

NASH

Your asshole area?

No, dicksausage. You know, the gooch. The taint. The devil's fucking driveway. That runway from your asshole to your balls. It's dangerous territory. One not many women want to visit.

ROMEO

Where do you come up with this shit?

RIVER

It's a King thing. But I wish I'd known because I'd have loved to see Oscar Daily's face when I told him the ointment was for King's devil's driveway.

NASH

#priceless

HAYES

My head is still spinning over this, but I do think it's rather fitting.

My devil's driveway was chafed as fuck, and the cow tit ointment is pure magic.

ROMEO

Words I never thought I'd hear.

HAYES

He's all ours. Ride or die, bitches.

NASH

Everyone is losing it. See you soon.

I shoved my hands into my back pockets and stretched my back, just as Saylor came walking through the door with her mouth hanging open.

"You finished?"

"Of course, I did. You've got the furniture coming today, right?"

"Yeah, but we could have all helped paint today while we got the furniture brought in." She shook her head, her smile bigger than I'd ever seen it.

*Totally worth giving up sleep for.*

"King, you're going to be exhausted. Were you here all night?"

"You know I never mind pulling an all-nighter to get the job done."

Usually, it was pleasing a woman, but in a way, I *was* pleasing a woman this time, too.

"How are you going to have everyone for Easter tomorrow? You're going to be exhausted."

"I'm fine. I've never required a lot of sleep."

"Well, I talked to Ruby, and I'm going to come early and help set up. I already told you I'll make the ham, but I'm going to take on more jobs. It's the least I can do." Her eyes scanned the room, and she looked so pleased it made my chest squeeze.

I glanced toward the window to see a truck pull up. Hayes was the first one here. *Saylor's brother.*

A reminder.

"I forgot to tell you . . . you can invite Jalen if you want tomorrow. Obviously, anyone is welcome. I just hope the dude puts on some pants." I chuckled, and she opened her mouth to tell me something, but Hayes came through the door before she spoke.

"Big day, Saylor girl. You ready?"

"Yes. We just went through this five minutes ago when we were at my house loading furniture." She chuckled. "But look at this place. King stayed up all night painting the bookshelves."

"And with a chafed devil's driveway at that," the fucker said, and I turned to look at Saylor, who had a puzzled look on her face.

"I'll tell you later." I shook my head, just as the rest of the group walked in.

"My girl is moving into her new shop!" Cutler shouted as he jogged through the door, holding a handful of flowers that he'd clearly picked for her.

"I sure am. And I'm going to put in a little cozy reading corner just for you." Saylor bent down to kiss his cheek. "My little baseball star."

"Yep. I'm really good. Pops thinks I'm going to be better than him," he said.

I glanced up at Nash, who was smirking where he stood behind Cutler. "Damn straight. Put in the work, and you'll keep getting better."

"I want to be like Pops and all my uncles when I grow up. Uncle King, can you teach me to paint like this?" The little guy gaped at the bookshelves as he walked closer to inspect them.

"Absolutely. We're going to start working on that desk

you asked for next week. First, we'll build it, and then we'll paint it."

Cutler reacted with a fist pump and smiled. "Yes. I'm going to have my own desk and be a businessman like Uncle River."

"Then we'll make it the best around." I high-fived my little dude.

"All right, let's get these trucks unloaded," River said, as he peeked his head in the door.

And that's exactly what we did. We spent the next several hours working our asses off. Everyone showed up. River, Ruby, Peyton, Bobby, Slade, Nash, Hayes, Cutler, Romeo, Demi, a few guys from the gym, and Ruby's brothers, Rico and Zane, even showed up for a few hours. The one person who hadn't shown up was Jalen. I didn't ask if she'd ended things with him because Saylor hadn't mentioned it, and I didn't want to look like some desperate asshole who was dying to know.

Even if I *was* a desperate asshole and dying to know.

Demi made us lunch and kept us loaded up with iced teas, and we got the place unpacked.

And when I got home, I didn't even shower. I fell into my bed with my clothes on, and I slept.

* * *

My alarm had me jumping from a sound sleep. I glanced at my phone, stunned to see that I'd been out for fourteen hours, even though I felt like I could sleep a lot longer. Ruby and Saylor would be over soon to help get things set up, and I was definitely in need of a shower to wake myself up.

I hurried as I let the water spray down on my back, and I fought the urge to grip my dick and give myself some relief. But I wouldn't do it.

It had been weeks. Probably the longest I'd ever gone without sex. I was suffering big time, but I just couldn't get my mojo back.

When I thought about sex, I thought about Saylor.

It was a fucked-up thing to do, and I knew it.

So, I'd gone without.

*No sex. No rubbing one out. No spanking the salami. No fucking relief at all.*

I was working crazy hours and keeping my mind busy. My hands busy.

But my dick . . . he was not happy.

I shook it off, got dressed, and reminded myself that no man had ever died from a bad case of blue balls.

Had he?

I sure as fuck hope not.

The doorbell rang, and Ruby and Saylor walked in carrying grocery bags. I helped unload their cars, and I was grateful that they took charge of the situation.

"I'll get the ham into the oven," Saylor said.

"Perfect. I'll go start hiding eggs for Cutler." Ruby paused as she took in the bags full of eggs that I'd gotten for the egg hunt. "My God. He's one little kid. There must be two hundred eggs here."

"He's one little kid, but he's also the best kid on the planet. I figured he'd want to find a lot of eggs. I've been stuffing them full of all his favorite shit the last few nights."

"You're a good man, Kingston Pierce." Ruby pushed up onto her tiptoes and kissed my cheek, before she grabbed one of the large bags and headed out the back door.

I turned to look at Saylor, who was bent over, ass in the air, sliding a ham into the oven. Her tan legs were on full display beneath her cut-off denim shorts.

*Motherfucker.*

My dick strained against my jeans, and I did everything

in my power to make my boner go away. I squeezed my eyes shut and forced myself to visualize my worst nightmare.

*White vans.*

*Beehives.*

*Dozens of clowns.*

"Um, hello? Are you okay?" Saylor's voice pulled me from my own personal version of hell.

"Yeah. Of course. What can I do?" I asked, clapping my hands together and causing her to jump.

*I'm jumpy. My dick is jumpy. My whole fucking body is jumpy.*

We hadn't been alone for more than a few minutes at a time in a while. I'd made sure of that. But now, here we were.

She was wearing a white tee, and I couldn't pull my eyes away.

She glanced down and looked at herself. "Is there something on me? Why are you looking at me so weird?"

"What? Me? No. I'd never look at you weird."

"Oh. Oh, you're probably wondering why I'm so underdressed." She shook her head as if she should have thought of this first. "Rubes and I brought clothes with us here to change into before the party starts. But I thought I'd be casual while we cooked and set up."

I was not concerned with her attire, but I sure as hell wasn't going to say that.

"You look great. You don't need to change on my account. It's a casual party."

"Well, it's also Easter." She grabbed another grocery bag off the counter and handed it to me. "How about you start opening all the paper plates and utensils, and we'll get that set up on the island. Ruby and I figured buffet-style with this size group was best."

"Yeah. That sounds good. Thanks for taking care of all that. Ruby said my white paper plates were not going to work." I chuckled as I started unpacking the endless crap that they'd gotten. I'd offered to pay when they'd called me to ask if they could pick everything up, but Ruby said River had insisted on covering this stuff since I'd be covering the rest.

We spent the next two hours getting the food going, and I loaded coolers full of drinks, which I set up on the patio before I helped Ruby get the rest of the eggs hidden for Cutler.

When I stepped back inside, Saylor came walking out of the bathroom wearing a short white sundress and a pair of cowboy boots.

My mouth went fucking dry.

This was it.

My dick was going to explode. Right here in the middle of my house, with no one touching him. He was ready for an epic release.

I'd either have to eventually allow myself to rub one out or reach out to one of my usual hookups and make it happen.

I couldn't go much longer like this.

This was bordering on a medical emergency.

Saylor smiled and then spun around. The back of her dress was completely open, her tan skin glistening against the white fabric. "You like it?"

I nodded, my tongue poking out to wet my bottom lip. "Yeah. You look great."

Her hair was in a ponytail that swung down her back, and she wore just the slightest bit of makeup—pink gloss on her plump lips—and her smile reached her pretty turquoise eyes.

"Thanks, King. This is going to be a great day. And thanks for including my mama. It means a lot to her. To me." She moved past me toward the kitchen, her lavender scent taunting me as she floated by.

"Of course. Barry better not show up, but your mom is

always welcome. What time is Jalen coming?" I asked, because I was dying to know what was going on with them.

"Oh. I haven't filled you in yet because you've been so busy with work. That's done. I officially ended things. I mean, we're still going to be friends. But nothing more." She shrugged before holding her arms up and waving her hands around. "I guess I'm single and ready to mingle."

Ruby laughed as she walked through the back door. "Oh, boy. Here we go again. She's back on the market."

"Truth be told," Saylor sighed, her eyes moving between us, "I think I might just want to be by myself for a while."

"Well, you know, there's nothing wrong with that. A girl can always *take care* of her own needs if she doesn't want to rely on a man to do it." Ruby winked and then bumped her shoulder into Saylor's, and they both laughed.

*What the actual fuck is this?*

Were they actually talking about getting themselves off?

Was the universe fucking with me intentionally?

"Oh, yeah? You think you can please yourself better than a man can?" I asked, hoping like hell that they didn't notice how gruff my voice sounded.

Ruby was busy looking at her phone now, and my gaze locked with Saylor's.

"It's not like I've been with anyone . . . *like that,* in a while anyway." Her eyes widened as a grin spread across her gorgeous face, and she reached for a grape and popped it into her mouth casually, like we were discussing the weather. "So, yeah. I know how to please myself, King. Don't you worry about me."

*Fuck me.*

Not even a white van filled with killer bees, and a serial killer clown driving said van, could help me now. There was no vision that could erase what was going through my mind. I was for sure going to blow if I didn't take care of business soon.

I popped a grape into my mouth and tried to mimic her casual demeanor. "Not worried at all."

Because it wasn't Saylor that I was worried about at the moment.

It was me.

# 9

## Saylor

I couldn't remember the last time I'd had a day that was this relaxing and fun. I'd been so focused on getting the bookstore open, getting the financing lined up, and working at the coffee shop to cover my living expenses.

But today had just been about family and friends and enjoying our time together.

Cutler had needed help to find the two hundred eggs Kingston had filled for him, and we'd all pitched in. Nash made endless fun of Kingston for going so over the top, but that was just who he was, and I knew Nash loved it. Cutler had done endless celebratory dances as he opened each egg to find all sorts of treats inside. There were coins and candy and stickers and a few mini baseballs. He'd filled a few with sunflower seeds, which had earned him a glare from Nash, but Cutler enjoyed every second.

I was surprised that Selena wasn't here, but I didn't want to ask why. It wasn't my business. Maybe she was just with her family today.

One of the best parts about the day was the fact that my mom was there. Hayes and I had encouraged her to come, but it was always tricky because Barry wasn't welcome, and she would usually choose to stay with him.

*She's always chosen him, hasn't she?*

"It's so nice that Pearl is able to be here," my mom said, as we finished eating.

River had gone to pick up his grandmother so she could spend a few hours with everyone outside of the nursing home.

"Yeah. She's the best. I'm so happy she could be here, too."

"The food was delicious. Do you think I can take a plate home for Barry?" she asked, and I hated how nervous she was when she mentioned his name.

To say there was a lot of water under the bridge was an understatement.

I just hated that this man had come between us.

"Listen, I don't think you need to say who it's for, all right? You can absolutely take a plate home for later."

"Hayes is being really distant," she said, and my gaze moved to where my brother stood, pitching balls to Cutler.

"He just doesn't understand your choices, Mom." I looked away for a minute before my gaze locked with hers again. "Barry has caused all of us a lot of pain. And I don't know why you can't see it or why you stay—and Hayes, well, he's protective. It's who he is."

She nodded. "I know. But he's been really good lately. He encouraged me to come today. He wants to see you, too, you know?"

I let out a long breath. "I can't have a relationship with a man who has hurt all of us. Continually. So that is not going to happen."

"I get it. But people can change."

"Sure. And he's been given lots of chances, and they've never lasted long." I held up my hand to stop her from defending him. "I love you, Mom. I will always love you.

But I won't be around him. He's burned this bridge too many times."

"But you're always so willing to forgive your father and try to mend that relationship. What's the difference?" Her eyes were hard now, and this is what I hated. This is why my brother didn't want to be around her when she was with Barry. She was defensive and mean when they were together. Like she'd been around all his negativity, that she brought that ugliness here with her.

At the end of the day, she'd always put him first. I'd grown up in a home where neither of my parents had ever put me or Hayes first.

*But my brother, he's always been that person for me.*

*He's always put me first.*

"The difference is that my father never hit me. He never put his hands on me or on you or on Hayes. That's the difference, Mom." I shook my head and glanced around to make sure no one was listening. Everyone was off in the yard, cheering on Cutler or sitting on the dock, looking at the water. Kingston took a few people out for a boat ride earlier, and everyone was looking sun-kissed and windblown. "But you're right, Dad has not shown up for us at all. I should just walk away, but I'd still like to know him. Know my half-siblings. So that's why I try, I guess."

"I'm sorry. I shouldn't do this today. It's Easter, and I'm grateful that you invited me. But I'm going to head out, sweetheart. Barry is home alone, and I told him I wouldn't be long."

Of course, she did. I scanned her body out of habit, looking for bruises. The abuse from her husband was not the way I'd always thought abuse would be. It wasn't consistent. He wasn't a scary man on the outside. Barry was fine—until he wasn't. Sometimes the rage came once a year, and other times, it was once a month. My mother claimed it hadn't happened in years, and I could only take her at her word. He'd gone to court-appointed anger management therapy more times than I could count. He held a decent job. They had a home that appeared to be clean and safe.

Yet I'd never felt that way when I lived under that roof.

Because living in an environment where you had to constantly be on edge, wondering when the rug would be pulled out from under you, was exhausting. And I didn't live through what she did. Barry had hit me a total of three times in my life, and all three times were due to me trying to break up physical fights between him and my mother.

I'd been a nervous kid. An anxiety-ridden, painfully shy teenager. And once I'd moved in with Hayes when he turned eighteen years old and agreed to be my legal guardian, everything had changed. And it only got better once I left for college.

After many years away from that toxic environment, I'd found my way.

My confidence.

My independence.

I didn't live in fear or worry anymore. And I wanted that same peace for my mother.

I couldn't begin to count the number of dandelion wishes I'd made for her.

"All right. Well, I set out a bunch of to-go containers on the counter, so help yourself to some food to take with you."

"Don't be upset with me," she said, and my chest squeezed. I looked up to see Hayes watching us, his eyes hard. I smiled, letting him know everything was okay.

"I'm not. I'm glad you were able to come, Mom. All I want is for you to be happy."

"I promise you, I'm the happiest I've ever been," she said, and I realized in that moment that I didn't know what happiness looked like for my mother. She struggled with depression. She mixed her prescription drugs with alcohol when things weren't going well with Barry, and I didn't have a single memory where she'd appeared to be genuinely happy. And that was something that had always haunted me. "I'll go make my rounds and say goodbye. I'll stop by the bookstore for the grand opening this week."

"Thank you. I appreciate it." I leaned forward and hugged her. "Love you, Mama."

"Love you, too, baby girl."

I pushed to my feet and spent the next hour sitting down by the water, talking with the girls.

"River's a little worried about King. He hasn't been himself lately at all. He seems really tense, which is so unlike him," Ruby said.

"Yeah. Romeo said he's been working a lot and is definitely more stressed than usual." Demi leaned back in her chair and smiled at me. "I'm so glad you convinced him to come ride with us last weekend. I've been trying for a while, and he finally agreed when you asked him. There's something about riding a horse that just helps you find your peace, you know?"

"I'm guessing it's kind of like riding a man, huh? That's where I always find my peace," Peyton said, as loud laughter filled the air around us.

"You have the crudest mind." Demi shook her head.

"I think he enjoyed himself. He said it's been a while since he's been on a horse. And I think the pressure of getting this bookstore open and the renovation at Brighton Ranch has been weighing on him, so things will slow down now." I crossed my cowboy boot-clad feet at the ankles.

"I haven't seen him out much in the last few weeks, which is also very unlike King. You know he's Mr. Social," Ruby said.

"Maybe he's been spending nights at home with Selena," I said, taking a sip of my beer as my gaze found him sitting in a chair by the firepit, talking to the guys. His broad shoulders strained against his black tee, and his long legs were stretched out in front of him as he tipped his cup to his lips. I'd noticed he'd poured himself a hefty glass of whiskey after dinner. Maybe he just really needed to relax.

"Oh, I think that's done. River said that ended shortly after the party at our house, that night he got stung by the bee," Ruby said, and I was surprised to hear that. He hadn't mentioned it to me, but maybe he didn't think it was any of my business.

"You never did tell us," Peyton asked, leaning in and waggling her brows. "When you pulled that stinger out, did you get a look at the goods?"

I rolled my eyes, as Ruby and Demi both groaned while trying to hide their laughter.

"Of course not. Everything was covered up just fine." I shook my head. "I'm going to go grab another beer. Does anyone want one?"

"Hell yes," they all said at the same time, and I chuckled as I looked back at the firepit and noticed how tense Kingston's shoulders looked. He didn't appear to see me, and it was getting dark outside now, so I came up with the perfect plan.

I quickly moved toward the house and hurried to the side yard, where I knew there was a patch of dandelions. I picked the brightest flower, glancing over to make sure he wasn't looking, but he had his back to me now.

I dropped my empty bottle into the recycling bin and pulled out four new beer bottles, leaving them there on the counter before jogging down the hallway toward his bedroom.

I was going to hide this somewhere he'd least expect it. I made my way into his bathroom and glanced around.

We'd never hidden one in the other's shower before. I stepped in behind the curtain, looking around for the perfect spot. I tucked it between the shampoo bottle and the body wash. Damn. It smelled minty like Kingston, and I breathed in his body wash.

"I'll be right out!" a voice shouted from the distance, and I pushed the shower curtain all the way closed and stayed perfectly still. It was Kingston's voice. Maybe he was just grabbing something from his bedroom.

Shit.

*This was a bad idea.*

Say something.

Get out of his shower.

Footsteps moved closer, and I heard the click of the bathroom door closing.

It's now or never.

*Oh my gosh. This is bad. Really bad.*

My hand reached for the curtain just as a groan sounded from the other side, and I completely froze.

His breaths were coming fast.

Labored.

"Mmmm . . . so fucking good," he whispered, and I squeezed my thighs together, because there was no question what was happening on the other side of this shower curtain.

There was nothing I could do now.

I squeezed my eyes shut as his breathing escalated.

I knew he'd had a lot to drink, so maybe this was what drunk Kingston did when he didn't have a woman here.

I could imagine his hand sliding up and down his shaft, and the little groans that escaped his mouth had me using a hand to cover my mouth to keep quiet.

I squeezed my eyes closed to remain in control, as desire tingled between my legs. I was thankful for the music in the background coming from the backyard.

His breathing escalated.

He was close.

Another moan from Kingston had me tucking my lips beneath my teeth and breathing slowly through my nose.

"So fucking wet. So fucking tight," he whispered, and I

swear wetness pooled between my thighs. I couldn't even see him, and this was the hottest thing I'd ever experienced.

"Oh, fuck, Saylor." A gruff sound escaped his mouth, and he groaned.

*Saylor.*

He'd said my name?

I was trying to process what I'd just heard, as a loud banging came from what I imagined was his bedroom door, as it sounded distant. I heard some fumbling around and then the sound of his zipper before the water turned on, and I imagined he must be washing his hands.

"You in there, asshole?" Hayes shouted, and now he was outside the bathroom door.

What in the world was happening?

This had been a huge mistake.

I was scared shitless and also more turned on than I'd ever been.

And now my brother was here?

"Jesus." The sound of the door whipping open had me holding my breath. If they found me now, I wouldn't be able to look at Kingston ever again. "Can a man not have a fucking minute to take a shit?"

"That was my question. That green bean casserole is not sitting so well. I need some privacy," Hayes said.

*Oh, dear God. This isn't happening.*

I just listened to my brother's best friend get off to thoughts of me, and now my brother was going to come in and take a giant crap a few feet away from me?

"Oh, hell no. You can use the guest bathroom. The door to the bedroom is closed, so no one will bother you in there. But this is my sacred place." Kingston's voice was all tease, and I'll be damned if he didn't sound completely relaxed now.

*Unfortunately, I'm the one wound tight at the moment.*

"Fine. Don't tell anyone where I am. I'm going to need a

little time to myself. You got any magazines in there?" my brother said with a laugh.

"You are such a pain in the ass." Kingston laughed. "Let me grab you my *Sports Illustrated* from the nightstand."

Their voices were getting further away, and I just waited. It was completely silent now, and I was fairly certain they'd left.

And I desperately needed to get the hell out of here. I let out a long breath and peeked out from behind the curtain, not hearing anyone.

I stepped out of the shower and moved to the doorway, stretching my neck to see if anyone was in the bedroom.

The coast was clear.

I moved to his bedroom window and saw Kingston take his seat by the firepit again, and his head fell back in laughter.

Yeah. He was definitely relaxed now.

I hurried out of his bedroom and back to the kitchen, where I grabbed the four beers and made my way outside.

My heart was racing.

I couldn't believe what had just happened.

Maybe there was another Saylor that lived in Magnolia Falls?

I mean, I would be lying if I didn't admit to thinking of Kingston Pierce more times than I could count when I fantasized alone in my room.

But this was King. He didn't look at me that way.

"Saylor," his voice called as I was walking past, and I glanced over to see them all sitting around the firepit, smiling. "You need to back me up over here."

I walked toward the fire, his dark brown eyes glowing in the light from the moon. "Back you up how?" I asked, and my voice sounded a little hoarse, so I cleared my throat.

"Did you break up with Jalen because of the Speedo?" Romeo asked.

I rolled my eyes and shook my head. "Absolutely not."

It sure as hell didn't help, but I wouldn't say that was the reason.

Kingston's hand moved to his chest like he'd been shot. "You wound me, Saylor Woodson. I was sure that was the reason."

Why did he care so much about Jalen?

Was he jealous?

"So, what happened?" River asked. "He seemed to be really into you."

"He's a great guy. I just didn't feel that way about him."

Kingston's gaze never left mine, and his tongue swiped out along his bottom lip, and I nearly combusted right there.

On Easter Sunday of all days.

In front of all our friends and family.

I was having an out-of-body experience.

Imagining my brother's best friend standing in front of his sink, stroking his—

"Is there someone else you've got your eye on?" Kingston's voice was all tease, slurring the slightest bit from the whiskey he'd been sipping over the last few hours.

I straightened. "No. I'm just going to be single for a bit. Kind of like you, King. Maybe I'll play the field for a while."

He gave me a slow nod as the guys all laughed. River glanced from me to his brother, and I saw his wheels turning.

"It's not so bad out here," he said, raising his glass to me and winking.

I clinked my beer bottle against his glass. "All right, I'm going to take the girls their beers. You guys behave over here, okay?"

More laughter sounded as I sauntered down toward the water.

"Well, looky here. Did you go to the Daily Market to grab those beers?" Peyton asked as I handed them each a bottle.

"No. Just got sidetracked chatting with people."

Ruby raised a brow. "You look a little flushed. Are you feeling okay?"

"Yes. Of course. Never been better."

I dropped to sit in my chair and turned my head to glance over my shoulder, finding Kingston's eyes on me again.

My teeth sank into my bottom lip as I stared back.

"Well, I feel ten pounds lighter and much better!" Hayes shouted from the distance, and Kingston's gaze turned away quickly.

Just like that . . . he wasn't looking at me anymore.

He was a loyal best friend when he wasn't alone in the bathroom with his thoughts.

# 10

## Kingston

To say I felt lighter was a massive understatement.

I felt like a million bucks.

I'd thrown a fabulous fucking party.

Given Cutler a magical Easter egg hunt that he'd remember for years to come.

I'd had a few too many drinks.

I'd gotten off to thoughts of my best friend's little sister.

And fuck me, if it wasn't exactly what I'd needed.

Here's the thing . . . fantasies are exactly that. They aren't real. So, after being harassed all day about my bad mood, I knew what I needed. Five minutes alone in the bathroom, with thoughts of Saylor.

Her sweet mouth.

Her tight pussy.

Dirty thoughts.

Filthy thoughts.

And that was okay. Because I felt better. I hadn't acted on anything. I just needed a release. I'd get my mojo back, find a woman who took my mind off her soon enough, and this would all be a hilarious memory that I took to the grave.

No one would be the wiser.

It was not disloyal to be attracted to Saylor. It would be disloyal to act on that attraction.

The leftover effects of the whiskey had me feeling damn good, too. I'd been making my way toward the bathroom to take a shower when my phone rang.

Nash's name lit up my screen.

"What's up?" I answered.

"What's up, Uncle King?" Cutler's voice had me grinning big.

"How are you doing, Beefcake?"

"Good. We just got home. I told Pops I had the best Easter ever. I can't believe how many eggs that bunny brought for me. You must have said something to him, or maybe you know someone?"

I barked out a laugh. "Nah. It's all you, dude. The Easter Bunny knows who deserves all the eggs."

"Like Santa Claus knows I'm a good boy because my elf, Tater Tot, told him to bring me that motorized Jeep?"

*This fucking kid, man.*

He'd named his Christmas elf Tater Tot, which had been hilarious on its own . . . but Nash having to do all this elf shit every night was the funniest part of all. The guys and I got really into it, coming up with ideas every day to help him knock it out of the park. I'd built a mini fireplace for his elf, and we'd told him that Tater Tot must have built it.

We hadn't had fairy-tale childhoods, so if we could give one to Cutler, we'd move fucking mountains to make that happen.

"Exactly. It's impossible for anyone to miss that you're the coolest kid on the planet." I stepped into my bathroom and leaned against the vanity as I listened to the sound of his laughter.

"'Cause I've got the coolest uncles and pops around. And now that I have all my girls by my side, it's even better."

"You've got a lot of girls, Beefcake. You better pace yourself."

"I like all the girls, just like you, Uncle King. 'Cause I want to be just like you when I grow up."

"I thought you wanted to be just like me?" Nash grumped in the background, and I laughed.

"But Uncle King is the coolest. Even my other uncles told me that. They said he gets all the girls, and he builds things with his hands."

I was laughing hard now, knowing Nash was irritated as hell.

"I build things with my hands, too," Nash said, trying to act like he was irritated, but I heard the humor in his voice. I'd never known a better father than Nash Heart. He showed up every fucking day for his boy. He sacrificed and put his own needs aside. I only hoped I would be half the father he was if that day ever came.

"But you don't get the girls, Pops."

A fit of laughter coming from Cutler filled my ear, and I guessed Nash had scooped him up and was tickling him. "Hey, I've got *you*, Beefcake. I don't need a girl. I've got all I need right here."

My goddamn chest squeezed at his words.

Nash was raising this little guy on his own. Cutler's mom, Tara, rarely came into town anymore, and he was doing this whole parenting thing solo. Well, with the help of his four misfit best friends.

"Okay, say goodbye to Uncle King. I've got to get this stink bomb into the bathtub," Nash said over Cutler's laughter.

"All right. I'll talk to you tomorrow. Have a good night." I ended the call and reached over to turn on the water and stripped down before stepping into the shower.

Would it hurt to give myself some relief one more time

today? Now that I'd let myself go there, it was all I could think about.

Something caught my eye as I contemplated things. My hand was literally ready—ready to give in to temptation once again. But there was a fucking dandelion right there, between my body wash and my shampoo.

I let the water beat down on my back as I thought about it.

When had she come in here?

There was no way in hell it was when I was in here.

I would have known if she was hiding in my shower, wouldn't I?

Well, my need to grip my dick was no longer my priority. I had a flashback to the glorious minutes I'd given myself, and sure, I'd thought of Saylor. But I hadn't said anything incriminating.

I washed my hair quickly as I thought about it.

I did have a habit of being somewhat vocal.

Women had always appreciated my charm right along with my filthy mouth.

*Did I say her name aloud?*

There was no way she was even in this bathroom at the same time. And the chance that I'd said her name aloud was slim.

I was overthinking this.

There was only one way to test the theory. I gripped my dick in my hand, hard. I didn't have the luxury to take my sweet time. I stroked up and down, squeezing my eyes closed and seeing her face.

*Her lips part as I drop to my knees.*

*I bury my face between her thighs and hike her legs over my shoulders.*

*I lick her sweet pussy, and she responds by tangling her fingers in my hair.*

*My tongue slips inside as she rides my face, and the sound of her falling apart against my lips is more than I can handle.*

My breaths were coming hard and fast as I found my release on a groan. "Fuck, Saylor."

*Fuck me.*

Well, I'd always been a verbal guy. No arguing that.

But the likelihood that she'd been in the bathroom was so minute. I had nothing to worry about. I cleaned myself up and turned off the water. I dried my hair off quickly before wrapping a towel around my waist and stepping out of the shower. My phone vibrated on the counter, and I glanced down.

DANDELION

Just wanted to thank you for today. It was such a great party.

She wouldn't be acting normal if she knew what I'd done in the bathroom. Hell, she probably wouldn't be able to look at me, much less speak to me, if she knew the thoughts going through my head twenty-four hours a day.

This was a good sign. I could definitely feel her out. I dropped my towel and went to my room to pull on a pair of briefs before climbing into bed and texting her back.

You know I don't mind hosting. You and Ruby did all the hard work. You let me off easy. By the way, I just took a shower and found a little something in there. You're getting stealthier.

DANDELION

I try.

I never saw you sneak away. How'd you pull that off?

DANDELION

I knew I needed to up my game because I can't have you showing me up.

Sneaking into a man's bathroom is risky.

DANDELION

There were no risks taken. You were busy smoking cigars by the firepit. It was a piece of cake.

Relief flooded. She hadn't heard a damn thing.

It was a good night. I saw you talking with your mom for a while. How was that?

DANDELION

It's hard, you know? She's staying with a man who has caused our family a lot of pain. I don't know how to handle that sometimes. I know that Hayes wants me to just draw a line in the sand, but I can't do that to her. I don't know why.

I leaned my back against the headboard and thought about it. I understood Saylor's need to fix things with her mother, but

I also respected Hayes's need to protect her from something toxic.

It's because you have a big heart. The best heart. Always have. You feel things deeply. No shame in that. But Hayes has witnessed too much. He's seen the way it's hurt you. What it's done to your family. So, I guess you're both right.

DANDELION

I struggle with the finality of drawing that line in the sand, you know? My brother is the best man I know (of course, you're right there with him 😉). I love him so much, but he has to let me figure things out for myself. I'm not a kid anymore. I need to navigate my own relationship with my mother.

I scrubbed a hand over my jaw.

I think walking in on that horrible scene all those years ago really traumatized Hayes, you know? Seeing you fall the way you did. You were unconscious, Saylor.

We'd never talked about what happened since she'd left my house all those years ago. Hayes went silent after that, too, aside from sharing his anger toward his stepfather. She'd shared more with me than he probably knew she had, during the months she lived at my house. And I'd never repeated anything that she'd told me.

DANDELION

I know. I remember it like it was yesterday. I still have nightmares sometimes about coming to and seeing Hayes on top of Barry. About being taken out of our home. All of it. But I lived it, too. And I should be allowed to deal with the aftermath the way I best see fit.

I understand that. He just loves you so damn much. In his mind, you're his only family, Saylor. Aside from all of us, of course. But you know what I mean.

DANDELION

And I love him so much it hurts. But he's not my father. He's my brother. It's just so messy, and I hate that things are so complicated.

It doesn't have to be. At the end of the day, you both love one another, and that's all that matters. That man would walk through fire for you.

DANDELION

That's why I want to prove myself to him. I know how much Hayes has sacrificed for me. It kills me when I think about it. All the things he's given up for me.

When they'd been allowed to go back to their parents' home after more than six months of living apart, things had been rocky. Hayes had ended up turning down a college football scholarship, and he'd started training to be a firefighter, working two jobs at the time, to get an apartment so that Saylor could live with him until she graduated from high school. He'd become her legal guardian at the time, with no argument from their mother. He'd sacrificed a lot—and had zero regrets.

He wouldn't want you feeling bad about any of that. That's what you do for family.

DANDELION

Well, you did the same thing for me, King. I don't know that I ever thanked you enough for that.

It was nothing. I'd do it again in a heartbeat.

DANDELION

I wouldn't have survived back then without you. And now you worked your ass off to get my bookstore up and going. What would I do without you?

You'll never have to find out. Remember, you saved me back then, too. Teaching me how to wish on dandelions was a game changer. 😉

DANDELION

Yeah? Well, River seems happier than I've ever seen him, which I know is what you always wanted for your brother. And now you got my bookstore up quicker than expected. How about you close your eyes and wish for something for yourself?

So, your theory is that if I close my eyes, I'm going to see what I want?

I reached for my whiskey that I'd set on the nightstand beside the bed and took a long pull.

DANDELION

Just trust me. It works every time.

I already have everything I want.

DANDELION

Stop being so stubborn. Close your damn eyes and tell me what you see.

I chuckled. She was cute as hell when she was bossy.

Fine. You know I never could say no to you. I'm closing my eyes now.

When I squeezed my lids closed, I saw Saylor's face.

Aqua blue eyes.

Pouty, plump lips.

And just like that, my eyes popped open as my dick sprung to life.

DANDELION

Well, what did you see?

I saw a glass of whiskey—and seeing as I have one right here in my hand, I guess my wish has already come true.

I shook my head, disgusted with myself.

I'd gotten off to her twice tonight, and now I was seeing her every time I closed my eyes.

It was time to pull my head out of my ass and get my shit together.

This ends now.

DANDELION

You're no fun. I thought you'd see something good.

She had no fucking idea just how good it was.

# 11

## Saylor

I'd spent these past few days getting all my books unpacked and organized on the bookshelves. The store was set up and ready to go. Peyton, Ruby, and Demi were dropping in to help me whenever they weren't working. They'd each given me an hour or two a day this last week, and I'd appreciated it so much.

I was opening the doors to Love Ever After as the only employee because I couldn't afford to hire anyone else just yet. We'd need to see how sales went before I could even explore that option.

"Are you sitting down?" Demi asked as she came through the connecting door from the coffee shop.

I chuckled as I looked up at her from where I sat on the stool behind the checkout counter. "I don't think I have a choice. I'm so tired that I don't think I could stand up if I wanted to."

"You've been pushing so hard." Demi paused as she stood on the other side of the counter and smiled at me. "You know how the doors are opening on Monday?"

"Yep. I'm working around the clock, so that's all I think about."

"Well, what do you have planned for the following weekend? The Saturday after your grand opening?"

"Just hoping to sell some books every day after the opening." There was no hiding the exhaustion in my voice.

Demi's teeth sank into her bottom lip, and her eyes widened. "I have a surprise for you."

"I could use one. Give it to me."

"Well, you met Brinkley, Romeo's sister-in-law, the day that Romeo proposed to me. Do you remember her?"

Romeo's brother, Lincoln Hendrix, was a famous NFL player, and his wife, Brinkley, was a sports reporter.

"Yes. She's great. I really liked her. She's a bridesmaid for you, right?"

"Yes. So you will be seeing even more of her. But that's not the big news . . . I'd told her about your bookstore a few weeks ago, and she said she had an idea that might be great for Love Ever After. She didn't tell me much about it at the time, but she called a little while ago to fill me in."

"What is it?" She had me perking up with excitement.

"I told you that Brinkley's sister, Georgia, is in the publishing business, and she was so excited to hear that you were opening a bookstore. Well, Brinkley and Georgia decided to call their cousin to see if she could come here on the Saturday after your opening to have a book signing. You'll never guess who their cousin is."

"What? Who is their cousin?" My heart raced with anticipation.

"*Ashlan freaking Thomas*. Only one of the most popular romance authors out there right now."

I was on my feet, running around the counter, my hands flying through the air. "Ashlan Thomas is coming to my bookstore for a book signing?"

We clasped our hands together and jumped up and down.

"Yep. She'll be here next weekend. She's going to have the books shipped directly here to your store in time for the signing. We need to start making sure everyone in town knows about it."

"I'll post it on all of my social media, and I can make a bunch of flyers tonight to hand out to all the businesses downtown, as well as make sure everyone who attends the opening knows she'll be coming. I can't believe this. Thank you so much."

"Of course. I would do anything for you."

"I know, but you've got the wedding coming up and your own business to run. I know how busy you are."

She put a hand on each of my shoulders. "And you've been there for me since the day you moved back to town. I appreciate you so much, and I want this bookstore to be successful. You deserve all the best things, Saylor."

My eyes watered, and I shook my head. Demi and I had grown so close, and I was honored that I'd be standing up for her on her special day. She, Peyton, and Ruby had become my best friends, and now I didn't know how I ever existed without them.

"Thank you so much."

"Okay. No time for tears. I've got to get to the gym, but I'll text you later and see what you want me to do. I can make a flyer for you tonight, and you can work on the social media posts. I know Ruby and Peyton are working on some fun surprises for you for the grand opening. We've got this." She gave me a quick hug and waved goodbye before heading out the door.

I walked around the counter and heard my phone vibrate.

KING

The opening is just a few days away. I've been swamped at work, but I stopped by on my way to the jobsite earlier. I found a book on your shelves that seemed like the right one to hide something for you, so see if you can figure it out. Use your detective skills, and you'll find it. And then . . . close your eyes and make a wish.

When were you here?

I hadn't seen Kingston since Easter Sunday. We'd both been busy this week, and we hadn't texted, which was very out of character.

I'd been avoiding him because I couldn't stop thinking about what had happened in the bathroom.

The way I'd liked the sound of my name on his lips when he'd groaned in pleasure.

That I'd found my own pleasure replaying the sound of his voice every single night since.

*But why is he avoiding me?*

He didn't know I'd heard him.

Very stealthy. I'm looking now. But I should tell you . . . Demi just told me that Ashlan Thomas is coming here next weekend to do a book signing. She's Brinkley Reynolds's cousin, and she's a famous romance author. So, it'll be hard for me to wish for more than that at the moment.

KING

That's pretty damn cool. After you find your surprise and you close your eyes, are you supposed to see Ashlan Thomas? Is that how your system works?

I laughed as my eyes scanned the bookshelves. He said it seemed like the right book for him to choose. My gaze stopped on the forbidden romance section. I moved closer, taking in the gold-foiled spine that read *Forbidden King*.

*I don't think there could be a more fitting title.*

I pulled the book from the shelf and smiled when I saw what was resting on top of the pages. He'd placed it there so it wouldn't get damaged, as it was a fluffball dandelion—the kind you made a wish on. I turned my phone screen around so it was facing me and held it up, making my lips look like I was blowing on the flower, and I snapped a selfie.

Very clever book choice.

KING

Jesus, Saylor. You can't send me pics like that when I'm on the jobsite.

My eyes widened at his text, and I opened the photo again and studied it. What was wrong with this photo?

What's wrong with this pic? I'm blowing on the dandelion.

KING

Exactly my point. Those fucking lips. Now close your eyes and make a wish. If I'm going to be suffering in discomfort, at least let it be worth you getting something out of it.

Realization set in. Did it just get hot in here?

This attraction was definitely mutual.

*Forbidden King.*

It was the reason we'd been avoiding one another, wasn't it? We just weren't saying it out loud.

I closed my eyes . . . and I sure as hell did not see a book signing at my bookstore.

I saw Kingston. Standing over me. Hands on his hips, with me looking up at him from where I had dropped to my knees.

Holy hell.

My eyes sprung open.

I squeezed my thighs together in response and looked down at my phone.

KING

Well, what did you see? Was it Ashlan Thomas at your bookstore?

It was not. I guess that title was very fitting for the situation. 😉

There. I said it. He'd admitted it, so I may as well do the same.

KING

Damn, Dandelion. Good to know. See you at the opening.

That was evil.

KING

You have no idea.

I'd forced myself to focus for the next three days until the grand opening. Kingston and I hadn't texted again, and I'd tried hard to keep my focus on work.

I was busy, after all.

Fantasizing about my brother's best friend was a complete waste of time.

I knew enough to know that Kingston would never act on anything. And it was a one-way road to heartache anyway. I wasn't looking for a fling. That wasn't really my style.

Though I'd never had a fling, so I'd never say never.

"You ready?" Demi asked as the door flung open, and I turned my attention to my girls.

Ruby, Demi, and Peyton had rallied around me to get things ready for today, and I was grateful.

They'd baked and stayed up late, helping me get this place ready for the grand opening.

"Yes. I'm as ready as I'll ever be." I blew out a long breath.

"You look like a sexy librarian," Peyton said, and Demi and Ruby both laughed.

"You look gorgeous." Demi gave me a hug.

"There is already a line forming outside. I can't even imagine next week when you have the book signing for Ashlan." Ruby took a bite of a chocolate-covered strawberry and groaned. "Damn, these are so good."

"I thought they were a good romance bookstore snack," Peyton said, admiring the chocolate-covered goodness she'd made for the opening.

"How do you figure?" Demi asked, with a wicked grin on her face as she reached for one and took a bite.

"Warm chocolate. Sexy men. Speaking of sexy men, I saw Coach in line outside with some flowers. Apparently, he's coming for your big day. You sure you don't want to drip some chocolate down his ripped abdomen and lick it off?"

"Girl, you've got a one-track mind," Ruby said before

waggling her brows. "But do you have some leftover chocolate that I can take over to River's tonight?"

My head fell back in laughter, and I patted down the skirt of my white and pink sundress. "You can take it all. I won't be needing it."

Jalen and I had remained on good terms since I'd been honest with him about our relationship being better off as just a friendship.

I glanced around the place one last time before I opened the doors. We'd gone with rustic wood planks on the floors, and the bookshelves were sage green, with four-inch thick molding and gorgeous detail, and the checkout stand that Kingston had built for me was topped off with a white quartz countertop. Janelle, who owned Sweet Magnolia a few doors down, had dropped off a vase full of pink peonies for me, and they were sitting on the counter, looking more like a piece of art.

"Hey, hey," Kingston called out, as he and all the guys came walking through the side door from Demi's coffee shop. "Big day today for our girl."

Hayes and River each had a case of bottled water in their hands. Romeo had two sleeves of clear cups, which Demi wanted to be placed next to the lemonade station she'd set up. Nash was holding Cutler's hand, and Kingston had a big bouquet of flowers.

"These are from all of us, and Beefcake picked them out from Janelle's shop." He handed them to me, and I didn't miss the way his eyes quickly raked over me from head to toe.

"Thank you so much," I said.

"Happy opening on your love bookstore," Cutler said, and my eyes widened as I took him in.

"Thank you. I like your hat."

"It's a fedora. It's very cool, right? I wanted to wear something special for your big day." He dropped his dad's hand, and I bent down to give him a hug. "I like having you live here all the time, Saylor. And I'm going to come to your bookstore and read all the books."

Nash cleared his throat. "How about we bring your magic fantasy books that we just got for you, and you can read those here?"

"But I want to woo my ladies. That's what Uncle King told me these books are about. He said they would teach me everything I need to know someday."

Nash put his hands over both of Cutler's ears. "For fuck's sake. Seriously?"

Kingston smiled, and my heart raced in response. His broad shoulders were straining against his white tee. His denim jeans showed off his finely toned ass and long legs. He had a pair of cowboy boots on, and his dark hair looked like he'd just run his fingers through it and walked out the door. He was sexy as hell, and I felt this pull toward him lately that was becoming more and more difficult to ignore.

"Take your hands off his ears and I'll explain," he said, a wicked grin on his face.

Nash removed his hands and raised an eyebrow as he waited.

"What I told my little man here is that romance books are books that women read, which means it's what they want. So, when Beefcake *grows up*, he should consider these books his . . . education on how to win over the ladies, so to speak."

"Wait. Is this your defense? He's six years old," Nash hissed.

Kingston shrugged. "Today, he's six years old. I was six years old . . . yesterday. I wish someone had told me about these books a long time ago. I've been reading every night now, and let me tell you, I am learning a whole lot about what women want." He winked at me.

"You hate reading," River said, shaking his head and laughing.

"Not anymore. I've been reading the *Landmark Mountain* series by Willow Aster, and these dudes have game. You guys could learn a thing or two from the Landmark brothers."

"You're reading a romance series? Who are you, and what have you done with Kingston Pierce?" Hayes said, after he set down the cases of water next to the cooler I'd filled with ice.

"Don't knock it till you try it." Kingston's gaze locked with mine. "You boys have a whole lot to learn."

"I'm sure all the women in Magnolia Falls will be very pleased that you've found a love for romance books." Hayes shook his head and laughed as he continued placing the water bottles into the cooler.

"I'm all about pleasing the ladies," Kingston said, his gaze never leaving mine.

Ruby cleared her throat, and I quickly turned to look at her, and she raised a brow. "I think it's time to open the doors."

I was grateful my brother was preoccupied, and everyone else was too busy having their own little side conversations to notice the way Kingston was looking at me.

The way I was pretty sure I was looking at him.

But Ruby definitely noticed.

I shook it off and moved toward the doors.

Today felt special.

*Like the first day of the rest of my life.*

I turned the lock on the door and pushed it open.

Here we go.

# 12

## Kingston

"Are you getting a commission for this?" Hayes asked, as he came to sit beside me on the pink velvet couch that Saylor had on one side of the bookstore. It was the first time I'd sat down since she'd opened the doors.

Everyone in town had come out to support her. It was great to see. No one deserved it more than Saylor.

I crossed my feet at the ankles as I glanced over at Cutler talking to Oscar Daily, who owned the grocery store in town, the Daily Market. Our boy looked like a cool cat with his fedora. The kid had more swagger than any six-year-old should be allowed.

"What can I say? I'm a natural when it comes to selling love. Who knew?" My voice was all tease.

"You were a born salesman." Hayes shook his head. "But tell me this . . . how does one sell love when they've never experienced it?"

"You are one naïve, bitter bastard." I laughed. "How does a plastic surgeon sell a procedure he hasn't had done to himself? How does a pharmaceutical rep sell drugs they don't need to take? How does a lactose-intolerant ice cream maker sell ice cream he can't eat? It's about believing in it, not experiencing it."

"How many lactose-intolerant ice cream makers do you know?" His lips twitched as he tried to keep from laughing.

"There are plenty out there. Let me tell you, dairy has been doing a number on my digestive system lately." I shrugged. "And how do you know I've never been in love?"

He raised a brow, resting his elbows on his knees. "Because I've known you my whole life. Are you telling me I'm wrong?"

"I'm telling you that I don't like being put into a box." I leaned forward, glancing over my shoulder to make sure no one was listening. "Unless by box, we're talking about a pussy, and then you can put me in there all day."

Loud laughter bellowed from him, and I couldn't help but smile. Hayes didn't laugh often, and I'd always been the one to make him do it when he did. It was an honor I wore proudly. Because Hayes Woodson was one of the best men I'd ever known. I liked to give him a hard time, but he was good to his core.

"Anyway, thank you, brother. You've stepped up for Saylor big time, and I'm grateful. You got this place up and built quickly, and I appreciate it. It means a lot."

"You know I'd do anything for her," I said, quickly backing up my words. "All of us would. She's family."

He nodded. "Yeah, I wanted to talk to you about that."

My stomach dipped. There was no way he could know what was going on in my head lately. I hadn't told a soul that I'd been getting myself off to thoughts of my best friend's little sister.

Those were words you didn't say out loud unless you had a death wish.

Hell, those were words I was never supposed to allow myself to think either.

I cleared my throat. "Go on."

"I didn't want to tell Saylor today, it being her big day and all. But Cook called me last night," he said, keeping his voice low. John Cook was the fire captain at Magnolia Falls Firehouse.

"Everything all right? Is he announcing his retirement?" I asked, because I knew that he'd be retiring in the next few years, and Hayes wanted that job badly. He was a Lieutenant now, and it was the next step in his career. And he fucking deserved it. The dude was the best out there.

"Nah. He's not there yet. But apparently, there are some bad forest fires dangerously close to Barley Creek outside of Rosewood River, and they need help. They are gathering guys from each station in the outlying towns to try to help. Cook wants to send a few of ours out there for the next couple of weeks, if necessary, and he wants me to lead the crew there."

"Damn. I'm sorry to hear that. You'll be safe, yeah?" I asked. I worried about him when he went into these types of situations. Hayes was trained for this, but that didn't stop any of us from worrying.

"Always. That's not why I'm telling you." He rubbed his hands together, and I followed his gaze to his sister. The dress she wore managed to be sexy as hell, with the thin straps resting on her tan shoulders. The front dipped low, outlining her perky tits, and I'd cussed myself out many times today for the thoughts I'd had. The skirt on her dress hit her mid-thigh, and the desire to drop to my knees and bury my head between her legs was strong.

I was a fucking asshole for having these thoughts.

But I'd save them for when I was alone later tonight.

"What is it?" I asked, keeping my voice low.

"I wanted to see if you'd keep an eye on Saylor while I'm gone. I'm heading out in about an hour. Ruby's over at River's every night, and Saylor's alone at their place. Lionel told me Barry's been to Whiskey Falls a lot lately, which means he's drinking again. And when that asshole drinks, it's never a good thing. He's got a chip on his shoulder that he isn't included in anything with us, and he sure as shit won't come to me about it. He'll go to her, which he wouldn't dare if he thought he'd run into me. But the minute he knows I'm out of town, he'll be looking for her. I want to make sure he stays the fuck away from my sister, you know? I just don't trust the dude. Never will."

"Yeah. Don't give it a second thought. I can keep an eye out. She and I talk often. I can stop by and make sure she's all right as often as you want me to." It was the truth. I would do anything for him. For her. But there was a lot of guilt weighing on me for the attraction I was fighting. I knew if I could just go out and get laid, it would probably go away.

But I hadn't been able to.

I didn't want anyone else at the moment, and that had never happened.

So, I'd just wait it out. That's why I'd been trying to keep my distance from her.

But it hadn't passed yet.

And Hayes needed me, and there was no hesitation. I'd always say yes.

"Thanks, brother. I know River's busy with Ruby, and Romeo is in over his head wedding planning with Demi, and Nash has Cutler."

"So, what are you saying? I have no life, and that's why you're asking me?" My voice was laced with humor, but I feigned irritation.

I'd never be irritated about helping Saylor.

In a lot of ways, it felt like my purpose.

I'd always wanted to be that person for her.

"Don't be a sensitive asshole. Of course not. I'm asking you because I trust you, brother. I trusted you all those years ago with her, and I trust you today."

A heaviness settled on my chest, just as River, Nash, and Romeo came over to sit with us.

"Hey now," I said, as they crowded me. "Give a man some space."

"Mrs. fucking Brighton just squeezed my ass. I'm done with these horny women today. Make room for me," Nash grumped, and everyone laughed. I was smashed between him and Romeo, and River and Hayes sat on the loveseat across from us.

Hayes filled them in about leaving town for a bit, and we all discussed his concern that Barry would find out he was out of town.

"King's going to keep a close eye on her, and he'll let you know if anything goes down. I appreciate you all having my back while I'm gone. I shouldn't be away too long."

River leaned forward, meeting each of our gazes. "*Ride or die. Brothers till the end. Loyalty always. Forever my friend.*"

We all repeated the words. It had been our mantra for as long as I could remember.

"You never need to worry. We've got you," Romeo said.

"King, you just say the word if you need us." Nash clapped me on the shoulder.

"Of course. I've got this."

But it was River's eyes that found mine and studied me.

There was a warning there.

*Don't cross the line.*

I'd never told my brother about my attraction to Saylor.

Nor had I shared just how deep our friendship ran during the time she'd stayed with us all those years ago.

There'd been no reason to.

Nothing had happened, therefore there was nothing to discuss.

I was a grown-ass man. I could handle myself.

We pushed to our feet, and Hayes was going to let Saylor

know that he was leaving. I'd promised to help her lock up here and make sure she got home safely. The place was thinning out.

He pulled me into a hug. "Thank you, brother. I owe you."

"You owe me nothing." I clapped him on the back, and everyone started saying their goodbyes.

"Uncle King, will you come ride with me and my girls this weekend again?" Cutler asked.

"How's the devil's driveway feeling?" Nash leaned against me and whispered in my ear with a laugh.

"It's finally healing," I said under my breath before turning to the little dude in front of me. "Yeah. I just need to make sure I grab a saddle this time."

The guys all laughed, and I gave a few high-fives, and they held their hands up in a wave and walked out the door.

Saylor turned around to look at me with a puzzled look on her face. "Are you staying to help me finish up?"

"Yeah. I thought you could use some help." I shoved my hands into my pockets.

Her gaze searched mine, and she looked upset. I knew she was worried about her brother. "Did you know he was leaving before today?"

"Nope. He just told us."

"And he asked you to watch out for me, didn't he?" she said, and she wasn't smiling the way she usually did. Saylor was stronger than most people knew. She was sweet and kind, but she also had this inner strength that I'd witnessed many times. She was protective of the people that she loved, her brother being at the top of that list.

"I'm not going to lie to you. You know he worries about you. And if I'm being honest, he has every right to worry about Barry. The guy is a drunk asshole."

She raised a brow, not hiding her irritation. "You know what? I think you and Hayes should worry about yourselves.

I think there's plenty to dive into there, don't you?" Anger radiated from her hot little body.

"I can't believe you're this mad about me looking out for you. It's not a big deal. You had a long day. We're friends." I shrugged. "And I'm not sure what you're talking about with me and Hayes, but have at it if it makes you feel better."

I glanced outside the window, noting it was completely dark now. It had been a long day, and I'm sure she was tired. She stormed around the other side of the counter and looked up at me with fire in her pretty gaze. She stood almost a foot shorter than me, blonde hair falling down around her shoulders.

"Let's unpack this, then. Hayes is a goddamn firefighter," she hissed. "And now he's going to fight a wildfire. But by all means, the concern should be on me and my romance bookstore."

I couldn't stop the chuckle that left my lips, and she narrowed her gaze. "I'm not laughing at you. You make a valid point, that's all. But Barry is here, and that was his concern. Not you."

"Then why don't you babysit Barry?" She crossed her arms over her chest, and my eyes moved to where her tits were pressed above her arms before quickly shooting back up to look at her.

"Because no one gives a shit about Barry as long as he stays the fuck away from you."

"That's what I thought. You guys are such hypocrites." She started slamming things into the register, and I didn't know where all this hostility was coming from.

"Hey now. Don't turn this on me. I'm helping out a friend."

"Are you?" Her tongue swiped out along her bottom lip, and I had to adjust myself when my dick throbbed against the zipper of my jeans.

"Am I helping out a friend?" I asked, not hiding the surprise in my voice. "Are we not friends anymore?"

"I don't know. You tell me."

"I think we're friends. I think we'll always be friends." I crossed my arms over my chest and studied her.

"So that's the only reason you agreed to babysit me?"

"Don't say it like that. You know I consider you one of my best friends."

"Yet you've avoided me since Easter. Was that because we weren't friends during that time?"

I shrugged. "I would never avoid you. We've both been busy. I didn't see you calling me this last week either."

"You're correct. Because I was avoiding you."

"You were intentionally avoiding me?" I asked, shaking my head in disbelief.

"Yep. I'm not too proud to admit it." She walked around the counter and tipped her head up to look at me. She held the dandelion I'd left on the counter in her hand. "To admit that I'm confused by what I feel for you."

"There's nothing to be confused about, Saylor. We're friends. Close friends."

"Do you get off to all your friends in the middle of a party in your bathroom?" she whispered, and my fucking mouth went dry.

*She'd fucking heard me.*

I wouldn't deny it. I couldn't look her in the eyes and deny it.

"Saylor."

"King," she mimicked me. "Answer the question."

"Fuck. I'm sorry you heard that. I'm a horny asshole."

She nodded once, her gaze locking with mine. "What did you mean when you chose the book *Forbidden King*? Are you forbidden, King?"

I looked away for a minute, trying to gather my thoughts. She was so close, and my body was reacting. My dick was throbbing uncomfortably behind my zipper. My heart pounded in my ears. "Obviously, being best friends with your brother makes us both forbidden, right?"

"So, I'm curious. Do you want to kiss me as much as I want to kiss you?" Her hand fisted in the fabric of my tee.

"That wasn't the question."

"Well then, I guess there's a new question for you."

I reached for the flower in her hand. I don't know why I did it. I ran the yellow petals along her bottom lip slowly. Back and forth. My free hand moved to cover the side of her neck, while my thumb grazed along her jaw. My mouth watered at the way her plump lips parted for me. "Do I want to kiss you? That's the question? Of course, I've thought about it."

Her eyes fell closed, and she whispered. "Then do something about it."

# 13

## Saylor

The feel of the petals grazing along my bottom lip, while his hand was wrapped around the side of my neck, thumb slowly tracing the line of my jaw . . . was overwhelming.

I'd never been so turned on from just a hand on my face.

This made no sense.

This attraction. This pull. It was like nothing I'd ever experienced.

"Can't go there, Saylor." His voice was gruff, and my eyes sprung open.

Mortification set in as I searched his gaze and realized he wasn't going to kiss me.

Here I was, panting over the man who was barely touching me, and he was turning me down.

The feeling was familiar in ways I couldn't begin to explain. This feeling in my life like I wasn't good enough. This battle I had with myself about not allowing anyone to make me feel that way again.

I stepped back immediately.

"Got it. Then let's stop playing games, okay?" I moved around the counter and locked the register before grabbing my purse.

He just stared at me with this look I couldn't quite pinpoint. I knew Kingston Pierce better than most. He was a good man with a big heart. He'd never intentionally hurt me.

But did that make the situation any better? Not really.

Did anyone intentionally hurt anyone? I don't know. But it wasn't much of a defense either.

I walked toward the door, and he followed me outside as I turned to lock the bookstore up. When I glanced over at him, he looked like he'd just committed a crime.

"I'm fine, King. You don't have to feel bad about it. I never expected anything to happen." I started walking, and he found his stride beside me.

"The only thing I feel bad about is you hearing me in the bathroom. That was so fucking wrong, Saylor. I just had a lot of pent-up frustration, and it was the release that I needed."

I tried to hide my smile as I turned to look at him. "Life of a playboy, huh? Always chasing your next release?"

"It's not like that." He stared straight ahead.

"Your house is in the other direction. You do not need to walk me home."

"So if I don't kiss you, I don't get to walk you home?" he teased, and I slapped him on the arm.

"No. It's not that. But I already told you . . . I don't need a babysitter."

"Well, you're stuck with me. So, deal with it."

I huffed and didn't respond. We walked in silence the rest of the way. When we made our way up the steps to my front door, I paused and turned around. "I'd say you've done your job. I'm good."

"Are you mad at me, Dandelion?" he asked, and he looked so tormented it took everything I had not to hug him. This was a pattern for me. Always trying to make everyone else feel better. Always putting other people's feelings first and my own needs second.

"I'm not mad. Not at all. I'm just . . ." I shook my head and looked away.

"Come on. Tell me what you're thinking. We've never held back from one another. We've always been honest."

"Okay. I have a father who didn't fight for me. A father who let me go live with friends instead of stepping up and helping me and Hayes when we were taken from our home. A father with a lot of money who just chose not to help us. Help me. And I tend to be drawn to that. You know, finding people that don't put me first. Grahame, my college boyfriend, is a perfect example. He loved me, but not enough to make me a priority. He always put football first. His family. His friends. And I finally had enough, but it took me a long time to realize that it's a pattern for me. Me trying to be enough, you know? So here I am again, about to kiss a man I've known forever, a man I'm fairly certain is attracted to me, too, and—I'm still not enough." I swiped at the tear that broke free and rolled down my cheek. "And I'm not doing that again. I just dated Coach who was crazy about me, and for whatever reason, I didn't feel it for him. Maybe I'm doomed because I have daddy issues."

"Saylor," he said, his voice strained as he moved closer. "That is not what this is."

"All right. I was honest with you. How about you grant me the same respect."

He nodded, reaching forward and tucking my hair behind my ear. "You want the truth? I'll give it to you. I'm so fucking attracted to you it's painful. I haven't been with a woman in months, and nobody knows that. I think about you all the time. But I've never been in a relationship. I don't know if I'm capable. But that is on me, not on you. You are enough, I can assure you of that. You are so much more than enough. I get off to thoughts of you every fucking day. Don't you ever say that you aren't enough, because there is no one that compares to you."

My breath hitched in my throat, and my eyes widened. "But . . ."

He shook his head. "It's not like I can date you and see where it goes. It doesn't work that way with us. Your brother is family to me. He's my best friend. He trusts me. The five of us have a bond. And it's not a line I can cross casually. So, I can't go there, and it's not because I don't want to. And it's not because you aren't enough. *It's because I'm not enough.* And if I fucked this up, it would affect a lot of people."

I shook my head in disbelief. "Do you hear yourself? That's so ridiculous. No one knows when they first date what's going to happen. I wanted to have feelings for Coach, and I just didn't. But I didn't run from it. I gave it a chance, and it didn't work out. I was honest with him, and we're still friends. That's what grown-ups do."

"To an extent, that's what I do with other women. I know how dating works. I've always been honest with the women I've dated and the women I've hooked up with. *But they are not you.* And you and me—we can't do what you and Coach did. We can't test the waters, because if it ended poorly, Hayes would never forgive me. The guys would tell me I was being selfish. And they'd be right. This attraction, these feelings, they'll pass. We've always been close friends, and if I fucked that up—I would never recover from that."

I shrugged. "Well, we can agree to disagree. It's no one's business. I don't need my brother's permission to kiss someone or date someone. Life is about making mistakes and learning from them. Chasing things that feel right and acting on them. Hayes has made his fair share of mistakes, too. I don't get to tell him what to do. I asked you to kiss me, King. I didn't ask you to walk down the aisle. You're making this too big a deal."

He moved closer, my back pressed against the front door. He moved both his hands to each side of my face now. His dark gaze searched mine beneath the moonlight.

"One kiss?" he asked, his tongue swiping out to wet his lips.

"One kiss. Then we'll laugh about it later and go back to normal. No one has to know. It's our secret. We've kept secrets before."

That was all it took, apparently, because his lips crashed into mine.

He tipped my head back the slightest bit as his tongue slipped in and tangled with mine. My arms wrapped around him, my hands twisting in his dark hair, tugging him closer. My entire body tingled, as he groaned into my mouth, kissing me like I was the air he needed to breathe.

My body sparked to life in a way I'd never experienced from just a kiss.

I was lost in the feel of his lips against mine.

Of his tongue exploring my mouth.

And he pulled back, eyes wild with need. "Well, it's official. I'm fucked."

I smiled up at him. "Not too shabby for a one-and-done."

"It was hot as hell, and you know it." He took a step back, shoving his hands into his pockets.

"I won't deny it. But I'm not the one who needs everyone's approval to act on it." I smirked. "Have a good night, King. I'm guessing a cold shower is in your future."

"You're enjoying this, aren't you?" he asked, as he walked backward down the walkway.

I held up my thumb and forefinger and kept them about an inch apart. "A little bit."

"Get inside. I'll text you later."

I laughed as I put the key in the door and stepped into the house. I dropped my keys on the counter and fell onto the couch.

I'd just kissed Kingston Pierce.

And it was the best freaking kiss of my life.

*He really is a forbidden king.*

It had been a day, and I moved to my feet, making my way to the bathroom before turning on the water to fill the tub. I hurried to the kitchen to pour myself a glass of wine.

The bookstore opening had gone off without a hitch, and I'd sold far more books than I'd anticipated, which meant I'd need to check inventory and restock items this week.

I'd had an emotional outburst with King, followed by the sexiest kiss of my life.

A girl could only handle so much in one day.

I poured a hearty glass of chardonnay and made my way to the bathroom and turned off the water. I placed my wineglass and phone on the little table beside the freestanding bathtub. The smell of my lavender bath salts filled the room as I stripped down and tied my hair up in a messy knot on top of my head. I slipped into the hot water and groaned at how good it felt.

I thought about my conversation with King. About how I was done settling for anyone who didn't want me to be their priority. I thought about how much my relationship with my biological father had affected my life. I resented him for it, but a part of me still wished for a relationship with him. I wanted to know my other siblings, too.

My father had reached out to congratulate me when I graduated from college. I had stopped trying, and now it seemed like he was making more of an effort. He lived just one town over in South Clarita Hills, and he'd asked if I'd be willing to meet for lunch, but I hadn't answered yet. Hayes wanted nothing to do with him, and I understood it, even if I didn't feel the same. I'd learned to have boundaries to protect my heart where my father was concerned. Hell, I had to have boundaries with both of my parents, which was a hard pill to swallow. Even as a young kid, I'd learned to be cautious when it came to my parents.

I'd never had the kind of security that most kids experienced with their parents. All of the security I'd known had come from Hayes. He'd always been the one at every sporting event. The one who met me after school and made sure I got home. My parents had never been there for me. But I'd learned to take care of myself, with the support of my brother.

My anger dissipated as I thought about Hayes asking Kingston to watch out for me.

He cared. How could I fault him for loving me and being the best brother?

My phone vibrated on the table beside me, and I grabbed the little towel there and dried my hand before seeing King's name light up on the screen.

"What are you doing?" he asked.

I chuckled and reached for the glass of wine beside me, taking a sip before setting it back down. "I'm soaking in a hot bath with a glass of wine. How about you?"

"Did you purposely just tell me that you're naked? Are you trying to kill me?"

"You asked. I answered." My teeth sank into my bottom lip. "Did you take a cold shower?"

"Yep. It didn't help."

My heart raced a bit as I thought about how to answer.

"Do you need a hand? I could talk you through it," I said, and my voice was all tease.

"It's not nice to fuck with a man in severe discomfort, Dandelion."

"I'm not messing with you. I'm offering assistance. It's harmless. We wouldn't be touching one another. We'd just be talking. The rest would be nothing more than what happened in your bathroom the other day. You would just know that I was there this time."

He cleared his throat. "It would have to work both ways. You all right with that?"

I reached for my glass and took another sip of wine.

*It would have to work both ways.*

I could live with that. I'd never done anything like this before, but I wanted to see where it would go.

"Sure." I tried hard to keep my voice even. "It's been a long day. I wouldn't mind taking the edge off."

"Do you touch yourself often?" he asked, his voice gruff.

"As often as I need to. How about you?"

"Every fucking day. Multiple times a day. Especially lately, since I've been abstaining from sex."

"And you're abstaining from sex because you're attracted to your best friend's sister and won't act on it?"

"Correct," he said, with no hesitation.

"It sounds ridiculous when you think about it."

"Well, this would still be abstaining, because we wouldn't be touching."

"Fair enough." I chuckled. "Let's just have a little fun. It's innocent, and no one will know about it."

"That was some kiss, huh?"

"It was."

"It was tough to pull back, Saylor. I wanted to push that door open and pull you inside. Run my lips down your entire body. I wanted to taste you and touch you and make you come so many times you wouldn't ever want another man to touch you."

*Wow. Hello, Forbidden King. We are not holding back anymore, and I am here for it.*

"What would you have done first, if you'd come inside the house with me?"

A slow moan left his lips. "Tell you to slip your hand between your thighs, where I know that sweet pussy is desperate for me."

*Oh. My. God.*

"Only if you do the same," I said, my voice gravelly and barely recognizable, and we had barely gotten started.

"No. If you want to do this, you're going to have to say it."

I'd never had phone sex or sexted anyone before, and I didn't have a clue what I was doing, so I would follow his lead.

I let out a long breath. "Wrap your hand around your dick and stroke yourself."

"Already there, and I can barely contain myself thinking about you touching yourself in the tub. It was torture, watching you all day in that little dress, thinking about what I wanted to do to you. And then kissing you and knowing what I'd do if I took you inside the house."

My fingers found my clit beneath the water, and I made little circles there, as my breaths were already coming hard and fast.

"Tell me," I whispered into the phone.

"I'd have pushed you up against the front door as soon as I got you inside. I wouldn't have been able to wait another second and would have dropped to my knees, my cock throbbing against my zipper at the thought of all that sweetness waiting for me."

"Oh my God. Tell me more."

"I'd have pushed your dress up around your waist and torn the panties covering that sweet pussy right from your body before I buried my face there. I'd spread your legs wide and lick you from one end to the next before hiking your legs over my shoulders and gripping that perfectly round ass of yours with both of my hands."

*Holy shit. This is hotter than I could have ever imagined.*

"King." I panted. "Keep going."

"I'd lick you slowly at first, taking my time tasting you while you rubbed that sweet pussy up against my mouth. And then I'd slip my tongue inside you and fuck you relentlessly. The way I've wanted to for so fucking long." His words were labored now.

"I want that. I want you."

I'd never been so turned on in my life, and I groaned as I held the phone with one hand and touched myself with the other.

"Do you want my fingers, Saylor? My lips on your clit, sucking you so hard you won't be able to stop from screaming?"

"Yes. I want it all."

"First, I'd slip my finger inside you. Just one to start, because I know how tight that little pussy of yours is. I'd slide in and out before adding another and fucking you with my fingers while my mouth moved to your clit, and I flicked you with my tongue."

My head fell back on a gasp as I bucked faster, my entire body tingling now.

White lights exploded behind my eyes.

"King," I cried out his name on a groan, as I went right over the edge.

"Let go, baby," he said. "So fucking good."

A guttural sound left his mouth, and my breathing was out of control as I rode out my pleasure to the sound of King going over the edge right along with me.

It had been the most erotic thing I'd ever done.

I wasn't embarrassed.

I was sated. And relaxed. And more turned on than ever.

We both stayed on the phone, panting, before our breaths finally slowed. I didn't know what to say as my eyelids closed and my head leaned against the back of the tub.

"Sleep well, King."

"I definitely will. Good night, Dandelion."

# 14

## Kingston

I pulled the door open at the bar and walked in. Last night had been . . . one for the books, so to speak.

I'd come so hard at the sound of her coming. And the thought of a naked Saylor in the bathtub touching herself while I said filthy things—that was all it took.

Her voice had been sated and raspy and sexy as hell when we'd said goodnight.

Then I'd texted to make sure she was okay, and she'd told me she was fine.

She'd enjoyed it.

And then she reminded me that it was a one-and-done deal, and we'd never speak of it again.

I was hoping like hell that this was out of my system now. I'd never forget the feel of her lips against mine. Kissing Saylor was better than I ever could have imagined. Her soft lips were made for mine. The way they parted for me, inviting me in to take the kiss deeper.

*Fuck.*

Apparently, this was not out of my system just yet. But we'd all agreed to meet at Whiskey Falls bar for country music night, and I'd be seeing her there. I hadn't been out in a while, but Saylor had reminded me that it was my job to look out for her, with a snarky comment about me being her babysitter.

Such a smartass.

I walked into the bar and the girls were already on the dance floor. Romeo held his hand up and waved me over. I stopped to say hello to Lionel who was behind the bar and having a great time being in his element. It was good to see him doing so well since having a stroke last year.

"Looking good, Lionel," I said, as I dabbed him up.

"You, too, King. Expecting to see you out on that dance floor."

"You know it." I held up a hand and made my way to the table where the guys were sitting.

Well, everyone but Hayes. He'd texted to let us know he'd made it to Barley Creek and wouldn't be able to talk much, but he'd check in when he could. We were all following the fire on the weather app he'd sent us, so we could get updates.

"There he is," Nash said, as he took a pull from his beer. "I was worried you were going to bail again."

"Hey now. Don't go throwing shade. I told you I'd be here. Cutler's having his first sleepover at JT's tonight, right?" Cutler had obviously slept at our homes before, and his best friend, JT, had spent the night at Nash's house. But the little dude had never slept at JT's house, so it was a big deal. Nash was protective as hell—we all were. But JT's parents were great, and our boy was excited to go over there.

"Yep. Jay and Susannah said they'd call me if there were any issues. But they were ordering pizza and watching a movie when I called to check in on my way over here. I'm sure he'll be just fine."

"So, no one is at your house." I waggled my brows. "You can actually take a woman home to your place for once."

"Shit. It's been a while. And as sad as it is to say, I'm fucking exhausted from this past week. I wouldn't mind sleeping for the next twelve hours, you know?" Nash said, setting his glass down.

"I hear ya. It's been a busy couple of weeks." I nodded.

"Well, I hate to add to your plates, but we all need to go get fitted for our suits for the wedding," Romeo said. "Maybe we can meet up midweek, and we'll just have Hayes go as soon as he gets back. He sent me his suit size, and Wally over at Stitch said he can work with that until he gets back."

"We got you, brother. Don't give it a thought. But when I had to go get some alterations for a suit I bought for court, it was a little awkward," River said, leaning in so no one would overhear what he was saying, while his gaze remained on the dance floor.

On his girl.

"What do you mean?" Romeo asked.

"He grabbed my junk. Moved it to the side like he was lifting my arm. But it was my dick."

All three of us erupted in laughter, and I made a mental note to fill Hayes in on this story the minute he returned.

"What?" Romeo asked, not hiding his discomfort. "Why did he grab your junk?"

"I don't know. I'd never been fitted for a suit, and I asked Ruby about it, and she fell over laughing, too. She said that wasn't normal. And he wasn't fucking gentle either." River shrugged.

"What did you do?" Nash asked, as his mouth hung open.

"I took my dick back, man. I wasn't going to tolerate that shit. I just held it in my two hands while he continued measuring my inseam."

I was laughing hysterically now, and it was difficult to get my words out. "Was it out in the open?"

"Fuck no. It was in my briefs. He didn't yank it out completely. But I wrapped two hands around it to protect it. And Wally didn't seem to care. He just wanted it out of the way. So what I'm telling you is . . . go in there with a game plan. Or wear a cup."

"So that he can't *yanky your wanky*?" I said over my laughter.

"Fuck you. You're the sensitive one. You would not be okay having your dick manhandled by a dude old enough to be our grandfather."

My gaze moved to the dance floor, where Saylor had her hands over her head. She wore a short, fitted denim miniskirt, a white spaghetti strap cropped blouse, and her favorite cowboy boots.

Fuck, she was cute.

Her hair was pulled back in some sort of knot at the nape of her neck, and her cheeks were flushed. She didn't drink often, and by the looks of the empty shot glasses on the table and the way they were dancing around and laughing on the dance floor, they were well on their way to having a good time.

"Don't you worry yourself about my dick. He's doing just fine." I winked as the song ended, and Ruby led the girls back over to the table.

My eye caught a guy waving Saylor over from a few tables over. It was fucking Coach. That dude needed to take a fucking hint. She stopped at his table and hugged him, and I didn't miss the way his hands landed on her hips, and he kept them there.

Demi was laughing about something to Romeo, Peyton was talking Nash's ear off, and Ruby was standing between my brother's legs with her hands in his hair as she swayed to the music.

"Coach has his hands all the fuck over Saylor," I hissed, and everyone turned to look at me before glancing over at her. She kept stepping back, and he was stepping forward.

"He's had a lot to drink tonight, and she does look a little uncomfortable," Romeo said.

"They're friends." Ruby eyed me suspiciously as I pushed to my feet. "Don't embarrass her by going all caveman on her. Just go tell her you want to dance and take her out to the dance floor so it won't be obvious."

I nodded. "Great idea. I've got this."

"Any excuse to fucking dance and keep the party going," River said, and he smirked at me.

*It is so much more than that.*

I walked toward her, and her gaze locked with mine. She'd obviously been drinking because her eyes and cheeks told a story.

"Hey," I said, pushing to stand between them so I was half-blocking Coach, forcing him to drop his hands. "This is our song. How about you come dance with me?" It wasn't our song. We didn't have a song. But it was one of my favorite country songs, so it sounded believable.

Her lips turned up in the corners, and her head fell back on a chuckle. "Sure. Let's dance, King."

Coach glared at me, and I tossed him a wink. There was just something about the guy that I didn't like. Maybe it was jealousy. I wasn't too proud to admit that it was a possibility. I didn't like the way he looked at her.

Like he was claiming her.

*I want to claim her.*

I wanted to claim every fucking inch of her.

"You having a good time, Dandelion?" I whispered against her ear, my hands finding her waist, our bodies swaying together.

"Yeah. I thought maybe you'd changed your mind and weren't coming?"

"I'd never leave you hanging like that." I loved the way she looked at me. Like I set the sun and hung the moon all at the same time. No one had ever looked at me the way Saylor Woodson did.

"You've left me hanging plenty of times, my forbidden King," she said against my ear, her words slurring a bit, and I tugged her close so her head could rest against my chest.

We just swayed to the music, her body pressed against mine, moving as one.

Her head fit beneath my chin perfectly, and I savored this moment.

The song came to an end, and I reached for her hand and led her to the table.

"Let's get you a water, and I think the guys ordered some food. Have you eaten yet?" I asked, as my fingers intertwined with hers.

"Is this part of your babysitting duty?" She giggled, and I rolled my eyes as I pulled out the stool where I'd been sitting and lifted her by the waist and set her down.

I put some tater tots and chicken fingers on a plate and set it in front of her. "Yes. I take my job very seriously."

I went to the bar to get her a water and brought it back and handed it to her. "Drink."

"Thanks, *Dad*," she said, as she and the girls burst out in laughter.

I didn't mind it. I was having a good time. I liked seeing this side of Saylor.

Seeing her relaxed and having fun.

She deserved that.

I had a couple of beers and followed Saylor out to the dance floor a few more times like it was my job to protect her.

Because, in a way, it was.

Everyone started making their way out, and we said our goodbyes. I assured the girls I would get Saylor home safely, and my brother made some snarky-ass comment, and I flashed him the bird.

She was walking beside me, leaning against my body as she told me all about the book she was reading. How the hero was obsessed with the heroine and how his sole purpose in life was to please her.

"I mean, I know you're impressive with the dirty talk, King. But this guy is next level." She chuckled.

Like clockwork, my dick heard the word 'dirty talk' and jumped to attention.

"Trust me. That was casual phone sex. I'm much more impressive in person."

Why was I telling her this?

"Oh, I don't doubt that for a minute," she said, waggling her brows at me.

We walked up the steps to her house, and when she reached into her purse for her keys, she lost her balance. She fell into me, and I caught her before she toppled to the ground.

A fit of laughter escaped her sweet mouth as I steadied her. "You never could handle your booze."

"I'm fine. Don't be ridiculous." She put the key in the door and tripped as she tried to walk inside, and I caught her again.

I was done with this, so I turned her around, bent down, and tossed her over my shoulder fireman-style, as she burst out into a fit of hysterical laughter.

Saylor Woodson was a fun drunk, no doubt about it. But I didn't want her falling over when she'd be staying here alone. I knew Ruby had gone home with River, so I kicked the door closed behind me and walked her down the hall toward her bedroom. I dropped her onto the bed, and she smiled up at me. Her crop top and skirt both managed to ride up higher than they'd been just a few seconds ago. I could see the lace of her panties, and I cleared my throat before yanking her skirt down.

Her teeth sank into her bottom lip, and she smiled. "Sorry about that. I'm fine, really. I just get a little clumsy when I drink."

"I know you do. That's why I wanted to make sure I got you home safely."

"Thanks." She looked away before turning back to me. "That was pretty sexy what we did the other night. Phone sex is my new favorite thing."

"Ahhh . . . first-timer, huh?"

"Yep. Never thought it would be my thing. But I think everything is my thing when it comes to you," she said, before springing forward and kissing my cheek. "I've got to go brush my teeth and get my jammies on. Do you want to go now or wait till I come out?"

"You go do your thing, and I'll grab you some water and a pain reliever, and once you're tucked in, I'll head out."

"Fine. But for the record, I like forbidden King more than protective King." She fluttered toward her bathroom like some sort of goddamn fairy.

I went to her kitchen and poured her a glass of water and found the Tylenol in a cabinet with the vitamins. I walked back to her room and set it down on her nightstand. I pulled her white-and-pink floral comforter down and tossed the ridiculous amount of decorative pillows covering her bed onto the floor. Something caught my eye from beneath her pillow that was lying at the head of the bed. The corner of a piece of fabric that I recognized immediately. I pulled it out, and my chest pounded.

The blanket I'd loved as a kid had been tucked beneath her fucking pillow all these years later.

I unfolded it, and right there in the other corner was the faded outline of my handprint I'd drawn for her.

She'd held onto it all this time.

# 15

## Saylor

I glanced in the mirror one last time and smiled. My teeth were clean. My face was washed. My cute purple stretchy headband with a bow at the top held my hair back as I applied moisturizer to my skin.

I looked down at my thin tank top and tiny shorts and shrugged. He'd seen me in a swimsuit more times than I could count. This had more coverage than that did.

I was definitely sobering up, but I still had the slightest buzz running through my body.

I pulled the door open and stopped when I found Kingston sitting on the edge of my bed, holding my favorite blanket in his hands.

Well, it was his favorite blanket first.

"You aren't going to try to steal that back from me, are you?"

He looked up, his dark gaze locking with mine, before he raked his eyes down my body, slowly devouring every inch of me.

"No. Just surprised you still have it."

I walked toward him, and he held up the two pain relievers,

and I popped them into my mouth before taking the glass from his hand.

"Thank you. And of course, I still have it. It's what I fall asleep with every night."

"You still have nightmares?" His voice was low and full of emotion.

I set the glass down and dropped to sit next to him. "No. Not very often. But I tuck my hand into yours every night, just like we did all those years ago. It's how I like to fall asleep."

He reached for my hand and intertwined our fingers, smiling. My stomach fluttered, and I tried to act unaffected.

But his nearness overwhelmed me.

The feel of his hand wrapped around mine, the slight buzz still coursing through my veins.

The memory of how he made me cry out his name in the tub the other night.

All of it.

It was a challenge not to be affected by King.

*My forbidden King.*

"It always kept the nightmares away when you'd fall asleep with your hand in mine," he said.

"It did. You scared all the bad guys away." I chuckled, even though he wasn't laughing.

"I remember those days like it was yesterday."

"Me, too," I whispered.

He shook his head and pulled his hand from mine. "All right. Let's get you into bed, and I'll head home."

Once he was standing, I crawled up toward the headboard and slipped beneath the covers. "How about you lie here with me for old time's sake?"

"I can do that," he said, kicking off his shoes and flipping off the lights before he moved to the other side of the bed. The mattress dipped low when he stretched out, staying above the covers while I was beneath them. We both rolled onto our sides so we were facing one another. I reached for his hand, just like I used to do every night all those years ago.

Kingston Pierce had always been my serenity.

My safe place.

And now he was all grown up, and he still felt like my safe place.

"Your hands are still just as small as they always were," he said, his voice deep and gruff.

"Or you just have really giant hands." I chuckled. I loved his hands. They were strong, and it was obvious he worked hard by the callouses on his palms.

"Did you have fun tonight?" he asked.

"I did. I probably drank a little too much," I admitted. "My dad called on my way out to Whiskey Falls. He wants me to come out and see him and Constance and the kids on Sunday."

"Really? I didn't know you still talked to him." His voice was quiet, void of emotion. He knew my brother despised my father, and rightfully so.

"Not very often. He reached out after I graduated from college, and then again after I completed my MBA."

"I didn't see him there either time," Kingston said, not hiding his irritation. Hayes and all the guys had come to my graduation for both undergrad and grad school.

My mother hadn't been there, because Barry had fallen off a ladder at the house the first time around. And then when I'd walked at the commencement for my MBA, my mother had not been able to take the time off work.

None of that mattered to me.

Hayes had always been there.

Kingston had always been there.

They'd all always been there.

"You're correct. But I don't think he felt particularly welcome knowing how much his son despises him." I closed my eyes at the feel of his thumb stroking my wrist. "But Hayes and I don't have to feel the same way about him. I'm not saying I forgive him for leaving us, but I still want to know him."

"You're so fucking good to your core, Dandelion." Kingston leaned forward and kissed my forehead. "So, are you going to go?"

I hesitated and let out a long sigh. "I want to. I really want to. And with Hayes being gone, I wouldn't have to even mention it and get him all pissed off. I could tell him after, and if it goes well, maybe I could convince him to come with me the next time."

"Why do I feel like there's a *but* in there?"

How did he know me so well?

"I'm just nervous about going by myself, you know? I feel like he and Constance and the kids have each other. And I'm the one walking into their world, and that makes me hesitant."

He was quiet for a long minute. "Why don't I come with you? Hayes wouldn't want you going alone, and you wouldn't feel like it was you against them if I were there. I'll just be there for support."

"You would do that?"

"I don't think you have a fucking clue just how much I'd do for you," he whispered, his hand still wrapped around mine. "But there is one stipulation."

"What is it?"

"You tell Hayes you're going, or I will."

I groaned. "This loyalty thing is out of control."

"That's the deal, Dandelion."

"Fine. I'll tell him. We can go on Sunday if that works for you."

"You got it. It'll be a little road trip. I'm assuming he still lives in Clarita Hills?"

"Yep. Thanks, King." I raised our joined hands and kissed the back of his.

He mimicked me and pulled our hands to his mouth and did the same. His warm lips set my body ablaze. I tipped my head back and kissed his jaw. "That means a lot."

He leaned down and kissed the tip of my nose. And then my cheek. His lips moved down my neck. Our joined hands broke free, and suddenly, his hands were on my hips, and he was tugging me forward. My fingers tangled in his hair, as his mouth found mine.

The room was dark, only the light from the moon aglow as we lay with my comforter between us, and I urged my body closer to his. His tongue slipped inside, and our breaths strained as he tugged on the knot at the nape of my neck, tilting my head back so he could take the kiss further.

Deeper.

Needier.

Hungrier.

My legs were frantically trying to kick away the fabric from the bedding that remained between us. In one swift move, Kingston lifted me over the comforter, bringing our hips together so I could rock against him. He rolled onto his back, and my legs settled on each side as I straddled him. His hands moved along my inner thighs, his thumbs finding the edge of my pajama shorts. He slipped his fingers beneath, dipping into my heat.

"So fucking wet, Saylor." A gruff whisper left his mouth as I bucked against his swollen erection between my legs. I rocked up and down shamelessly, desperate for release, as we kissed for what felt like hours. I was so worked up, and an overwhelming sensation took over. Kingston's thumb continued to stroke me, and as if he knew exactly what I needed, his thumb moved to my clit. He pressed with just the right amount of pressure, forming little circles, as every inch of my body started to shake. Our breaths were the only audible sound in the room, and he groaned into my mouth . . . and that was all it took.

"King," I cried out, as bright lights exploded behind my eyelids.

I was dry-humping him like an animal in heat, and I didn't even care. Nothing had ever felt this good, and we weren't even having sex.

His hands found my hips as he guided me back and forth along his hard length.

I fell all the way forward, panting like I'd just run a race, and he just stroked the back of my neck while I continued gasping.

When my breathing quieted and my body stopped shaking against him, he nipped at the lobe of my ear. "Are you all right?"

I lifted my head, making out his dark gaze in the little bit of light coming through the window. "Never better."

He chuckled. "That was hot."

"My body clearly reacts to yours. I've never done . . . that. You know, while making out with a guy."

"Can you not say the word *come*?" He laughed as his hands slipped beneath the waistband of my shorts and squeezed my butt. "Damn. This ass is what fantasies are made of."

I felt his length beneath me, and I rolled off of him and went to reach for the button on his jeans. He wrapped his large hand around my wrist and stopped me.

"Nope. Tonight was about making you feel good. I've broken enough rules for one evening. I need to get home." He kissed my forehead and pushed off the bed. He came around to my side and searched for the blanket before glancing down at the large handprint inside that he'd drawn all those years ago, and he laughed.

He was so tall, with broad shoulders and his hair a

disheveled mess—I'd never seen anyone sexier. He tucked the blanket beneath my chin, leaned down, and kissed my forehead.

"You can't stay?" I asked, regretting the words as they came out of my mouth. I already knew the answer.

"I've already crossed the line, Dandelion. I need to go while I can still look at myself in the mirror."

I rolled my eyes and pushed forward before moving to my feet. "I'll walk you out. You guys and your stupid pact. It's ridiculous really."

He wrapped his fingers around my wrist when I huffed past him. "Hey, don't do that. You know that I lost my parents before I was old enough to remember them. So that pact, those guys, you . . . that's my family. My reason for waking up every day."

My eyes closed as guilt took over. I was being selfish. I wanted this piece of Kingston I'd probably always wanted since the first time he held my hand as I fell asleep.

*I want his heart. All of it.*

But it was something he couldn't give to me.

I nodded as I turned to look at him, my teeth sinking into my bottom lip. "I'm sorry. I'm being a horny asshole, aren't I?"

"It's all right. Horny Saylor might be my favorite." He tugged me closer, his hand finding my ass cheek and lifting me just enough to feel his erection. "Don't mistake my leaving with me not wanting you. But you can't always have what you want."

"Did you just quote the Rolling Stones?"

"Possibly." He gave me a chaste kiss, pulled his hand away, and made his way to the door. "I'll stop by the bookstore tomorrow with that little library mailbox thing you asked me to build you. It just needs one more coat of paint, and it'll be ready."

"Thanks, King."

He pulled the door open and turned around. This sexy grin

spread across his handsome face, eyes heated as his tongue came out to wet his lips. "For what?"

I gave him a puzzled look. "The library mailbox you built for me?"

"Oh, I thought you were thanking me for letting that greedy pussy of yours rub against my dick."

My mouth fell open. "You have a filthy mouth."

"And you fucking love it, don't you?"

"Please. I barely noticed," I said over my laughter as I shook my head.

He leaned forward and kissed my cheek. "If you touch yourself thinking about me again tonight, I want you to text me and tell me."

"Not happening. You have an awfully big ego."

"Maybe. But it's not nearly as big as my dick." He winked and walked right out into the night.

I groaned and closed the door, locking it behind him before padding back down the hall.

I climbed into bed just as my phone vibrated on my nightstand. I looked down and read the text.

KING

Touching yourself yet?

Not a chance. I'm not an animal.
Goodnight.

But as I squeezed my eyes shut, I felt his lips on mine. I felt his hands on me. I could smell his minty scent on my sheets.

My hand moved beneath the waistband of my shorts.

Damn you, Kingston Pierce.

*My forbidden King.*

# 16

# Kingston

Can you die of a bad case of blue balls?

HAYES

Listen, if this forest fire hasn't killed me, I think you can survive not getting laid for a few days.

NASH

I've gone without sex longer than you, so you came knocking on the wrong door for sympathy.

I didn't ask for sympathy. I asked for medical advice.

NASH

I have to take Cutler to see Dr. Dolby

today for his allergies, so I can ask him if you want.

RIVER

The fact that Dr. Dolby is still alive is a miracle in itself. He's got to be ninety years old by now. He was around before modern medicine was a term people used.

ROMEO

Hey, don't hate on Doc Dolby. The dude has helped me so much. He's more like a healer.

RIVER

My point exactly. He was alive in the 1800s, and they probably called him a healer before he went to medical school.

Can we please circle back to my dick? I'm serious. I wake up hard. I go to sleep hard. I'm concerned.

NASH

Go get laid, you whiny little bitch. I wake up hard and go to sleep hard every day. It's called life, brother. We don't all get to be pleasured every second of our day.

I knew I shouldn't have asked about this on the group chat. I should have googled it.

ROMEO

Ride or die. This is where you come with your problems.

NASH

Says the dude getting married in a few weeks. Of course, he's all Zen and acting like the Dalai Lama. He lives with a woman. His needs are met every day.

ROMEO

Touché. It's damn good over here. I'm sure River would agree.

RIVER

Fuck yeah. I just want to make it official. Ruby said she'll go to Vegas with me after Romeo and Demi's wedding. She doesn't want to take their rain cloud or some shit.

Steal their thunder, you dickoyster.

RIVER

Whatever. Just be prepared for a call that I'm hitched. No fancy ceremony for us. Just a little Vegas wedding with a cutout of Elvis in the background and no drama.

ROMEO

Sounds pretty damn good to me. My mom is driving me crazy with all the questions lately. By the way, Hayes, we had our fitting this week, so you'll get alterations when you get back. Which better fucking be before the wedding.

HAYES

Wouldn't miss it for the world. But this fire is blazing, and I'm fucking tired. How's my sister doing, King?

She's doing good. The bookstore is kicking ass. You have nothing to worry about.

NASH

Yeah, King's been a good boy, keeping an eye on her. Hence, the reason he isn't getting laid. He's taking his job very seriously.

HAYES

I didn't say you couldn't go out and get laid. I just said to make sure that dickhead Barry stays away from her.

Saylor is not the reason I'm not getting laid. I just haven't felt like going out. I've lost my mojo.

That wasn't a complete lie, although Saylor was the reason that I wasn't getting laid. But that was because I only wanted her, and that couldn't happen. But the rest was true.

RIVER

This happened once before, remember? We were all worried about you because you weren't going out.

NASH

Dude. That's when he had a bad case of the shits, and we found out that he was lactose intolerant. His blue balls were fine back then.

ROMEO

Is that when he nearly shit his pants at The Golden Goose?

You are a bunch of insensitive pricks. Midge has since stocked dairy-free cheese for me at the diner. And I have a sensitive stomach. My dick was highly active and working just fine during that time.

HAYES

My advice. Go get laid. You'll be cured.

I'll google it.

A bunch of emojis came through, and I laughed as I set my phone down and walked through the cemetery, making my way to where my parents were buried. Side by side. Both my parents had been born and raised in Magnolia Falls, and they'd raised me and River in the city, but this place had always been home for them.

I dropped to sit in the grass and tipped my head up to let the sun beat down on my face. I came here often. I didn't have memories of my parents while they were alive, but I'd been coming here since I was old enough to walk on my own to visit them.

I'd heard every story there was to tell from those who had known them, and from those details, I'd gathered I was a lot like my mother. River, apparently, took after our father. Our parents were ridiculously in love, and they were fabulous parents in the short time they were with us.

My brother remembered them and grieved them.

My grandparents suffered the loss of them, and I'd felt that throughout my life.

They'd poured their hearts and their pain into raising River and me.

My parents' accident was a reminder to me about how quickly life can take away the ones you love.

I'd always been more of a light-and-easy guy. I didn't take things too seriously. It was a choice I'd made a long time ago.

I glanced over to where the leaves rustled in the tree a few feet away, and a patch of dandelions bloomed near the trunk.

Fuck. I was in a situation, and I didn't know what to do about it.

"Wish you guys were here," I said. It amazed me to learn that you could miss someone that you didn't even remember. I guess some people lived on in your heart and were etched into your soul. "Happy Anniversary. I'm glad that, at the very least, you two get to be together."

I pushed to my feet and walked the short distance to my grandmother's nursing home.

*Pearl Arabella Pierce is my person.*

She raised me, she loved me, and she believed in me. Always had. Always would. When I struggled, she was the first person I turned to. She knew things about me that no one knew.

The guys were my family. I relied on them.

But for advice, my grandmother was who I talked to.

When I walked through the doors of Magnolia Haven, I waved at a few of the ladies that I played cards with once a week and made my way down the hall. Grammie's room was the last door on the left, a corner suite with views of the garden, which was important to her. River did a good job keeping up with planting flowers for her, and I normally just provided pure entertainment.

It's what I was good at.

"Hey there, beautiful," I said, as I waltzed in and kissed her on the cheek. Grammie sat in the reclining chair, looking out at the garden.

She clapped her hands together once and smiled. "My boy. I knew you'd come today. Were you at the cemetery?"

She knew me. Knew that's where I'd be today.

"I was. Had a little chat with them like I always do."

She smiled as I dropped into the chair across from her. "What's on your mind, my boy? You've been quieter lately. Visiting more. That means that head of yours is spinning, am I right?"

"I'm fine. Just been a little off the past few weeks."

"Tell me about it. What's going on?" she asked as she studied me.

"Everything is good. There's nothing to worry about."

"That's not what I asked. Come on now, you know you can tell me anything."

I leaned back, rubbing a hand over the back of my neck.

"I haven't felt much like going out, and I've just been pouring myself into work, which makes me tired. I'm not used to being grumpy, you know?" I shrugged. I sure as shit wasn't about to tell her I was sexually frustrated. I'd have to find a way around it, because I did need her advice. She'd never steered me wrong.

"Yes. Grumpy is more your brother's cup of tea." She shook her head and chuckled. "But you don't always have to be happy either, Kingston. I think that's part of your struggle right there."

"What do you mean?"

"Well, we like to tease River about being grumpy, but he's always been very honest about his feelings. When he's in a bad mood, he doesn't hide it. When he's happy, you know it. I never knew with you what you were feeling growing up, because no matter what was happening, you were always okay. It's who you are. But no one is always okay. So, I've learned to drag it out of you."

I let out a long breath. "I think you and Gramps had plenty on your plate as it was. You didn't need me to fall apart. You lost your son and his wife, and you raised your grandsons, all while grieving the loss. And River being hospitalized after the accident for months couldn't have been easy on you. I didn't remember them, so I was the only one who wasn't affected. The least I could be is happy, right? I was too young to understand the loss."

Her eyes widened. Had we never talked about this?

"Just because you didn't understand the loss at the time, doesn't mean it wasn't a huge loss throughout your life." She reached for my hand and squeezed it. "It's okay to be sad that you didn't get to know your parents for very long before they passed away. It's okay to grieve for what you never had. And it's okay to not be in a good mood all the time. So how about you stop pretending with me and tell me what's going on."

"You know the guys are everything to me. Ride or die and all that good stuff. I would never do anything to mess that up. We've been loyal, through and through."

"But?"

"I'm having these feelings, Grammie," I whispered as I leaned forward.

"What kind of feelings, my boy?"

"I don't know, that's the thing. It's never happened to me before, so I can't say for sure." I shook my head, not certain I even wanted to say it aloud. But I was dying inside, and I needed to talk to someone. The guys would all tell me not to go there, and I knew they'd be right.

"Talk to me, Kingston."

"I've been spending a lot of time with Saylor. You know I worked on renovating her bookstore, and Hayes asked me to keep an eye out while he's gone fighting this wildfire. Sometimes when I'm around her, I just—feel things. Things I shouldn't feel for my best friend's little sister, you know?"

*Please read between the lines and don't make me spell it out.*

"Ahhhh . . . she was here yesterday. Do you know that sweet girl comes to see me almost every single day on her way home from work? She brings me a new book or a sun tea from Magnolia Beans or some pretty flowers that she picked along the way. She's a special one. I understand why you're struggling, but it's silly to make this harder than it has to be."

"I think it's definitely complicated."

"Why? You ask women out all the time. You've never been shy."

"Grammie," I said, gaping at her as I leaned forward and rubbed my hands together. "This is Saylor. She's not just *some woman*. I can't casually date her. Hayes would cut my—" I paused and thought over my words wisely. "Hayes would have my head."

She leaned back in her recliner, and a wicked grin spread across her face. "That's because he doesn't know the truth."

"Well, apparently, I don't know the truth because I don't know what the fu—what the heck to do with these feelings. So please, enlighten me."

"Oh, my boy, you really don't know, do you?"

I threw my hands in the air. "I really don't. Are you going to quit torturing me?"

"The reason you're hesitant is because you love her, and that makes everything different."

*I don't know shit about love. I know that I want to do dirty things to Saylor Woodson. And I know that is wrong.*

"That's old-fashioned thinking, Grammie. I don't know anything about love when it comes to romantic relationships. But I know that I don't, er, want to be just friends with her. Does that make sense?"

She chuckled. "I get it, sweetheart. I think you've loved Saylor Woodson since she came to stay with us all those years ago. You didn't act on those feelings because you love her. You're terrified of love, Kingston. Because you lost the first, most important loves of your life—your parents. You've watched everyone you love grieve since you were a toddler. So, you've spent your life being easy and happy and keeping things simple, but that wasn't only to protect us. It was to protect yourself. Your own heart. You knew loss before you knew love."

"What are we talking about? This is not about love. This is about the fact that I'm uncomfortable because—" I threw my hands in the air in frustration. "Grammie. I can't sleep with other women because I'm thinking about Saylor. All the fu—freaking time. It's a physical need. Nothing more. And Hayes would kill me if I acted on it."

"I disagree." She shrugged and reached over to grab her teacup and took a sip as if we were discussing the weather and not the shit show that was currently my life.

"You disagree? That's your answer?"

"Yes. If it were just a physical need, you'd fill it. You'd go out there and do what you do, which you know I don't agree with. But that's a chat for a different day. This isn't physical, Kingston. That's why you're struggling."

I groaned. "I don't think you understand what this is."

"And I don't think *you* understand what this is." She raised a brow, setting her teacup on the table. "I've been around a lot longer than you. I know these things. So I'm going to give you the only advice I know to give, all right?"

I leaned forward, elbows on my knees, as I clasped my hands together. "Okay."

"Don't run from it. It's rare to find someone who affects you like this. Who consumes your mind and your heart. It's what I shared with your grandfather. It's what your parents shared. And it's what River found with Ruby. Don't run from it, sweetheart."

*This is her advice?*

"I was looking for something a little more specific. Like, go ahead and cross the line, and you won't be a terrible human being who backstabbed his best friend," I huffed. "*Don't run from it?* Come on, Grammie. What the hell does that even mean?"

"Oh, my boy. The joy you bring me is just too much sometimes." Her head tipped back in laughter. "What I'm saying is, trust your heart. It's telling you something. Don't cross the line unless you talk to Hayes. Tell him how you feel."

*Oh, hey, buddy. I can't stop thinking about fucking your sister. Are you cool with that?*

"I can't tell him that I want to sleep with his sister." There, I said it.

She was completely unfazed, as if she'd expected me to say this. "I definitely would not recommend saying that. Try dating her first, Kingston. Tell him you have these feelings, and you want to date her."

"I've never lasted long with anyone. I don't do relationships, you know that. And Hayes would never be okay with me having a casual . . ." I paused to think of the right word to say.

"Tryst?" she asked, her eyes dancing with excitement.

"Fling."

"No, I can't imagine he'd be too pleased with that. I guess you're going to have to rethink your no-relationship rule. Because if you want to cross the line with Saylor Woodson, all those rules would be thrown out the door."

No shit.

That was the problem.

I hugged her goodbye, not feeling any better than I had when I'd arrived.

# 17

## Saylor

The bookstore had been open for a few days, and we'd been busy from the time the doors opened until they closed. Today would be no exception, because the infamous Ashlan Thomas was coming to Love Ever After, and it's all everyone in town was talking about.

"Even Midge freaking Longhorn is excited about this," Ruby said, as she helped me finish putting out the cookies and treats that I'd ordered for today.

"Yeah, that's because Midge got back together with her ex, Doug. So she's in her romance feels," Peyton said, as she added some strawberries to the large glass dispenser we'd filled with water.

"Who knew Midge even had feelings?" Ruby laughed.

"Yeah, she already called this morning to ask what time the doors were opening. Apparently, she's reading everything Ashlan's ever written."

"Damn. Romance books really bring the world together, don't they?"

"Well, for the sake of my business, I hope you're right."

"I'd say your first week in business was a huge success," Ruby said.

My phone vibrated, and I looked down to see a text from Demi.

DEMI

We're here.

Ruby chuckled at how nervous Peyton and I were, just as the door from Demi's coffee shop opened, and they walked into the bookstore. I'd met Demi's future sister-in-law, Brinkley Hendrix, before, but I hadn't met the other two women.

"Hey, are you ready for the big day?" Brinkley asked.

"Yes," I said, and my voice shook, which made it clear I was nervous.

Demi smiled and then turned to the women standing beside her. "You all know Brinkley, and this is her sister, Georgia Lancaster. She is in the book world, as well, and her family owns Lancaster Press. And this is the infamous Ashlan Thomas. Well, that's the name she writes under. Her real name is Ashlan King."

"It's so nice to meet you both, and I'm happy to see you again, Brinkley. I can't thank you all enough for doing this," I said.

We took turns making rounds and hugging one another, and they appeared to be as excited as we were about the event.

"This is so cute," Ashlan gushed. "I need to take pictures of this setup. My girls would love how adorable this all looks."

"Are they still bummed they couldn't come with?" Brinkley asked.

"Yes. But Hadley had soccer practice, and Paisley had dance class, so Jace was taking them to their activities today. Monroe is just happy to be along for the ride with her sisters."

Ashlan smiled, and it was easy to see how much she loved her girls.

"They sound adorable. And how's your little guy doing?" Demi asked Georgia.

"Oh, he's doing so great. About to have his first birthday next month. I can't believe how fast it's going."

They both opened their phones and showed the photos of their adorable kids. I was immediately relaxed, and all the nerves over meeting Ashlan were gone.

"There is a huge line forming out front," Peyton said as she looked out the window.

"Let's do this." Ashlan took the chair behind the table that I'd set up for her to sign books at. She'd had a few boxes of books sent here for the signing, and we were ready for business.

I pushed the door open, and my eyes widened when I realized the line wrapped around the block. Everyone was here to meet her, and I couldn't be happier.

Romance was alive and well in Magnolia Falls.

Ashlan was a champ, signing books while making small talk with readers.

When Midge approached the table with Janelle from Sweet Magnolia, I was just bringing Ashlan a fresh glass of sweet tea.

"So give me the dirty details, Ashlan. Where do you get your inspiration for the sex scenes?" Midge asked, and I shot her a look, making it clear that I was horrified.

Janelle's head fell back in laughter. "Midge, that's a bit much, even for you."

"Come on, now," Midge said. "She writes romance. We're all grown-ups here. I follow you on social media, and I've seen that hot husband of yours."

"Oh my gosh, Midge. Stop." Demi shook her head and then used her hand to contain her laughter.

"It's fine." Ashlan shrugged. "I get my inspiration everywhere. But yes, my husband is one sexy man, isn't he?"

"Damn, she's getting better at handling these questions," Georgia said to just me and Brinkley, who were standing to the side now.

"She's so easy to talk to. I can't thank you both enough for setting this up." I was beyond grateful to them for putting this together.

"Don't give it a thought. You're family to Demi, which makes you family to us. And our cousin Ashlan is as nice as they come. I knew she'd do it in a heartbeat to help you kick off your grand opening," Brinkley said.

"This is so fun. And we were thrilled to come to Magnolia Falls for the day." Georgia was as down to earth as her sister. Demi had told me that Georgia's husband had a private plane, and they'd flown in for the day with Ashlan from Honey Mountain.

Apparently, it was nothing for Brinkley, whose husband was one of the most famous quarterbacks in the NFL, and she flew all over the country with him as well.

"Well, it means the world to me. And I'm glad we'll have time to grab dinner before you head back tonight." I was looking forward to relaxing and hanging out afterward, as I'd been anxious about getting everything ready for today. But if I were being totally honest, I was very distracted about tomorrow. I'd be going to see my father and his family, and I was nervous about it. The fact that Kingston was going with me made me feel much better, but that was another issue I was struggling with, too.

I was attracted to him.

Ridiculously attracted to him.

We'd already crossed the line multiple times, and I was frustrated that he wouldn't just give in to it and let things happen naturally. Just like any other relationship. There were no guarantees. But it bothered me that he thought Hayes should have a say in this.

We were both adults.

Two consenting adults.

"Saylor, I've got a question for you." Midge walked toward me, with Janelle and Peyton right behind her, and they were both already laughing.

"Should I be worried?" I asked.

"Don't mind these two prudes." Midge shrugged.

"I can assure you that no one has ever called me a prude," Peyton said, not hiding the fact that she was offended by the comment.

Demi came up behind her with a big smile on her face. "She's right. No one has ever called her a prude."

Midge waved her hand around as if they were all annoying her. "Anywho, I'm wondering if you could label the books by spice level as well as genre?"

"You want me to label the shelves by how sexy the books are?"

"Correct. Sometimes a woman wants something spicy to liven things up in her own bedroom. And other times I want something serious. Closed door. So how about you help a girl out?" Midge crossed her arms over her chest.

"Midge Longhorn, you have lost your mind since you got back together with Doug." Janelle chuckled and shook her head.

"You might be right, but a lot of people are pleased to see that I'm in a much better mood than I used to be."

"This is you in a good mood? You snapped at me for not getting you a glass of ice water quick enough, just fifteen minutes ago, and then you called me a prude," Peyton said.

"Well, you weren't very fast, and I was calling Janelle a prude, too." She raised a brow.

More laughter. Brinkley and Georgia were watching with complete fascination.

I noticed Ashlan out of the corner of my eye, and she was walking up beside me. The crowd had died down, and I was relieved to be closing up soon. I turned my attention back to Midge.

"I don't know if giving a spice level to all the books would work, honestly." I shrugged because it was the truth.

"And why is that? I've heard that people use a chili pepper system." Midge pressed. My God, the old horndog could judge her own heat level on her books.

I was flustered by how to answer her, and I tried to think of a good response, just as Ashlan put a hand on my shoulder and leaned in. "I think the reader should make that assessment for themselves, because the heat level is very subjective. Some readers give me one chili pepper, and others give me three or four."

I smiled at her in thanks, because it was clear that Midge thought Ashlan walked on water. "You know what? You're right, Ashlan. I can't trust some stranger to decide if it's sexy enough for me. Your books have just the right amount of steam. Doug and I listened to your latest release on audio together last night." Midge whistled. "Let me tell you, we had a very good night."

"Oh, wow. Good to know." Ashlan's face turned bright red, but she shook it off quickly.

Brinkley and Georgia were laughing hysterically, and we all joined in.

Midge and Janelle left shortly after, and we spent the next few minutes cleaning up.

"Let's go get some food and cocktails. I'm starving," Ruby said.

Everyone agreed, and we locked up and spent the next hour and a half laughing endlessly about everything from

Midge Longhorn to the fact that Oscar Daily had come in and bought a book, but he'd worn sunglasses and a baseball cap to hide his face.

I was grateful that I'd completely forgotten how nervous I was about my upcoming road trip to see my dad tomorrow.

Ruby spent the night at our house to keep me distracted, even though I told her multiple times that I was fine. She would be moving out soon, and I knew she'd only agreed to keep renting the other room to help me out. She stayed at River's almost every night. But we'd stayed up late talking, and I was grateful that I was so exhausted when my head hit the pillow that I didn't have time to second-guess if I was doing the right thing.

My phone buzzed in the morning, and Hayes's photo filled my screen. I'd sent him a text in the middle of the night to check on him because they couldn't seem to get this wildfire contained, and it was still blazing with a force.

"Hey," I said as I ran my fingers over the charm on my necklace out of habit. "How are you doing? Are you okay?"

"Hey, Say." I heard the exhaustion in his voice. "This fire is still out of control, but we're not backing down. Just had a few minutes to check in and saw you'd texted pretty late last night."

"Yeah, I woke up in the middle of the night and checked the app, and I just got worried. How long are you going to have to stay there? Are you eating? Sleeping?" I dropped to sit on the bed and chewed on my thumbnail. I hadn't slept well because I'd woken up shortly after falling asleep last night because I was anxious about Hayes, and I'd checked the fire update. That had me tossing and turning for hours.

"I'll be here for probably at least two more weeks. Maybe longer. It depends on what the weather decides to do. This damn wind keeps shifting, so every time we make progress, the weather makes things worse again. I'm eating and sleeping just fine. Don't worry about me. I'm good. Tell me about the book signing."

"Says the man who never stops worrying." I chuckled, but it was forced. Because I was worried, and I had a valid reason to worry. He was the one in the middle of a wildfire. "The book signing was so great, Hayes. Everyone in town came out to meet her, and she was amazing in every way. Charming and sweet and funny. The bookstore has been really busy since we opened the doors. Today is my first day off in a while."

"I'm proud of you, Say. You were determined to do this, and you made it happen. What are you going to do on your day off?"

I cleared my throat. I knew I needed to do it. The last thing I wanted was for my brother to worry about me going to see my father and his family, but I knew Kingston wasn't joking when he said he'd tell him if I didn't.

"If I tell you, can you just trust me on this?"

"If you're going anywhere near Barry, I am going to lose my shit."

"I have not seen Barry at all. Mom came to the book signing, and it was nice to see her. She looks good. And losing your shit has never helped anything."

"Tell me."

"I'm going to see Dad and Constance and meet our half-siblings. He invited me for lunch. And before you freak out, I told King that I was going, and he insisted on coming with me. He takes his babysitting job very seriously," I said, making no effort to hide the sarcasm in my voice.

I wasn't even slightly annoyed that Kingston was coming with me, but my brother didn't need to know that.

"I'm glad he's going with you. I'm surprised he didn't tell me about it when I spoke to him yesterday."

"He told me that if I didn't tell you by the time we got on the road, he'd be calling you."

"Ride or die. That's the way we roll. Of course, he'll drop everything and make sure you're all right. That's my brother right there. But I don't understand why you make such an effort for a man who hasn't been there for you. An entire family who hasn't been there for you."

A lump formed in my throat at his words.

"Everything is not black and white, Hayes. Dad made mistakes—I'm more than aware. But I don't give up on people. We have half-siblings that I would at least like to meet. They didn't do anything to us. Can you not give me a hard time about this? It's just something I want to do."

"Yeah." He yawned. "I can do that. All I care about is you being okay. I know I'm a closed-minded prick sometimes, Saylor. But you've just always been so good to the core, and I guess I just want to protect you from the big, bad world. I don't want to see him hurt you again. That's all it is. I don't hate his other kids because I don't know them. I don't like him because he left our mother and us and had an affair and started a new life with a new family—without giving one fuck about us. He made no effort to know us. He chose them." I heard the frustration in my brother's voice, and it hurt me, too. "And damn, Say, I was busy trying to be the man of the house after he left. Mom couldn't handle jack shit at the time."

A tear ran down my cheek, and I tried to compose my voice. "I know. And I want you to know that you have been more than a brother to me, Hayes. You've been my protector, my best friend, and the only solid parent I've ever really had. And I'm grateful for that. Having you for a brother is the best thing that's ever happened to me. But you have to trust me to make decisions for myself, okay?"

"Yeah. I can do that. Just let me know how it goes. I'm glad you'll have King with you. That dude can make the worst situations seem like a party."

"Yes. He will definitely lighten the mood. As much as I was pissed off that you basically forced him to babysit me, I'm happy he's coming with me."

"Me, too. Be smart and be safe, okay? You got your necklace on?" he asked, his voice not hiding his concern. The necklace was an inside joke, as he'd always told me he'd protect me from all the evil out in the world, and when he wasn't with me, I'd have my evil eye necklace to do it for me.

"Of course, I do. I only take it off when I sleep. And I've got this. You're the one heading into a blazing forest fire. Let's worry about you being safe." I tried to keep my tone light. "I love you, Hayes."

"I love you, too. Don't ever forget it."

"Well, don't say it that way. That makes me think you're going into this fire and not coming out." I shook my head.

He chuckled and covered it with a cough. "Fine. I love you. I'll call you later."

We ended the call, and I just sat there, worried about my brother and nervous about what I was walking into today.

"Hey, hey! Are you ready for a road trip? I've got the snacks in the car already." Kingston filled the doorway as he leaned against the frame, looking sexy as hell in his dark jeans and white tee. His navy baseball cap was turned backward, which just worked for him, and he held his gold aviators in his hand.

"I told you I'd bring the snacks." I pushed to my feet and walked toward him.

"I told him that you bought the snacks already, too!" Ruby shouted from the kitchen.

"I'm more than aware that you were bringing your version of road trip food. But I don't want fruit-flavored water and sliced oranges. I want an ice-cold fountain drink full of sugar, beef jerky, spicy potato chips, and red licorice."

"That'll give you a stomachache." I walked past him

toward the kitchen, where I'd packed up the healthy treats for our drive.

"You seem edgy. Are you nervous about today, Dandelion?" He asked.

I *was* actually worried, but not for the reasons he thought.

Because being alone in the car with a man I was painfully attracted to was going to be a hell of a lot harder than seeing my father after all these years.

# 18

## Kingston

The drive to Oak Grove Hills took a little over two hours. Saylor Woodson was my kind of road tripper. She appointed herself the DJ, and we had similar taste in music. A lot of country and a few good old-school 90s rap songs.

She was a fabulous navigator, even if she repeated everything the Google Maps woman had already said.

Her choices in snacks were pretty lame, but my stomach was gurgling from all the shit I'd eaten, so she was clearly a hell of a lot brighter than me.

We'd talked about the book signing yesterday, Romeo and Demi's upcoming wedding, and she'd asked endless questions about the new renovation I was currently working on out at the Halseys' ranch.

I pulled into a fancy-ass gated subdivision and got in line to check in with the guard. I leaned forward to take in the giant mansions that stood beyond the gates.

"Wow. I know you said he married a woman with money, but these are outrageous, right?"

She chewed on her thumbnail. She'd gotten quieter in the

last few minutes since we'd exited the freeway. "Yeah. I've never been here, so I don't know."

I glanced over at her. "Hey, relax. You've got this. If it sucks, we'll bail."

"Okay. I like that idea." She looked out the window when a car moved through the gates, and we pulled up closer to check in. "Maybe we should have a code word."

"Like a safe word?" I waggled my brows, and she chuckled.

"Sure. If it's not going well, we can say the word to let the other one know we need to leave."

"Hmmm . . . what's a good safe word? Titties? Pussy? Orgasm?" I said, and she shook her head as her cheeks flamed pink.

"It's our turn, Casanova." She pointed for me to move forward.

"Hello, sir. May I ask who you're here to see today?" the guard, who was dressed in a military-looking outfit, asked.

"Yes, you may. We're here to see the Woodsons. I'm King, and this is Saylor," I said as he stepped back from the car and made his way toward the small guard shack. He picked up the phone and spoke to someone before returning with a card for me to put on my windshield.

"They're expecting you," he said, completely void of expression.

"I would hope so. They're in for a real treat with this one." I thrust my thumb at Saylor and winked at her. "So, what are they like? Are they any fun? Can you give us a little insight?"

"King, stop," Saylor said over a fit of laughter as she squeezed my arm and waved at the guard.

The dude surprised me when he lifted his sunglasses and leaned down. "They are an *interesting bunch*. Have a nice time."

I saluted him as I drove through the gate and followed the GPS through the swanky-ass neighborhood. It pissed me off that their father had this kind of money, and he hadn't stepped up when they'd been removed from their home. He hadn't helped pay for Saylor's college education or done anything to support Saylor or Hayes since the day he'd left, outside of paying the minimum child support. I knew she was thinking it, too. Hearing that someone had a lot of money and seeing it with your own eyes were two completely different things.

I needed to lighten the mood because I could feel the tension radiating from her hot little body. "Okay. What's our safe word?"

"How about Beefcake? You can say it when you cough like, *Beefcake*," she said over a muffled cough, which made me laugh.

"He'd be honored to be our safe word." I turned left per the directions.

I pulled in front of the palatial palace that Donald Woodson called home. The bastard lived like a fucking king.

"Wow. This place is huge. That's a six-car garage, and the front porch looks like something out of a gardening magazine," she said as we both got out of the car, and I reached for her hand on instinct. I knew she was nervous, even if she wouldn't admit it.

"I don't know. It's a little too neat. Too perfect. If I say *Beefcake,* you need to trust me, and we both agree to get the fuck out of this place, okay?"

She chuckled again, and I loved that I always knew how to help her relax.

"Thanks for coming with me, King." Her voice was just above a whisper. When we walked up the three brick steps leading to the grand entrance, we both turned as a cloud of smoke was coming from a few feet away, and a strong smell of marijuana wafted around us.

"Are you the infamous Saylor?" A dude sitting on an Adirondack chair who'd just released another round of potent weed raised a brow.

He wore dark skinny jeans, a black hoodie, and black military boots. His hair was jet black and hanging over one side of his face, and his skin looked like he hadn't seen daylight since . . . birth. The sun was shining, birds were chirping, and the porch looked like some sort of Norman Rockwell painting. Yet, this dude stood out like a sore fucking thumb rocking his best Addams family look.

"Um, yes, hi. I'm Saylor, and this is my friend, King." She moved toward him, extending her hand in greeting.

He didn't realize she was going for the handshake, and he quickly offered up his joint. "I'm Phoenix. You want a hit? It's some damn good shit."

"Oh, no. I'm good. All smoked out for the day." Saylor chuckled, clearly trying to play it cool, which made me laugh. She wore a white tank top and a long, flowing floral skirt that came to her ankles. She looked gorgeous, like she'd fit right in this picture-perfect home, minus her half-brother who'd clearly just arrived from the pits of hell.

"You look like a dude who can hang. You want in?" He flung his head to the side so the stiff piece of hair covering his eye shifted a bit as he looked me over.

"I'm all set for now." I smirked.

"All right," he said, looking back at Saylor. "I guess you're my long-lost sister, huh?"

"Something like that."

"Well, here's a tip, sis. The people behind those doors—they're a lot, so buckle up. Destiny is a real piece of work, but she's the one who pushed for this meeting, and what Destiny wants, Destiny gets." He took another hit, and I was fairly certain I had a secondhand high from standing this close to Puff the Magic Dragon.

"Thanks for the tip," she said, taking a step back. "Are you coming inside?"

"As soon as I'm fully high and chill enough to enjoy the show."

I raised a brow. What the fuck were we walking into?

Saylor held up a hand and gave him a slight nod as we walked toward the door. I leaned down close to her ear. "Is it too soon to say Beefcake?"

She swatted my chest as she rang the bell. "I'll take a pothead over a haughty snob any day of the week."

The door opened, and a man wearing what looked like a tuxedo stood in front of us. "Welcome. Do come in. May I take your hat, sir?"

"That's a hard no. I like to keep everything I arrived with on my body in case I need to make a quick exit, you know?" I chuckled, and the older man just gave a curt nod while Saylor tried to cover her laugh.

She glanced at me as she stepped inside, and I followed. The entry was grand, with black-and-white marble flooring that must have cost a pretty penny. As a contractor, I knew what materials like this would run someone, and I'd never seen an entryway that was quite this large or grand. There was an oversized round table in the middle of the foyer with a large floral arrangement sitting on top and an enormous crystal chandelier hanging overhead.

"Is that my little girl?" A man came around the corner wearing a colorful polo shirt with pink flamingos all over it. His dark hair was thinning on top, and he pulled her into a hug. "Saylor, look at you. You're so grown up."

*That'll happen when you don't see your kid for over two decades, dickhead.*

"Hey, Dad," she said awkwardly, and I noticed the way her body stiffened as he held her there.

I extended my hand as I narrowed my gaze and studied him. "I'm King. I'm a good friend of both Saylor and Hayes."

The dickweasel loosened his hold on her and extended his arm. I quickly assessed the fact that his hand was soft and completely lacking any signs of ever doing an ounce of work. I intentionally squeezed harder than usual and noticed the way he winced, and I internally patted myself on the back.

He was a weak motherfucker, no question there.

I was here for Saylor. This was important to her. But that didn't mean I had to like the asshole. I knew the pain he'd caused. I knew he was a piece of shit. I just hoped she'd figure it out, too.

A clacking against the marble floors had me dropping his hand as we all turned to see a girl walking our way with her eyes set on Saylor. She looked to be about sixteen years old, maybe younger; it was hard to tell with all the makeup she was wearing. Her blonde hair hung down to her waist, and she wore a black short skirt and tall heels that made her look like she was playing dress-up. But it was the white tee that read *DESTINY* in capital letters across her chest, along with the bright pink fur coat around her shoulders, that caught my eye. What was with the clothing choices of the people in this home?

"Is this her?" She snapped her fingers in her father's face before shouting in a painfully high-pitched, loud voice that would have any dog in a ten-mile radius running for the hills. "I said, *is this her?*"

Saylor glanced at me, and I leaned against her ear, whispering with a desperation that she wouldn't be able to miss. "*Beefcake.*"

Of course, she ignored me. So much for safe words.

"Yes, Destiny. This is Saylor. Your older sister."

"Hi," Saylor said, startling a bit when Demon Barbie began circling her.

"I know. And I have to say, she's exactly what I hoped she'd be," Destiny said before pausing to tug hard on Saylor's hair.

"Ouch," Saylor gasped, and I moved forward to stand between them.

"What the fuck was that?" I hissed.

"Oh, look at you. She brought some man candy. Can I call you Daddy, big boy?" the little tyrant asked. I was in some sort of twilight zone because Donald Woodson just smiled like this was perfectly normal behavior.

"Absolutely not. And if you touch her head again, I will have no problem doing the same to you."

Destiny made this odd growling noise and then ran her long, sharp nails along my chest like a motherfucking cat in heat.

"Easy, boy. I was just seeing if she had extensions in her hair. I'm impressed that's all yours, sis."

Saylor looked completely shell-shocked as she stared at Destiny with confusion. "Yeah. This is my hair. So, let's not pull it again, okay?"

"Oh, she's not the passive wallflower you described, Donald." She shot a look at her father, and normally I'd be wondering why she'd called him by his first name, but this girl was definitely beating to her own drum, so it wasn't too surprising at this point.

"I asked you to call me Dad when we have company." Donald shook his head and smiled like his evil spawn didn't just assault everyone in the room. "Come and have lunch. Constance has a nice meal planned for us."

I took Saylor's hand in mine as we followed them through the house, passing what looked like a grand library and a formal living room before stopping at a dining room that was fit for the royal family.

The tuxedo dude was standing there, and Donald asked him to let Constance and Phoenix know that lunch was being served.

The table was set with what I assumed were expensive

plates and cutlery, accompanied by crystal glasses. I was hoping for a burger or some chicken fingers, but I had a hunch that lunch was going to be something very different.

"You're sitting there." Destiny pointed to a chair and motioned for Saylor to take her seat. And when I moved to the chair beside her, Destiny fisted my tee in her freakishly sharp fingernails. "*No, Daddy.* You're on the other side of me. I'm sitting between you two."

She turned around to pull out her chair, and Saylor's eyes widened as she looked at me, and I mouthed the word *Beefcake* for a second time since we'd arrived.

I wanted to get the fuck out of here, and I was grateful that she hadn't come here alone, because this was proving to be the palace from hell.

"Hello, you must be Saylor." A woman who looked like an older version of the terrifying teen beside me approached the table.

"Hi. Yes, I'm Saylor, and this is my friend, King."

"I'm Constance. Thank you for coming. This was very important to my Destiny." She took her seat across from Saylor just as Puff the Magic Dragon came skateboarding into the dining room with a cloud of reefer surrounding him.

I leaned forward and met eyes with Saylor, and she gave me that look I knew all too well.

*What the fuck is happening?*

She wanted to stay, so I was going to try to enjoy myself. Our glasses were filled with water, and they'd offered wine and champagne, which both Saylor and I declined, because, well, it was noon, and we were definitely getting the hell out of here as soon as possible.

The first course was served by not one, not two, but three women in full black-and-white uniforms. They set down a plate with some weird-ass orange goopy-looking eggs on top of a piece of salmon.

"Enjoy your salmon and caviar," one of the women said, and I used my finger to flick the orange shit off the salmon.

Destiny raised a brow and smirked. "So, are you dating my sister?"

"Yes. We're very serious. Marriage is definitely in our future."

Saylor put a hand over her mouth and turned her attention to Constance, who was snapping her fingers to get us all to look her way.

Apparently, snapping was the way they communicated in this hellish place.

"You are your mother's daughter, aren't you? You don't resemble your father at all," Constance said, and the way she spoke to Saylor rubbed me wrong. Hell, who was I kidding? This whole experience rubbed me wrong.

"She does look like Stella, but she's got my eyes," Donald said proudly, as if it was his claim to fame, or as if he'd had anything to do with the beautiful girl that he'd abandoned.

"She has my eyes!" Destiny shouted, and everyone startled.

What was with the fucking outbursts?

When her fists hit the table, some of her pink fur detached from the coat and fluttered around me. I waved my hand around to push it away as I coughed over a little piece that had gotten into my mouth.

"I actually think I look the most like my brother, Hayes," Saylor said. "So, tell me, why has it taken so long for us to all get together?"

Ahhh . . . the million-dollar question.

Finally, a voice of reason.

Donald paled a bit, but Constance looked unfazed, though it could be her overly injected face because it lacked all expression. Her eyebrows hadn't moved since she'd entered the room and her lips were so plump they looked painful.

"We've just been living our lives, dear. But Destiny was determined to meet you."

I looked up to see Phoenix looking at me with a wicked smirk. He'd warned us to buckle up, and clearly, he'd meant it.

# 19

## Saylor

"That's not entirely true. I wanted to see you, as well. Tell us about the bookstore that you opened," my father said, and I studied him for a long moment.

I'd held onto a memory from when I was young for such a long time. It was my father holding my hand at the Magnolia Falls fair. He'd bought me cotton candy and bent down to give it to me, and he'd laughed when I'd tried to tear a piece off. I wasn't even certain that it was a real memory after all these years. Maybe I'd dreamt it or made it up in my head after he'd left.

Because the truth was, I didn't know this man.

And I'd been uncomfortable since I'd walked through the door.

This was not my family.

These were not my people.

But I was here, and I'd make the best of it. At the very least, I could get some answers.

"I opened a bookstore in town just over a week ago. So, it's still new, but I'm enjoying it."

"And you didn't have to go to college to do that?" Phoenix asked.

"I went to college. I just finished my MBA this past year," I said, noting the way they all looked at one another. "However, it wasn't a requirement to have a degree to open a bookstore, but I wanted to have an understanding of how to run my own business."

"I thought you said none of them went to college?" Destiny shouted, and I was about done with her outrageous, high-pitched hissy fits.

I was on edge every time she spoke.

"I said that her mother and her brother didn't go to college, and I thought Saylor had dropped out, as well," Constance said, as her icy gaze locked with mine, and she forced a smile.

A growl came from Kingston, as if he'd heard enough, and I leaned forward and looked at him. That's all I'd ever had to do with him. He understood me without any words being said.

*I've got this.*

"I see. Let me clear things up for you. My mother met my father when they were *both* in college." I paused when one of the ladies in uniform cleared my uneaten plate of fish eggs. "My mother got pregnant by *my father*." I shot him a look, because the asshole had obviously been telling lies about everyone and everything.

"Correct." He cleared his throat and asked for a refill of his wine.

"I wasn't finished," I said when he started to speak again, and he clamped his mouth closed. "My mother dropped out of college to raise my brother, *your son*, Hayes."

"The oldest boy," Constance said, looking at her two children, and I raised a brow as our eyes locked.

"I am not done speaking, Constance." I waited for her to look at me. "Yes, my brother is your husband's oldest child. One of the kids that he abandoned. But I think, in the end, we were actually the lucky ones." I paused to chuckle, not hiding my anger. "Hayes didn't go to college because he went to school to be a firefighter so he could provide a home for me. Because he's a really good man. He didn't want to leave me in a bad situation with my mother's second husband, so he sacrificed his own life for mine."

"He's the best, and so are you," Kingston said.

"Thank you. I feel lucky to have a brother who knows what it means to be a man." I turned to look at my father, and he quickly stared down at his plate. "I hope that's shame that you're feeling right now. And I hope you feel it every single day until you take your last breath."

"Excuse me," Destiny said, in a normal tone for the first time since we'd arrived. "But this meeting was not about *Donald or Constance or you*, Saylor. This was about me. So, I'd appreciate if you'd stop with your little trip down memory lane. You seem to be just fine. Today is about me having a sister. Something Donald and Constance promised me."

I fell forward in laughter. "Are you kidding me right now? You don't get to decide that you want a sister and then have a tantrum and pull my hair and behave like a ridiculous child. That's not how this works."

"Are you going to allow her to speak to me like this?" she yelled again as she looked at her parents, and Constance shoved her chair back.

"You will not speak to my daughter that way." Constance pointed her finger at me.

"*Beef. Fucking. Cake*!" Kingston shouted, and everyone turned. "Put your fucking finger down now, and don't you ever point it in her direction again."

"Excuse me?" Constance gaped. "How dare you speak to me like that in my own home."

"Phoenix, I think your mother could use a little hit from that joint, if you know what I mean, buddy. I see why you're sitting out there, trying to check out before you enter crazy town. What do you say, Dandelion? Time to blow this popsicle stand and go get some chicken fingers and road trip food?"

I chuckled. "Yes. I've definitely had enough. Don't reach out anymore, Dad. I should have stopped trying when you left all those years ago, but I'm finally at peace with it now. Thanks for the closure."

"Atta girl. Let's get out of here." Kingston held his hand out and waited for my fingers to intertwine with his.

"What is happening!" Destiny shrieked, and I stepped forward and placed one finger from my free hand on her lips, and her eyes widened.

"I'll tell you what's happening. I'm leaving. If you want a relationship with me, you can reach out on your own. But the way that you have behaved today—you wouldn't last in my world for two minutes. Call me when you grow up."

Phoenix moved to his feet, his head falling back in a full fit of laughter. "Fucking balls to the walls. I love it."

"Phoenix," Constance hissed.

Phoenix held his hand out and high-fived me and King on our way out of the dining room.

And we waltzed right out the front door, and I made no attempt to hide the smile on my face.

This was what I'd longed for all those years?

To know this man? This family?

*Note to self: Be careful what you wish for.*

Kingston opened the passenger door, and I slipped inside. He leaned over and buckled my seat belt for me, as if he thought I was too shaken up to do it myself.

I let him because I was still processing the scene I'd just walked out of.

He got into the car just as I caught something out of my peripheral, and my father came jogging toward the car. I put my window down and looked at him.

He reached for my hand. "I'm sorry, Saylor."

"You should be." I tugged my hand away and rolled up my window as he stood there watching as we backed out of the driveway.

It didn't hurt to see him fade into the distance.

It felt like closure.

And I knew without a shadow of a doubt that this was goodbye.

No more wondering or hoping.

"Are you okay?" Kingston asked, after we pulled out of the development.

"I actually am. Thanks for going with me. I don't think I'd have believed it myself if there weren't two of us witnessing that madness with our own eyes." I shook my head in disbelief. "What even was that?"

"That was—a shit show. I kind of like Phoenix, though." He chuckled.

"Yeah. He was nice enough. But Destiny? The screaming? What is my father thinking?"

"Honestly. I think your father went for the money, and he totally traded down. They may have a big house, but that place was terrifying," Kingston said, as he pulled down a side street as if he knew where he was going.

I laughed. "Constance had the most frozen face I've ever seen, and my father just lets her say whatever the hell she wants. He knew I graduated from college. Not to mention the way they talked about my mother and my brother. That was the final nail in the coffin for me." I ran my fingers over my necklace.

"Me, too. And Demon Barbie definitely gouged my chest with those freaky claws, not to mention the fact that I've got pink fur lodged in my throat."

I chuckled because it was impossible not to. If I didn't laugh right now, I'd curl up in a ball and cry. Because the truth was, my father hadn't wanted to see me today. His spoiled, belligerent, teenage daughter wanted a sister—so he'd called me.

It should hurt, but it didn't.

It was sort of on par with the man who'd left all those years ago.

I'd finally seen him for who he was.

"I did patch you up after the bee sting, so I'm sure I could do the same for the damage Destiny did," I said, turning to him as he pulled into a drive-thru.

"All right, Dandelion. I'd love to have you patch me up." He waggled his brows. "Now, let's eat some chicken fingers and put the house of horror in our rearview."

"Sounds like a plan," I said.

We pulled over and ate lunch in the car and then got on the road back to Magnolia Falls.

"You seem like you're handling things okay, huh?" Kingston asked.

"Why do you think I'm breakable? I know my brother does, too. But just because Hayes and I have different ways of looking at things, doesn't mean I can't handle disappointment. My father hasn't seen me in over two decades. Did you really think I had high expectations? I just wanted to meet them. Meet my half-siblings. See if there would be some sort of connection if I saw my father in person after all these years. But how can I be let down when the man has never shown up for me or Hayes?"

"You're much stronger than people think, Dandelion," he said, as we closed the distance to Magnolia Falls.

"Hayes still sees me as a kid. And I can't even fault him, because he's always had my back. But we look at things very differently. He is very black and white, and I think there is always a little gray area to hope for the best, you know?"

"I get that. How are things going with your mom?"

"She's come into the bookstore a few times. We're working on it." I shrugged, glancing back and taking him in. His baseball cap was still turned backward, and he had just the slightest bit of scruff on his jaw. My eyes zeroed in on his plump lips, and I remembered the way they felt against mine.

He was ridiculously sexy.

I couldn't get that kiss out of my head.

I'd never ached for a man the way I ached for Kingston Pierce.

"That's great. I think I understand that gray area, too. It's okay to hope for good things to come out of tough situations."

"Yeah? So you're on my side on this one?" My voice was all tease.

"I'm always on your side, Saylor." He ran a hand over the back of his neck. "I think losing my parents the way I did and missing out on knowing them was about as bad as it gets. But being raised by amazing grandparents was the bright side of a horrific situation."

I nodded. He always played it so cool. But I knew that he felt that loss every single day. "Your grandparents really did step up. I just went to see Pearl yesterday. She really is the best."

"We definitely agree on that." He winked at me before turning his attention back to the road in front of him.

"Do you think that losing your parents the way you did is the reason that you don't do relationships?" I asked, because what did I have to lose at this point?

He didn't respond for several seconds, and I wondered if I'd pushed too far. "I don't know. I do like to keep things light. According to Ruby, who loves to get inside my head—" he laughed, "—learning at a young age how quickly someone can be taken from you, could potentially cause someone to be hesitant about going too deep with someone in the future. But I'm in deep with my grandmother and my friends and you."

"Well, you won't go too deep with me." I stared out the window.

"That's not true, Dandelion. I don't think I've ever gone deeper with another person than I have with you."

His words hit me hard. I hadn't expected that.

"I know." I shrugged as I took in all the wildflowers covering the field in front of me. "But taking things further is something you aren't willing to do."

"I've already crossed the line so many times with you, I'm not sure where the line is anymore." He cleared his throat, staring straight ahead. "I understand why Hayes would be angry."

I rolled my eyes. "And why is that? It shouldn't be any of his business."

"You're wrong about that, Saylor. Half the reason I love him so damn much is because of the way he is with you. You deserve that type of love, and you didn't get it from your parents. He stepped up. And he knows my track record. He knows that if I ever went there with you and fucked it up, it would be over for me and him. If I hurt you, he couldn't be in my life."

"You would never hurt me, King. You've always been there for me."

"Because we haven't gone there. You deserve someone who loves you and knows how to treat you right. You deserve the prince on the white horse." He glanced over at me, dark eyes filled with emotion.

He was so damn hard on himself.

"That's the thing. I'm not looking for a prince on a white horse. I don't need to be saved or rescued. And to be honest, I just got out of a long relationship, and it wasn't a great one. Grahame never made me his priority, but at the same time, he was overbearing and possessive. I was always explaining myself, and dealing with his jealousy was exhausting. I'm not looking to get into anything serious. Maybe I just want to have some fun."

"I do bring the fun," he said, his voice gruff and sexy.

"You sure do. I'm not looking to jump back into a relationship. I'm young. I'm single. And I like hanging out with you."

"I like hanging out with you, too," he said as he pulled down my street.

When he put the car in park in my driveway, I turned to face him. He looked serious now, like he was struggling with something.

"It's fine, King. I get it. You can't go there. Thanks for going with me today. If you want to have some phone sex later, give me a call."

We were both laughing as I reached for the door handle, but his fingers wrapped around my wrist to stop me.

"Maybe I'm not ready to say goodbye just yet."

I raised a brow. "Neither am I. What do you have in mind?"

"The sun's about to go down. You want to go for a swim in the lake?"

My breath hitched, and I nodded.

The sunset, cool water, and a half-naked Kingston.

Yes, please.

# 20

# Kingston

What the fuck was I doing? I should have just driven away. But I didn't want to.

We'd spent so much time together now, that I was thinking about her when I wasn't with her.

And I was wrestling with it all the fucking time.

I thought about talking to Hayes and telling him how I was feeling. I hadn't brought it up to any of the guys, but they'd noticed how much time I spent with her, especially since Hayes had left town.

I didn't feel right discussing it with them before I talked to him.

And what would I even say?

*I can't get enough of your sister, and I get off to thoughts of her in the shower every fucking day. I think about her every fucking minute of the day.*

He'd laugh in my face, and he'd have every right to.

My track record was not good. But I'd also never felt this way about anyone.

So maybe I'd talk to her about it once we were out in the water.

Admit that I was feeling things I'd never felt before.

"You got lucky finding this house on the canal. It's perfect for swimming," I said, as I followed her outside. "You don't have the boats over here."

She'd slipped into her pink bikini, and I was doing everything in my power not to stare. Her tan skin glistened in the last bit of sunlight, and when we got down to the little dock sitting by the water, she dropped her shorts.

"Are you going to swim fully clothed?" She turned around and smiled at me.

I yanked my tee over my head and kicked off my shoes. I didn't miss the way her eyes raked over me as I shoved my jeans down my legs, leaving me in nothing but my black fitted briefs.

Her eyes widened, and I followed her gaze down to see my erection straining against the fabric. I was hard every single time I was around this girl, and there was no hiding it when I was standing here with just thin cotton covering my eager dick.

"I told you it's been a while, so it is what it is," I said.

She chuckled before pulling all that pretty blonde hair up into a messy knot on top of her head and wrapping some kind of hair tie around it. She stepped down the few steps into the water and gasped as she let go, keeping her head just above the water. I followed her in and yelped as I adjusted to the cold water.

"It actually feels good after sitting in the car all day." I swam behind her as she glanced over her shoulder.

"Come check out this cool little cove I found the other day."

I moved beside her, rolling onto my back and tipping my head back to wet my hair.

"Where are you taking me?" I asked, before I rolled back onto my stomach just in time to see her ass above the water as she kicked ahead of me.

"Just trust me." She swam a little further before coming to a stop under a huge tree, which formed a large canopy over the water. "Look at this. Someone hung a swing over here. And look through the branches. The sun's about to set, and we have the perfect view. Have you ever seen anything more beautiful?"

She held onto the rope hanging off the tree as she stared straight up at the orange-and-pink-filled sky—but I was staring right at her.

"I can't say I have."

Her head straightened, and she caught me looking at her as I pushed to stand, finding the bottom with my feet, and I moved in front of her.

I gripped the sides of the shabby wood that she'd pulled herself to sit on, and she held onto the rope on each side. "You want me to push you?"

"Nope." Her voice was just above a whisper.

"You know what we were talking about in the car?"

"Yes." She reached out with one hand and stroked the hair away from my face as I moved to stand between her legs.

"I sometimes wonder if maybe I've always been single because the only girl I really ever wanted was the one I couldn't have." My heart raced as I admitted to her what I'd been wondering since my grandmother called me out on it.

"But you can have her. You've just decided to become ridiculously moral all of a sudden."

"He's my best friend, Saylor," I said, as she reached for my shoulders and pulled herself forward. My hands found her perfectly round ass, and I stepped back from the swing, and her legs wrapped around my waist. "We have a pact, the five of us. You know that."

"King, you are overthinking this. Let's just see where this goes. You are putting so much pressure on yourself. On this." She motioned between us. "We've been friends for a long time, and we're attracted to one another. I know who you are. I'm not asking you for forever. I'm asking you for right now."

"I need to talk to Hayes. That's what I was thinking about on the drive. I think I should talk to him."

She groaned and made no attempt to hide her irritation. "Right. Because when you're testing the waters and have no idea what to expect, you should definitely ask permission from my overbearing brother first."

"I can't lie to him."

"I'm not asking you to lie to him. I'm asking you to treat me like an adult. When you get together with a woman, do you go to her family and ask if you can kiss her first?"

"Well, I've already kissed you, haven't I?"

"You know what I mean. The minute you tell Hayes anything is going on, there is going to be all this pressure on us. Everyone will be watching, and it will change things. What if we just explore this attraction and see where it goes? It's no one's business. Once Hayes knows, he'll get all broody and weird, and it'll make things awkward for everyone. And who knows? We could lose interest in a day, and then we made it a big deal for nothing."

Her fingers were tangled in my hair, and nothing had ever felt more right.

I knew I was being a selfish prick.

I wanted her so badly I could barely think straight lately.

"A day, huh? You think you'll get bored of me that quickly?" I teased.

She shrugged, her teeth sinking into her bottom lip. "Sure. It's probably just a phase. An itch we need to scratch."

"We'll see about that. But I'm not fucking you until we tell him," I said, trying hard to keep myself in control.

Hayes would lose his shit if things went that far. But we'd already crossed a line that I knew he wouldn't be okay with.

Maybe if we just stayed right there and didn't let things go too far, it would be okay.

She was right. Maybe this would all pass in a few days, and then we'd have gotten everyone all worked up for nothing.

"Don't be so sure I'd be willing to. I just want to kiss you right now. Just you and me and no one else telling us it's a bad idea."

I nodded as her forehead fell against mine. "Okay. But if this isn't out of our system quickly, then we talk to him."

"If you still can't get enough of me when Hayes comes back home, then we can talk about telling him." She laughed, and I buried my facc in her neck.

"You think that's funny. You might be the one who can't get enough," I said, nipping at her ear.

She pulled my head up, and her aqua-blue eyes locked with mine. There were pops of gold and amber with the last sliver of sunlight shining down on her. "Show me what I've been missing."

And that was all I needed to hear. I tugged her mouth down to mine, and I kissed her with a need I couldn't begin to wrap my head around.

I tilted her head as her lips parted, and my tongue slipped in.

I tasted and explored her sweet mouth as her hips started grinding against mine. One hand stayed at the back of her head, and the other moved to her hip, and I guided her up and down my throbbing cock. Even in the cold water, I was ready to explode. She slid up and down my erection, and I groaned into her mouth. And we stood there, under the canopy of leaves, kissing and rubbing up against one another.

I'd had a lot of sex in my days, but nothing beat the feel of Saylor Woodson against my body.

Against my cock.

Even if I wasn't inside her, this was the best sex I'd ever

had. Her hard nipples pressed against my chest, and I couldn't fucking take the little moans coming from her mouth.

"Oh my God," she groaned as she started moving faster.

Her head fell back, and I kissed down her neck as she continued riding me.

"Come for me, baby," I said, as both of my hands found her hips, and I ground her harder against me, feeling my dick grow between her thighs.

"Yes, King," she cried out.

I pumped harder. Even with the fabric of my briefs and her bikini bottoms between us, I could feel everything.

Every. Fucking. Thing.

Now her head was back up, and she had her hands on my shoulders, eyes wild and sated as she continued to grind against me. Up and down my shaft. Faster. Our breaths filled the air around us. Desperate and needy.

"I want you to come for me," she whispered, and that was all it fucking took.

"Fuck," I hissed as I came hard.

And she kept moving before she fell forward, her head resting on my shoulder.

My arms were wrapped around her, and I held her there as we waited for our breathing to calm.

Her fingers traced over the tattoo on my shoulder. "Tell me why you have a dandelion on your Ride or Die tattoo. And tell me the truth this time."

I walked a few steps toward the large boulder sticking out of the water, and I settled against it, keeping her right where she was.

I pulled back, forcing her head to rise and tipping her chin up so her gaze would meet mine. "Because it was supposed to be a reminder. Our pact with the five of us . . . it's strong."

"I know that. And I would never do anything to come

between that. But we're two consenting adults. I don't understand why you added the flower all those years ago?"

"Because I had these thoughts about you before you left for college."

She sucked in a breath. "And the dandelion was a reminder of me?"

"Yes. Of what I couldn't have."

Her gaze softened. "You should have talked to me. I'd thought about you so many times, but I never thought you felt that way about me."

"I'm going to fuck it up, Saylor. I'm not good at this. You deserve a hell of a lot better than me. I know it. Hayes knows it. Why don't you believe me?"

"Because I think I've always been yours, in a way. My forbidden King."

"Forbidden for good reason, and don't you forget it," I said, grazing my lips against hers.

"So, if you're such bad news, how come you haven't been having sex these last few weeks? I mean, we haven't been together, yet you've admitted you haven't been with anyone else."

"I don't fucking know. Trust me, I've tried. I think you broke me." I shrugged, and her head tipped back in laughter.

"I think you broke me. Because I'm not sick of you yet, and I want to do that again."

"Yeah?" I asked, my voice gruff and needy. "I've already come in my briefs like a hormonal teenager, with that hot little pussy of yours rubbing up against me."

"Does that mean you're done?" She nipped at my bottom lip. "You've had enough and we'll pretend it never happened?"

"Not even fucking close. I haven't tasted you yet."

"You've got one filthy mouth, Kingston Pierce." She pulled back and studied me. "But I'm here for it. Let's take this slow and see how we feel tomorrow."

"I think you're going to be begging for my lips on your pussy the minute I'm gone." I chuckled.

"We'll see. I might just wake up and be over it." She smiled and raised a brow.

My gaze locked with hers. "You're so fucking beautiful. Sometimes it's hard for me not to stare at you."

Her breath hitched, and she stroked the scruff along my jaw. "We've already established that we won't be having sex. But everything else is on the table, so you don't have to flatter me. I'm all in for as long as we agree to do this."

"Let's get one thing straight right now." I wrapped my large hand around the side of her neck, my thumb grazing along her jaw. "I will never bullshit you. We've got to be on the same page if we're going to do whatever the fuck this is we're doing."

"We're just getting one another out of our systems. I'll probably tire of you by the time we get back to the house." Her voice was all tease. "But I agree. We need to be honest. That way, no one will walk away hurt."

"I would never forgive myself if I hurt you, Saylor."

"Stop overthinking it. You just gave me the sexiest make-out session I've ever had. Only second to the last make-out session I had with you. A few more orgasms, and I won't even remember your name." She smiled, but I knew she was trying to play it cool.

We both felt this pull.

It was dangerous.

Forbidden.

But I couldn't stop it if I wanted to.

I'd tried for weeks to stay away.

Yet here I was.

With Saylor Woodson in my arms.

# 21

## Saylor

"Who keeps texting you?" Peyton asked.

"Oh, it's just my mom asking about having lunch this weekend." I stretched the truth. She'd texted once, but all the other texts had been from Kingston. He'd left after we'd made out again at my house when we said our goodbyes last night.

And then we'd ended up talking on the phone for hours until we couldn't keep our eyes open.

I'd never been with a man who I was this comfortable with. We could talk about anything and everything.

He told me all about the kitchen renovation he was doing, and he was so passionate about it. He took pride in his work, and he loved what he did.

We talked about childhoods, my lack of stability, and his guilt that his grandparents had lost their chance to retire and enjoy old age because they'd raised him and his brother. I assured him that it was the greatest joy of their lives, because anyone who knew them knew it was true.

And then we read a few chapters of the latest romance book of his choosing. He was dabbling in historical fiction and telling me how he thought he would have thrived back then if he'd been alive.

But who was he kidding? The man would thrive in any time period.

"How are things going with your mom?" Ruby asked.

"We're making progress." I fiddled with my cocktail napkin. We'd met at Whiskey Falls for a quick happy hour drink and a few appetizers. "I've told you guys that my mom struggles with depression, so it's a daily battle for her most of the time."

"I understand that. Slade struggled for a long time when he was younger, and I think a lot of that led to him turning to drugs and alcohol to deal with it. But he's really making progress and learning that it's okay if you're struggling. You just need to talk about it." Demi sipped her martini, her eyes filled with empathy.

"That couldn't have been easy for you growing up in a home with a mom who struggled with depression, and you didn't have the tools to help her back then." Ruby studied me.

"You've got your therapist hat on." Peyton chuckled. "I know you aren't a therapist, but you're an emotional problem solver, Rubes. Just own it."

Ruby chuckled. "Whatever. I'm just saying that it couldn't have been easy for you or Hayes."

"I think it's why she chooses the partners that she does. Maybe she's drawn to the toxicity. I'm fairly certain she and my father had a volatile relationship, as well. And after he left, things only got worse. It's also why my brother wanted to get us both out of that house as soon as he could."

"Yeah. I know he can be overly protective, but it's coming from such a good place, you know?" Demi said.

"I never doubt that. He just needs to be reminded that I'm not a little kid anymore."

"He's definitely protective." Ruby took a sip from her wineglass. "And that was nice of King to go with you to meet your dad and his family. Even if they were batshit crazy."

I'd filled them in on how odd the whole experience had been, and they'd been pretty floored by all of it.

"Yeah. He's the best." I could feel my cheeks heat, and I tried my best to act casual. I couldn't get him out of my head. The way he'd kissed me out in the water. The way he'd made me feel.

"You two sure spend a lot of time together," Demi said, as she waggled her brows.

Kingston and I had made a deal to keep this between us, and I'd asked him not to talk to my brother about it, so this wasn't something I could share with anyone.

And I was fine with it, because it was something that I only shared with him.

"We're good friends." I popped a tater tot into my mouth as all three studied me.

They didn't push.

It was obvious they suspected something was up. I wasn't going to blatantly deny it, but I wasn't going to offer it up, either.

Kingston had never been in a relationship. And now he was fooling around with his best friend's little sister. The minute Hayes found out about it, he would freak out, and this whole thing would blow up. I just wanted a chance to see where this went before all the noise brought it to a quick end.

I knew I was playing with fire, but I was willing to get burned for this man.

That's how strongly I felt about him.

"Just be smart, all right?" Ruby whispered to just me, her eyes giving me that knowing look as Demi and Peyton added more food to their plates.

"I wish you'd just jump the man's bones. He's so hot. I

don't know how you hang out with him all the time without anything going on." Peyton sipped her cocktail and shrugged.

At least only one of them appeared to be suspicious.

"Never crossed my mind," I said, and we all laughed because they knew that was a big, fat lie.

No one could meet Kingston and not think about it.

There was just something about him.

"Speak of the devil," Ruby said, and I turned to see him walking toward us.

"Ladies," he said, his hand landing on the small of my back. "Did you forget to invite me to happy hour?"

Everyone chuckled, and my heart raced because I knew he was here for me.

*He can't stop thinking about yesterday either.*

"Are you out trolling tonight, King?" Peyton said, her voice all tease.

"Nope. I seem to have retired my trolling days, Peyt." He reached over and took a tater tot and popped it into his mouth. "I was just on my way home from work and thought I'd grab a beer."

Ruby was looking between us, but Demi and Peyton seemed to buy it.

Hell, *I* was buying it. We had plans to meet up later, but I hadn't expected him to show up here.

Lionel, Ruby's father, brought a beer over and made small talk with Kingston while we finished our drinks. He'd pulled up a barstool in between me and Peyton and made himself right at home.

"Okay, so we're all set for the bachelorette party, right?" Peyton asked. "Even if you want it to be tame, we're still going to make it fun."

"I know you're bummed, Peyt. I'm more than aware that you wanted it to be some wild Vegas trip, but it's just not my thing. So, we'll come to Whiskey Falls and dance and have some fun. But I promise, when you get married, we'll do all the crazy things, okay?"

"Fine," she huffed, and we all laughed.

Kingston's hand found my thigh beneath the table, and I sucked in a breath. Our shoulders were touching because the table wasn't large, and his hand climbed up my thigh without any warning. I jumped a bit and cleared my throat to cover it.

"Yes. We'll go all out for Peyton's bachelorette. I think this sounds fun, though, even if it's tame," I said, trying hard to pull myself together while his thumb was grazing along my inner thigh.

"And we've got the bridal shower in a few weeks that your mom and grandmother are throwing, so we've got lots of wedding stuff coming up." Ruby raised a brow at Peyton, as if to say that this was Demi's day, so she should do what she wanted.

"Snooze fest." Peyton rolled her eyes and then barked out a laugh. "I'm kidding. The shower will be so fancy and fun, and your mom did mention a mimosa fountain. I can live with that."

"Ahhh . . . and this is the party that I'm not invited to?" Kingston asked, with a wicked grin on his face.

"Well, I told her that you and Cutler were a little disappointed, and she said she was going to make an exception for her two favorite guys. But you have to come late so you don't sit through all the girly games." Demi smiled.

"Ahhh . . . Beefcake and I made the cut. I love it."

"Damn. I hope you guys crash the bachelorette party to liven things up." Peyton raised a brow.

"I know we're having the bachelor party on the same night, but we don't plan quite the way you all do. We just pull it together as we get closer. I think we're doing it at my house, and we'll do whatever Romeo wants."

"Well, at least we know where to go when ours ends." Peyton waggled her brows.

Kingston's hand moved between my thighs, and I sucked in a breath when he grazed his thumb along my most sensitive area.

*Oh. My. Gosh.*

I wrapped my hand around his wrist and pulled slightly because I wouldn't be able to control myself if he continued touching me like this. He pulled his hand away and winked at me as he continued making small talk.

Lionel came over to tell us that Kingston had already paid our bill, and we all thanked him and pushed to our feet. We hugged goodbye and walked toward the door. River was waiting outside to pick up Ruby and had offered everyone a ride. Kingston said he was on his way home, as well, and he'd walk with me.

River nodded, and I didn't miss the look between him and Ruby. I just waved goodbye, and we started walking when they pulled away from the curb.

Once they were out of view, I turned and smacked him on the arm. "What was that?"

"What?" He put a hand on my back to keep me walking.

"You can't do that to me in the middle of a bar. I could feel my cheeks turning pink, and everyone would have known what you were doing if I hadn't pulled your hand away," I said, throwing my arms in the air.

"And wasn't that kind of thrilling? Our little secret? Knowing that I couldn't wait to touch you. To taste you. It's all I've thought about all day. So yeah, I went to that bar, and I fought the urge to throw you over my shoulder and tell all of them exactly what I had planned."

I came to a stop, hands on my hips, as I turned to face him. "And what exactly do you have planned?"

He smiled, and I squeezed my thighs together. This man

was too good-looking for his own good. His thick hair was slightly disheveled, dark eyes heated and raking over me, and his smile did crazy things to me.

"I plan to strip you bare, spread you wide, and taste every inch of you. To make you come so many times you can't see straight. Does that sound all right?"

*Ummm . . . yes, please.*

"I think I can live with that." My teeth sank into my bottom lip, and I tried hard not to laugh at how awkward I was. "That's a pretty big plan, but still no sex, huh?"

"Nope. Not until we tell Hayes what's going on." He ran a hand through his hair. "I mean, he won't be happy with me that we've done anything, but at least he won't murder me."

"You do know how insane this is, right? You won't have sex with me until you get my brother's blessing?" I shook my head and started walking. "This isn't the 1800s."

"I hate to break it to you, Dandelion. But I don't think there has ever been a time period where the dude asked the brother if he could have sex with his sister." He barked out a laugh. "This isn't about me asking him for permission to fuck you. Trust me. I'm not stupid. He'd never be okay with that. This is about you and me figuring out if this thing is over before he even gets home. It's not about the sex. It's about doing the right thing regarding a guy who's like a brother to me."

I rolled my eyes and kept walking. I wanted to be irritated, but as much as it annoyed me that he was so worried about Hayes and how he'd react, I also sort of loved him for it.

My brother was a really good man. He didn't love many, but those that he loved, he'd walk through fire for. So, I understood why Kingston was worried.

"Again. We're two consenting adults. And let's just see if you're still coming around in a few days. It's very possible that you'll be tired of this by the end of the week." I chuckled as we turned down his street, after he asked me to come to his place.

"How about you? Were you hoping I'd stop by the bar? Were you thinking about last night the way that I've been thinking about it all fucking day?" He pulled his keys from his pocket.

"I thought about it all day, King. I'm not denying it." I followed him inside when he pushed the door open.

"Fuck, Saylor. I'm so fucked." He pressed my back against the door. "I don't know what you're doing to me. I've never wanted someone more than I want you. Not even fucking close." He dropped to his knees, catching me off guard.

"What are you doing?"

"I'm going to taste you right here in my entryway. And then I'm going to carry you to my bedroom and take my time with you tonight and do all the things I've dreamed of doing for a long fucking time."

He pushed my skirt up around my waist, and my head fell back against the door when he tore my panties right off my body like he couldn't wait another minute. "King," I whispered as his fingers trailed up the inside of my thighs.

"Spread these pretty little legs for me, Saylor. Let me see that perfect pink pussy, baby."

My breathing was already erratic, and my legs started trembling.

"Hey, look at me." His voice had my head springing forward and my eyes opening.

"Hi," I said, my voice just above a whisper.

"Is this too much? Your legs are shaking."

I shook my head. "No. I-I've wanted this. I just have never done, er, this before."

"Never done what?"

"I've never had a man . . . you know, taste me. Grahame

and I just didn't do that kind of stuff." I attempted to cover my face with my hands because this was mortifying, seeing as I was a grown woman. But I definitely hadn't had a lot of experience in this department. King reached up and pulled my hands down. "There's nothing to be embarrassed about. I'm honored that I get to be the first man lucky enough to taste you. To please you this way. And I promise you, Saylor, this will feel really good, okay? I've got you. Always. Do you trust me?"

"Of course, I do."

"All right. If for any reason you don't like it, or we're moving too fast, you just tell me to stop. There's no rush."

I nodded, and my fingers tangled in his hair as he buried his head between my thighs. His tongue swiped along my seam, and I gasped at the sensation.

He continued licking and teasing me over and over. His hands came around behind my butt, and he lifted me up, pulling my legs over his shoulders so he could support me.

He looked up at me, eyes blazing with need, lips wet with my desire, and he smiled. "Sweetest pussy I've ever tasted."

And then he covered my clit with his mouth, slipping a finger inside of me while my hips found their rhythm. I was grinding up against his face, tugging at his hair, desperate for more. He slipped in another finger, and the pressure had me gasping. My breaths were coming hard and fast, and I couldn't get enough.

"Kingston, it's too much," I whispered.

"Never too much, baby," he said when he pulled his fingers out. And just when I thought it couldn't get any better, his tongue slipped inside me. Sliding in and out, as his thumb moved to my clit, knowing just what I needed.

Bright lights lit up behind my eyelids, and my entire body was overcome with the most euphoric feeling I'd ever experienced.

I cried out his name as pleasure tore through me, and I rode his face into oblivion.

I had no shame.

I was lost in this man.

My forbidden King.

# 22

## Kingston

I'd carried her down to my room, and we were lying on my bed together, as I'd listened to the sound of her breathing go back to normal.

I'd always been a man who enjoyed sex. I loved it, actually. It was my favorite kind of escape.

Pleasing the woman I was with had always been something I did before I chased my own pleasure.

And I always delivered.

But pleasing Saylor Woodson was beyond anything I had ever experienced.

Watching her fall apart.

Hearing all the little gasps and moans—it was the hottest thing in the world.

Because it was her.

*Everything* was different because it was her.

This was not a fucking fling. This was so much more, and we both knew it.

I understood why Saylor didn't want her brother to know or have anyone involved, because she thought it would be too much pressure.

But the truth is—these feelings . . . that's where the pressure comes in.

It's scary as hell to feel this deeply about another person.

Fuck. White vans, bees, and clowns had nothing on this shit.

This was terrifying. Because if I messed this up, I knew I'd never recover.

There was no doubt she was it for me.

I was convinced that Grammie was right all along. I'd most likely fallen for her all those years ago, and nothing else had ever compared.

But how could I have loved her before I ever kissed her or touched her?

I didn't fucking know.

But I knew that I did.

"You're awfully quiet," she whispered, as her head lay on my chest.

"Just thinking about things."

"Yeah?" She rolled onto her stomach, and her hand drifted down my body as she stroked my dick over the denim of my jeans, and, of course, it was hard as a rock. "I am, too."

"You don't need to do that." I wrapped my fingers around her wrist to stop her.

"King." She paused as her gaze locked with mine.

"Saylor."

She smiled. "Don't be a prude. I want to touch you, too."

"I promise you, no one has ever called me a prude. You think I don't want you to touch me?" I released her hand. "I just didn't want you to feel any pressure."

She continued moving her hand up and down, and I sucked in a breath. "I don't feel pressure. I think about touching you all the time." She pushed up on her knees and reached for the button on my jeans and then the zipper.

I lifted enough so she could shove them down my thighs

before pulling on the waistband of my briefs and tugging them down, as well. She licked her lips as she looked up at me.

"Fuck, Saylor. I'm going to come before you even touch me if you keep looking at me like that." I groaned.

She wrapped her hand around my length and stroked me a few times before tipping her head down and wrapping her lips around my dick.

*Holy shit.*

Her tongue swirled around the tip, and she took me in about halfway, her hand pumping at the base as she bobbed her head up and down.

"Just like that, baby. Fuck, nothing has ever felt this good," I hissed through my teeth, trying to hold back the release that was already building.

"I love seeing my dick slide in and out of that sweet mouth of yours. Those fucking lips do crazy shit to me," I said, as my hips bucked faster.

She worked me in and out for the longest time as I tried hard to hold back. I squeezed my eyes shut, enjoying the feel of her lips, her tongue, her perfect fucking mouth.

"Mmmmm," she said on a moan, and that's all it fucking took.

I tried to pull her head back. "Baby. I'm going to come right fucking now."

But she gripped my hips harder and stayed right there as I unloaded into her mouth, emptying myself as she hollowed her cheeks and took me deeper.

A guttural sound left my lips as she continued to take every last drop.

When she pulled back, she wiped her mouth with the back of her hand and gave me this cocky smirk.

"Oh, you know how fucking good that was, don't you?" I tugged her down to lie on my chest.

"I've never enjoyed that before. But everything is always different with you."

"Well, there's lots more to do," I said, kissing the top of her head.

"So everything is on the table, aside from sex."

"Yeah," I said, tipping her chin up to look at me. "What did you have in mind?"

"Have you ever taken a bath with a girl?"

I laughed. "No, I never have. Is that what you want to do?"

"Well, you've got that massive tub, and the tub is so small at my place. I thought maybe we could take a bath together."

"Fine. But I get to undress you. I've never seen you completely bare. I've been dying to see those perfect tits of yours. The amount of times I've thought about them is not normal."

"Really? I never thought they were that noteworthy," she said with a laugh. "I mean, they aren't too small, but they aren't huge either. But I guess they are pretty perky." She stared down at the fabric covering her chest.

Goddamn, she was so fucking cute.

I pushed to my feet, shoving my pants and briefs all the way off before reaching over my shoulder and tearing the tee over my head. Her eyes trailed over my body, and I puffed my chest out.

"Of course, you're completely comfortable in your birthday suit," she said, adjusting her skirt in place.

I raised a brow. "And you're not? I've seen you in that fucking pink bikini. I swear I can't get the vision of you out of my mind. Come on, let me see you, Dandelion."

I moved closer to her, zero inhibitions about standing here buck-naked with her. She raised her hands over her head, and I pulled the white cotton tank off of her and tossed it onto the floor beside her feet. I ran my fingers over the lace of her white bra, grazing the hard peaks that were begging for my lips. I bent forward and covered her breast with my mouth, fabric and all. I flicked her nipple with my tongue, and she shivered in response.

I loved how her body responded to me. To my touch. To my mouth. To my words.

I'm sure it would be no different with my dick, but we weren't going there right now.

I reached behind her back and unsnapped her bra and let it drop to the floor. I studied her perfect tits as my calloused fingers grazed over each one.

"You're so fucking gorgeous," I said, cupping her breasts in each of my hands before leaning down and circling her nipple with my tongue before moving to the other side to do the same thing. She arched into me, her breaths coming fast again.

So damn responsive.

I continued sucking and licking as my fingers tugged her skirt down. She had no panties on because, well, I was an impatient fucker and I'd destroyed those.

I'd definitely be replacing them. I'd never torn a woman's panties off her body, but if they were on right now, I'd do it again.

"King," she whispered, as my fingers moved between her legs.

"Always so wet for me," I said, as I slipped one finger inside, and her head fell back as I nipped at her nipple, making her gasp. Her hips started moving, and I pushed another finger inside her. Her walls tightened around me as she rode my hand.

Her hands moved to my hair, and she tugged my head up, and my lips covered hers. I kissed her hard while I fucked her with my fingers.

She tightened around me, her hands pulling on my hair as she cried out my name.

I continued working her until she rode out the last bit of pleasure.

Her eyes were wide, and her teeth sank into her bottom lip before her head fell forward and rested on my chest as if she couldn't look at me.

"Hey. That was hot as hell. I love getting you off."

"Well, this is definitely not the norm for me. So, thanks for all the orgasms." She chuckled, and I wrapped my arms around her and hugged her tight. "I'm just getting started. Let's go take a bath."

Saylor turned on the water, and I grabbed some clean towels.

"Can I pour some of these bubbles in?" she asked, as she bent over the tub to reach for the bottle that I'd gotten as a gift a while back.

I leaned against the vanity and watched her. "Of course, you can. Keep bending over and giving me a shot of that pretty little pussy, and you can do whatever you want."

She looked over her shoulder, and her jaw dropped open. "Do you talk to all the women you've been with like that?"

"Well, I've never bathed with a woman. And I've never thought a pussy was perfect like yours. I've never seen tits as pretty as yours either. So the answer is no."

Her cheeks pinked as she poured the bubble bath in and screwed the cap back on. She held her hand out to me. "You get in first."

"I've never been a big bath guy, but sitting in the water, naked with you, makes it a lot more appealing." I dipped my toe in and howled at how hot the water was.

"Stop being a baby. It's not that hot." She laughed.

I climbed in and sat down, spreading my legs wide for her to come sit between them.

Her back rested against my chest, and I closed my eyes, breathing in all her goodness.

"You know when I told you that I kept your blanket all these years because it kept the nightmares away?"

"Yeah."

"That's not entirely true." Her voice was low, just above a whisper. "I just liked the idea of you being close to me."

"I guess, in a way, that's what the dandelion that I tattooed on my shoulder was for me," I admitted.

"But it was also a reminder to stay away from me." She flipped over in the spacious tub like it was her own personal swimming pool.

"It was. But it was a reminder of you at the same time."

"Are you sick of me yet?" she asked, her voice light and playful.

"Nope. That's why I brought you here."

Her brows pinched together. "What do you mean?"

"Well, I want you to spend the night. I can't risk staying over at your place with Ruby dropping in at any time. If we're going to be sick of one another soon, I want to enjoy this time together."

"Wow. No sex, but we're having a sleepover." She smiled up at me.

"I never slept as well in my life as I did those months that we shared a bed. Isn't that weird?" I asked her, because it had always puzzled me.

I didn't like sharing a bed with women after sex. I was too antsy. I liked my space and wanted to stretch out when I slept. But the memory of sleeping with Saylor's hand in mine had always given me a sort of peace that I couldn't explain.

"No. We comforted one another at a really hard time in our lives. You were worried about River, and I was a mess about everything going on with my family. And we were there for each other."

"Always will be. No matter how much I might mess this up, just know that I will always be there for you."

"I never doubt that, King. That's why no one needs to know what's going on—with our friendship or our history. Your connection with my brother and mine with your grandmother. It puts a lot of pressure on things. And I want this. Whatever this is that's going on between us right now. For us. For me. For however long it lasts. I'm happy when I'm with you. Always have been."

*This girl, man. So earnest and genuine.*

"Well, I'm yours until you tire of me." I winked.

"Deal. I'm guessing I'll be over it before the sun comes up," she said over a fit of laughter, resting her cheek against my chest.

I wasn't sure what I was doing.

My best friend was off fighting a beast of a fire, and here I was playing with fire.

Knowing that when you play with fire, someone always gets burned.

# 23

## Saylor

I would never have guessed that the bookstore would be this busy after opening its doors. Every day was just another surprise, and proof of why Magnolia Falls was the best small town around.

The locals had rallied around me, and it meant a lot. Even people I'd never expected to see at a romance bookstore had come in to show their support. I was grateful, even if some were slightly awkward.

"I've got some questions for you," Will Goldy said. He was the science teacher at Magnolia Falls High School. He hadn't been there when I was in high school because he wasn't much older than me, but I'd known him most of my life.

"Sure. What do you want to know?"

He was flipping through a historical romance book, and he turned to face me. "How much romance will I find in this type of book? I'm here more for the education, the historical relevance, you know?"

*That's what they all say, Will.*

"Right, yes. Well, I've read this series, and it's fabulous. There is a lot of detail about Scotland, and you really feel like you're living in the 1700s when you read these books. But there is also an epic romance, which is the focus of this book."

"I'll take it," Midge Longhorn said from the other side of the store. I bent down to scratch the top of Noodle's head because she brought her dog with her everywhere now. "That sounds like a really good one."

"Are you interested in Scottish history?" Will Goldy asked, his chin held high like he was trying to have an intellectual conversation.

Midge snorted. "No. I'm interested in hunky Scottish men getting it on with their heroines."

Will's cheeks pinked, and his eyes widened. "Midge. That's slightly inappropriate."

"Will, you've been coming to my diner since you were a toddler when you had the nickname Booger. I knew you when you were still shitting in your diapers. This is a romance bookstore. Lose the pretentious attitude or take a hike."

His mouth dropped open, and I used my hand to cover my mouth and stifle my laughter. It wasn't lost on me that Will Goldy had come to a Magnolia Falls council meeting when I was getting my permits in place. He'd tried to stop the store from opening, but he'd lost that battle.

Will made all sorts of gaspy sounds, making it clear he was completely offended. "I am far from pretentious. I just choose to read things that stimulate me intellectually."

"And I choose to read things that stimulate me in other ways," Midge said with a wink, and I shook my head and chuckled.

"Okay. Let's agree to disagree. All the books in this store are primarily romance. But this section over here is clean romance. That means they are closed-door sex scenes. Nothing is explained; you are just to assume things happened." I walked him over to the section at the other end of the store.

"Also known as *boring*," Midge sang out as she grabbed

the historical romance books and set them on the checkout counter. "Those will be perfect for you, Will."

"I'm thinking these might help me with my dating life," he admitted as he pulled one from the shelf.

"Oh, yes. You can get some very romantic ideas from the pages of these books," I said, as the door swung open and Oscar Daily waltzed in.

"Saylor. I need a book about how to fix a grandfather clock. Do you got one of those?" he asked, scratching the back of his neck as he moved toward the mafia romance section.

Midge raised a brow and smirked. "Well, you sure as hell aren't going to find it over there."

"I told you that I don't sell those types of books, Oscar." I walked to stand beside him after I finished ringing up Midge. "You can probably just google it and find something online."

"Yes, that's right." He shot me a look, and I realized exactly what he was here for. He'd bought book one in this mafia series last week, and he'd said it was for his daughter, but I had a hunch he wasn't being completely truthful.

"Did Sabrina enjoy the first book in the series?" I asked, pulling book two from the shelves for him and holding it out.

"Uh, yeah. She liked it. I guess since I'm here, I may as well get this one for her, too."

"Pfft. These men and their embarrassment over reading romance books. It's ridiculous," Midge said.

I made my way behind the counter as the three of them argued back and forth. Oscar insisted the book wasn't for him. Will insisted that he hoped the book he'd chosen would teach him about cooking because the hero was a chef. And Midge gave them both a hard time and called them out repeatedly.

It was a relief when they were gone, and I moved to the back hallway, where the new shipment of books was stacked in boxes along the wall. I started unloading the new inventory when the bell chimed and the door opened.

I looked up to see Barry step inside. I wasn't afraid of the man. He would never do anything in public. He saved everything for behind closed doors. Everyone in town thought he was this charming man, but I knew who he was. And after Hayes and I had been taken out of our home as teenagers, the rumor mill ran rampant. He hated that people wondered what he'd done.

"Hey, I didn't expect to see you here." I settled my hands on my hips, and he stopped in front of me, but it was impossible to miss the anger radiating from him.

"Well, if I don't come here, I won't ever see my daughter."

*My daughter.*

The man had never been a father to me. He'd come in and made a bad situation worse. He'd found a woman who struggled with depression and made her feel like she couldn't function without him. He was controlling and possessive, and I'd never liked the man. Not from the first time we'd met.

"What can I do for you, Barry?"

"For starters, you can talk to that asshole brother of yours. He's the reason that our family is broken." He ran a hand over his jaw and shook his head. "People fight. Kids get spanked, and it's not a big deal. It sure as hell doesn't mean that you cut them out of your life. He's hurting your mother, which means he's hurting me. And I'm about done with it."

"Really?" I made no attempt to hide my sarcasm, and my fingers instinctually moved to my necklace. "Are you really going to come into my store and talk poorly about my brother? Are you really going to minimize the hell you've put my family through? People fight, yes. People don't get physical. They don't raise a hand to their wife. To their daughter. To their son. And you did that. You can't blame Hayes for saying that he had enough. And I'd watch what you say about him because he's not a little boy anymore. He's looking for a reason to have a go at you, so be very careful, Barry."

"Un-fucking-believable. A few backhanded swats and you're all high and mighty, like that doesn't go on in families all the time. It's called discipline, Saylor. You asked for it when you got hit. You involved yourself in a fight that wasn't yours. That was between me and your mother." His beady gray eyes narrowed. His shoulders squared, and his hands formed little fists at his sides.

I noticed these things because I'd been trained to notice. When you live in a home with a man who is unpredictable and violent, you quickly learn how to read the signs.

I raised my chin, making it clear I wasn't afraid of him. "You were choking my mother, and I tried to stop you. You were the cause of all of it. You hurt her, and then you hurt me. I was a goddamn teenager, Barry. You threw me down, and I fell through a coffee table. I was knocked unconscious. That is all on you."

"Oh, for fuck's sake. You shouldn't have gotten involved in adult business. That's on you, Saylor. And with you living back in town and refusing to come over when I'm there, it's causing a strain in my marriage. Your mother is being distant and barely speaking to me lately. And I'm about fucking done with it, do you hear me?"

I never heard the door open or the bell chime. Kingston was there and moving between us in a blur. "Barry, I'm going to give you one fucking minute to walk out of this store before your teeth are in your throat."

Kingston shifted me behind him, his hand remaining on my arm to keep me there.

"Is this a fucking joke?" Barry chuckled this maniacal laugh and pointed at Kingston. "It's a public place."

"I'm not asking you twice. The choice is yours. Personally, I'd enjoy knocking your teeth out. I've wanted to do it for more than a decade. Give me a fucking reason." Kingston moved forward, his hand dropping from my body as he crowded Barry.

"You and your fucking friends think you're better than me. I make more money than all of you put together. You're a bunch of fucking losers."

"Keep chirping, Barry Boy." Kingston moved forward, and with every step he took, he forced my stepfather back, closer to the door.

"You disappoint me, Saylor. No fucking loyalty to the people that raised you. That piece-of-shit father of yours was not the one who put a roof over your head. That was me."

A lump formed in my throat as two tears sprung from my eyes and rolled down my cheeks. "You disappoint me, too, Barry."

Kingston bunched up the fabric on Barry's dress shirt and kicked the door open with his foot before shoving him outside.

"I could have you arrested for putting your hands on me, you little punk."

"Go for it. I'll have my lawyer explain why you aren't welcome here." Kingston chuckled. "And stay the fuck away from her, because we're all watching. I promise you that."

The door closed, and Kingston rushed me, placing his large hands on each side of my face. "Are you hurt?"

"No. He didn't touch me," I croaked, as the tears broke free and streamed down my face. My family was such a mess. I had a father who wanted nothing to do with me and a stepfather who terrified me ninety-five percent of the time. My mother was drowning in her own bullshit, and then there was Hayes.

He'd always been my rock.

"You're okay, Dandelion." He wrapped his arms around me and held me tight.

"I'm fine. He didn't do anything," I said, pulling back and shaking my head. "I just hate that my family is such a mess."

"Hey." He placed his hand beneath my chin and tipped it up so my gaze would meet his. "Your family is who you make it. Hayes, me, River, Romeo, Nash, Beefcake, Demi, Ruby, and Peyton. My grandmother. That's your family. And we're not a mess at all."

I swiped at my face, hating that I'd let Barry get to me. "I know. I'm fine."

"Saylor. You don't have to be fine on my behalf. That man is fucked up. He said some terrible things. You're allowed to feel bad about it. But he's not your family, and you need to know that. He doesn't get to come near you. I'll show up every fucking time. I promise I will."

"How did you know he was here?"

"I have some friends keeping an eye on him, letting me know if he is seen in the vicinity of your bookstore. I heard he was downtown and knew he was coming to see you. Something in my gut told me that was true."

Nash came through the door, eyes wide, as he looked around. "What happened?"

"He was here. Did his best to make her feel bad. And now he's gone."

"Oh my gosh," I groaned. "You didn't both need to come down here."

Before they could respond, River and Romeo came hurrying through the door.

"Fuck. I was training someone and didn't have my phone on me. I saw Nash's call and came running over here. What happened?" Romeo asked as he stalked around the bookstore as if Barry was hiding in the bookshelves.

"Same. I was with a client and then saw the call." River ran a hand through his hair.

"She's all right. That fucker took his shot. But he's gone, and I think he got the message loud and clear," Kingston said, but his gaze never left me.

Romeo's phone rang, and he looked down. "It's Hayes. His ears must be burning."

I knew they wouldn't reach out to him about it until they knew if he'd come here. But my brother had always had a sixth sense about these things, so I wasn't shocked he was calling.

I heard Romeo filling him in, and then he asked to speak to Kingston.

"Yeah. I've got you, brother. Don't you worry. I won't let her out of my sight." Kingston stood in front of me, stroking my shoulder with his calloused fingers. "Yep. She can stay at my house if you're concerned."

"Give me the phone," I said, shaking my head and taking the phone from Kingston's hand. "Let me talk to him."

"You all right, Say?" Hayes sounded really tired, and I immediately regretted giving him anything to worry about.

"I'm fine. He didn't do anything other than tell me how horrible we are for cutting him out of our lives." I let a long sigh leave my lips. "Kingston scared him off. I don't think he'll be back."

"This fucking guy. How many chances does he think he should get?"

"I know. He clearly hasn't changed. I made plans to have dinner with Mom this week, and I think he's just mad that he isn't invited. It'll be fine."

"Can you do me a favor?" Hayes asked, and the man rarely asked for anything, so it was hard to deny him when he did.

"Yes."

"Can you sleep at King's and stay in his guest room for the next few days? Just to be safe. Barry is a loose cannon. You mix that with booze, and who knows what that fucker will do."

"Hayes, I'm fine. You're the one in the middle of a gigantic forest fire. Stop worrying about me."

"Tell me you'll do this. Just for a couple of nights. I'll be home soon. I just need to know you're all right."

I looked up to see Kingston watching me. "Yeah. I'll do it."

"Thank you. You can stay in his spare room. Hopefully, he can go a couple of nights without bringing anyone home. I'd hate for you to have to hear that shit." He chuckled, and it was the first time he'd seemed relaxed since he'd called.

"I'll ignore any noisy sex sounds coming from King's room, okay?"

The guys all barked out a laugh, but Kingston shot them a warning look.

"All right. I'll talk to you later. Love you, Say."

"Love you."

I ended the call and didn't miss the glimmer in Kingston's eyes.

I was going to be staying with him for the next few nights, and we didn't even need to hide it.

# 24

## Kingston

RIVER

You still with us, Hayes? Haven't gotten an update since yesterday morning. You getting that fire under control?

HAYES

Good timing. Just heading back out. We're finally making progress. I should be home in a week or so.

ROMEO

I just watched the live footage on the news, and that is one bitch of a fire.

HAYES

Tell me about it. We had a close call last night with the wind shifting. But I'm here today, so clearly, I survived.

Dude. Do not joke about death.

HAYES

Don't be so sensitive, you dicksausage. I'm fine. How's my sister? Has Barry stayed away?

Yeah. She's staying here, but I barely see her because she works long hours. Barry has stayed away. He obviously knows you've got people keeping an eye on her.

It wasn't a complete lie. She was working a lot. But I saw her every minute that she wasn't working. And we most definitely hadn't grown sick of one another the way we'd both expected we would. If anything, I couldn't get enough.

NASH

He's not going to do anything. He'd be signing his own death certificate. Plus, she's an adult. She would report him if he laid a hand on her, and he'd be arrested.

HAYES

Yeah. We aren't kids anymore. We actually have a voice now. I just don't want him to put her through that. She's been through enough. She deserves a break.

RIVER

Dude, she seems happy. Her store is thriving. She's got a bodyguard who doesn't take a day off. (Don't get a big head, King. But you've been really good about it.) So, how about you take care of yourself and come home in one piece, all right?

ROMEO

Do you all notice that River is much more logical now? Ruby is clearly rubbing off on him. Normally, he'd say: Saylor is fine. Don't die. See you soon. But this . . . this is very Zen of you, brother.

RIVER

I have to agree with Romeo. You've gotten so deep in your old age.

RIVER

HAYES

Damn. I missed this. Thanks for the much-needed entertainment.

NASH

You'll be back for the bachelor party, so we'll be very entertaining there, I'm sure.

RIVER

Looking forward to it. Hey, King, I hear you're having lunch with my girl and I'm not welcome. Fuck you.

Such a jealous little asshole. She asked me to have lunch, and I said yes. Saylor is working today, Nash has baseball practice with the all-star Beefcake, and Romeo will be taking dance lessons for the wedding.

ROMEO

Thanks for outing me, you dickcock.

They don't call you Twinkle Toes for nothing, brother.

ROMEO

I think I like Twinkle Toes.

NASH

It's definitely a tougher name than Golden Boy.

ROMEO

Listen, I don't like dancing. But Demi's mom insisted we take these damn ballroom dancing lessons. Demi promised me that I could just sort of stand there and she'd lead and do all the hard work. I'm just going to show up and look good.

RIVER

Nice fucking try. You're taking lessons. Move your goddamn feet and do whatever Beans wants you to do. We promise not to give you a hard time until we're alone, and then we'll razz the shit out of you.

HAYES

I can live with that. If she wants you to dance, just do it. You danced all around that ring in the fight. How hard can this be?

ROMEO

Touché.

NASH

Because ballroom dancing and boxing are so similar?

I've got to go. I've got a hot lunch date.

RIVER

I hope Midge puts the wrong cheese on your sandwich and you shit your pants, you lactose-intolerant dickgoober.

HAYES

I like dickgoober. Storing that one away for another time. I've got to get back out there.

Be safe, Hayes.

RIVER

Ride or die, boys.

NASH

Friends till the end.

ROMEO

Watch your back, and get your ass back home in one piece.

When I walked into The Golden Goose, Midge and Ruby were chatting at a table, and my brother's girlfriend waved me over.

"Midge, you're looking less grumpy today. I take it Doug is treating you well?"

"Very perceptive, King. Maybe it's all those romance books I'm reading lately." She smirked before walking away.

"I think you are the only person she actually likes," I said, sliding into the booth and giving Ruby a kiss on the cheek.

"What can I say? I'm a real peach these days." She laughed and did this little shimmy in her leather coat. Ruby Rose put on a good front of being a complete badass, but she had a heart of gold.

"You really are. And my brother is having a fucking meltdown that he wasn't invited to lunch. You've really turned him into a whiny little pussy." I paused when Letty came over to take our order.

Ruby chuckled. "Oh, trust me, I know. He couldn't wrap his head around the fact that I was going to lunch with you and didn't invite him."

I leaned back in the booth when our drinks were set in front of us, and I reached for my soda and took a sip. "All right, so what did I do? Did I fuck up?"

"You're not in trouble. Why would you assume you fucked up?"

"I don't know. Have we ever had lunch alone?"

"No, but that doesn't mean we can't," she said, shaking her head and smiling.

"So, this is just a catch-up lunch? There's no agenda?"

"I mean, I may have a slight agenda."

"Give it to me, girl." I raised a brow.

"You are so ridiculous sometimes. This is not a big deal. I've noticed that you and Saylor hang out a lot. I just wanted to touch base with you on that."

I rubbed my hands together when Letty arrived with our food and announced that it was made with my special cheese, which made Ruby laugh.

I took a bite of my sandwich before looking at her again. "Why not go to Saylor about this?"

"I have. She's really tight-lipped. And I get it because Hayes wouldn't be okay with it, right?"

"Correct." I nodded, not wanting to say much because I hated lying to the people I loved.

"That's not what I'm here about, King. I'm here because I care about you, and I care about her. So, I wanted to ask you a few things because I thought you might be feeling like you have no one to talk to. I want you to know that you can talk to me, okay? And we could do it in a way that wouldn't be saying anything that you don't want to say."

I barked out a laugh. "Okay, Rubes. What would you like to talk about?"

"Well, let's just say I have a situation at work that I could use your help on."

"Sure. What is it?" I reached for my soda again.

"One of my teenagers is having a fling with his best friend's sister. If you were a psychic, would you think it's just a fling and he's going to break her heart? Or would you say the feelings probably run deeper? Because the girl, she's something. She's really special, and I would hate to see her get hurt."

*Unbelievable.*

Ruby had always been more observant than everyone else. She was basically a therapist out at the juvenile detention center where River and Romeo had spent some time as teenagers.

"If I were a betting man—which I'm not—I'd say that it's probably not a fling. I don't think he'd go there if he thought it was just a physical thing. I'm guessing he has deep feelings for her, but he doesn't know what to do with them."

And damn if it didn't feel good to talk about it without admitting anything that could get my dick cut off.

Her lips turned up in the corners, and her eyes watered a bit, which was very out of character for Ruby. It made it obvious that she'd been worrying about this for a while. "That's what I was hoping. But why would he be hesitant about feeling that way?"

"Well, maybe he's never had a relationship that wasn't casual. And no one he's ever been with has been his best friend's sister, so it complicates things. How does he figure out if he's even capable of being that guy when he isn't allowed to even go there without being a hundred percent certain that he won't mess it up? It's not like he can test the waters as if it were a normal relationship." I bit off the top of a french fry. "Your teenager is totally fucked."

"Well, here's the thing. He's a really good guy. Like, one of the best I've ever known." She smiled, and I chuckled. "So, he should figure out why he's so fearful of relationships. Is it because he can't be monogamous or because he's afraid of loving someone? Two valid reasons right there."

I finished chewing. "That's nice that you like him so much. I'll bet he's really good-looking, too."

"He's all right. He's got this older brother, though, and that guy is hot as hell." She fanned her face, and we both laughed.

"Lucky him. So, the monogamous thing is not an issue. I'm guessing this guy doesn't want to be with anyone else."

"Interesting. So it's all about the fear, isn't it?"

"I didn't say that. I just said it wasn't about being monogamous. At least it wouldn't be for me, but obviously, we aren't talking about me." I winked.

"Obviously not."

"For me, I have never been in a long-term relationship, and it isn't because I can't be monogamous. It's because I hadn't found anyone that I wanted to be monogamous with. But it sounds like your troubled teen has found that person, so hats off to him."

"So if it's not about being monogamous, it's got to be about fear. It's the only valid explanation."

"Fear of what, Dr. Rose?" I waggled my brows and feigned disinterest, when I was dying to know.

"Fear of failure. Fear of loss. Fear of letting anyone down." She leaned forward, gaze locked on mine. "You see this kid I'm working with . . . he lost his parents at a young age. He and his brother both handled that loss differently."

"How so?" I took a bite of my sandwich.

"Well, his brother was a real closed-off grump, but he eventually came around. But this kid that I'm working with . . . he never has a care in the world. He's a perpetual good time."

"Damn. This is my kind of guy. I'm sure he gets all the girls, huh?"

She nodded, a wide grin spread clear across her face. "He sure does. But you see, I think he's got real feelings for this other girl."

"His best friend's sister?"

"Correct. And he's scared shitless."

"Because his friend will probably cut off his dick if he finds out how he feels. I mean, look at his track record."

"Well, I mean, that's not really fair. Who has a great track record before they find their person? I didn't. River didn't. Romeo didn't. Demi didn't. No one has a great track record before they commit to someone, do they?"

"They have relationships that last longer than five minutes. And I'm guessing your teen, well, he's been a bit of a playboy, right? So his best friend won't think he's capable of changing, and it's a fair concern."

"Then, if it's important to him, he'll have to convince his best friend that it's the real deal."

"Maybe the girl he's talking to won't want to get the brother involved until they know what it is."

She sighed. "I understand that. It is no one's business, but it won't go over well to keep this kind of secret either. That's what's going to get you into trouble—er, him into trouble. If he feels this way, he needs to talk to his friend. Before it all blows up in his face."

"True. But perhaps as much as he's worried about his friend finding out, maybe he's more concerned with her needs right now. And she doesn't want her brother to know, so he's trying to be respectful."

She studied me for the longest time. "This just isn't about not knowing how to have a relationship because you've experienced a lot of loss. This is deeper, isn't it?"

"I don't know what you mean."

"This is no fling at all. I think my teen is in love with his best friend's sister." She tilted her head to the side and smiled. "He's probably been in love with her for a long time."

"He probably has, Rubes."

"Damn. I thought I was coming here to smack some sense into you, but you're the one who smacked some sense into me."

"I don't know about that."

"Don't let this go too far, King. It's going to blow up if you don't figure it out soon enough. Your brother is noticing, and so is Demi. You two are not as sly as you think you are. It's hard to miss it when we're in the same room with you. Hayes will sniff this out in a hot minute, and he needs to know this is not you taking advantage of her."

"I know. I'm going to talk to her about it. We've been trying to figure things out. Waiting for one of us to tire of the other," I said, done with pretending we weren't talking about me. "But I'm not tiring of her. I'm fucking crazy about her. She's all I think about. And I can't tell a fucking soul because I feel like a disloyal asshole."

"You need to get this straight. There are two people you need to talk to first, and that's Saylor and then Hayes. In that order. She deserves to know how you feel first, and then she has to understand that you owe him the respect of talking to him. He's a great guy, King. He'll understand if it's from the heart."

I closed my eyes and blew out a breath.

"I know. I just don't want to fuck it up."

"Well, start by being honest. Tell her how you feel. Make sure she feels the same, which she obviously does, but that conversation needs to happen. I mean, she's been staying with you every night since Barry's visit, and we all know he's not a threat at this point. You like having her there. She likes being there. So have the damn conversation, and then be a grown-up and go to her brother and tell him you're in love with his sister."

"You make it sound so easy."

"Trust me, being vulnerable is never easy. But loving someone . . . it's worth it, King."

I nodded.

I knew she was right.

Loving Saylor was the easy part.

Convincing her brother I was worthy . . . that would be tricky.

# 25

## Saylor

"Saylor? You here? It smells damn good." Kingston's voice called from the entryway of his house.

I chuckled. "Yep. I told you I was cooking you dinner."

He walked into the kitchen as I finished slicing the bread.

Damn.

He was wearing a white tee and a pair of jeans, and he looked so damn sexy that sometimes just being around him took my breath away.

"I like seeing you in my kitchen, Dandelion."

*I like being in your kitchen.*

In his home.

In his life.

"What are you making?" He wrapped his arms around me and tipped my head back to kiss me.

Nothing about this was a fling anymore.

This was not only a full-fledged relationship, but it was the best one I'd ever had.

Tonight, I wanted to talk about it.

"You know I love themes, right?" My words were all breathy when I pulled back from his kiss.

"Yes. I still don't fully know what it means, but I'm getting there."

"Well, tonight's theme is fondue. We're having dairy-free cheese fondue with all sorts of things to dip, from bread to steak to vegetables. And then we have chocolate fondue, where we can dip pound cake and bananas and marshmallows into the chocolaty goodness."

"Damn, baby. You had me at dairy-free cheese." He laughed before moving to the sink to wash his hands.

I finished carrying the last tray of bread to the table, where the fondue pot held the cheese in the middle. The chocolate fondue was on the kitchen island, and I'd move that one over when we were ready.

"How was work?" I asked as he came over to sit beside me. I handed him his little fork, and I dipped a piece of bread into the cheese and let it cool before popping it into my mouth. Kingston looked completely enamored with the whole thing. "Have you never done this?"

"No, and you make it look so sexy the way you keep smirking and blowing on the bread. Fuck. I love fondue." He dipped a piece of steak into the cheese and did not wait before biting down with his teeth and groaning at how good it was. "Work was fine. Busy. How about you?"

"It was good. I got to sneak off and pick up Cutler from school, and he came to the store to do his homework and hang out with me. It was really nice. We got some lemon bars from Demi, and he told me all about his day until Nash got there to pick him up."

"Why do you look so sly, like you know something I don't?" He popped a piece of bread into his mouth and leaned forward and tickled me, before tugging me onto his lap.

"Let's just say that Beefcake has a lady. You better not tell anyone because it's a secret."

"Beefcake has another girl? My God, how many ladies can that little dude have?" He held up his fork with the filet mignon on it, covered in the delicious cheese. "Try this."

I placed my mouth over it and bit down. "Wow. That is really good."

I pulled my chair closer and sat back down so our legs were literally touching as we took turns feeding one another. Laughing about our day. Talking about the upcoming bachelor and bachelorette parties for Demi and Romeo. About Cutler's playoff game and the elephant in the room . . . my brother, who was coming home in a few days.

I was relieved that he was finally done, and the fire was almost completely contained.

But I was worried that this little bubble we'd created would be coming to an end. We were always together. When we weren't, we were on the phone with one another.

"Hayes called before you got here, and the fire is finally under control," I said, noticing the way his shoulders stiffened, and he nodded.

"Yeah. I talked to him earlier, and he said he'll be home in a few days. I'm so glad this is almost over for him."

"Me, too. So that's what I wanted to talk to you about." I cleared my throat, suddenly feeling nervous.

"I wanted to talk to you, too."

Oh, God. Did he want this to be over?

"How about you go first, then?" I said, because if he wanted this done, I wasn't going to pour my heart out to him and embarrass myself.

"Okay, well, I want to show you something first." He pushed to his feet and shoved his hands into his pockets. "Can you come out to my workshop with me?"

"Of course. Let me turn off the chocolate." I unplugged both fondue pots and took his hand. We walked out the back door to the barn-looking structure that Kingston had turned into his woodworking shop. It's where he did most of his creating and building. He'd been spending a lot of time out there, working on a few projects that they had going on right now.

"Did you finish the desk for Cutler?"

"Yep. He's coming over this weekend to paint it after his game. But that's not what I wanted to show you." He led me to the back of the shop, and I came to a stop in front of a tall bookcase standing in front of me. I'd never seen anything more beautiful. It was painted in a very light sage green color and with a hand-painted dandelion with a darker green stem and white fluffball on one side, and some words scrolled around it in beautiful script. I moved closer and ran my fingers over the words as I read them. "Some see a weed. Others see a wish."

"This is stunning." I moved around to the other side, and there was a pair of dandelion fluffballs on that side, as well. There were white petals in the shape of hearts fluttering around the stem, as if they'd already been blown. I read the script on this side aloud, as well. "Love is in the air."

The detail and molding on this bookshelf were absolutely stunning, and I couldn't stop staring at it.

"I knew you wanted to have shelves of your own to keep the books that you've collected at home." He turned his baseball cap around backward before shoving his hands into his pockets again.

Was he nervous?

"This is for me?" I shook my head, blinking to try to keep the tears away. "This is what you've been working on?"

"Yeah. I wanted to surprise you."

"You always surprise me, King," I whispered, because he did. He had. He continued to surprise me every day with how thoughtful he was. How sexy he was. How vulnerable and protective and sweet he was. All at the same time, most days.

He took me around to the back of the bookshelf, and there was a handwritten note with a sharpie.

*Dandelion, I finally know what I want to wish for . . .*

*Love, King*

The date was written below, and he smiled at me before speaking. "When I close my eyes, I see you. Every fucking time. Whether there is a dandelion in my hand or I'm sitting in my car or I'm on a jobsite. *I. See. You.* It's always been you. When I tattooed this flower on my body beside *Ride or Die*, it was because I knew then what I was too afraid to say aloud."

"What?" My voice shook as tears streamed down my face.

"That I love you. I've always loved you. These last few months—this is what I've been wishing for. She's standing right in front of me."

"King," I said, shaking my head because I was overwhelmed by how much I loved this man. "I love you. That's what I wanted to tell you tonight. I've been in love with you for a while now, and I've just been so afraid to say it. To feel it."

He pulled me close and wrapped his arms around me, and we stood there hugging out in the woodshed for the longest time before I tipped my head back. "Does this mean you'll finally have sex with me?"

He laughed hard and reached his hands behind my backside, grabbing my ass and lifting me up. "Hell yeah, it does. But we're talking to Hayes right away. This is not a fucking fling. It never was."

"Agreed. And he comes home in a few days, and we'll tell him in person. So how about you stop holding back? I love you. You love me. Carry me inside and have your way with me."

I saw how conflicted he was in his gaze. "I wish we could tell him right now. I'm ready to tell everyone. I'm done with all the secrets."

"Me, too."

"I want everyone to know that you're mine." He nipped at my ear.

"I think I've always been yours, Kingston Pierce."

That was all it took. He was practically running toward the house as my head fell back in laughter, and he kept one hand on my bottom and one tangled in my hair as I tucked my head into the crook of his neck.

When we got inside, he carried me straight to his bedroom and dropped me onto the bed. "Do you know how many nights I've thought about this?"

"Probably as many as I have."

"I've had you in my bed dozens of times, and I've explored every inch of your beautiful body, and I've never been inside you. And I've fucking thought about it so many times, Saylor."

"Me, too."

He crawled onto the bed and kissed me. "Do you have any idea how badly I want you? Want this?"

"I do." I smiled up at him, my hands trembling as I pushed his shirt up and over his head. He unbuttoned the navy spaghetti strap blouse I was wearing and smiled when he opened it to find there was no bra beneath. His fingers traced over my breasts; my nipples were already hard and wanting.

"So fucking beautiful," he whispered, before he moved to his feet and pulled my cowboy booties off, dropping them to the floor. I sat forward and unbuckled his jeans, kissing his chiseled abdomen as I shoved his pants and boxers down in one swift movement. His dick sprung to life—hard and long and thick.

He kicked off his shoes and his clothes and then reached for the waist of my skirt. He tugged it down my legs as his tongue swiped out to wet his bottom lip, his gaze traveling over the length of me.

"I know I owe you some new panties, but I have no patience," he said, tearing the lace with ease as I chuckled. I didn't mind it.

I had no patience when it came to King either.

He leaned down to grab his jeans and pulled his wallet out before the foil packet appeared in his hand.

"I've never been with anyone without a condom, and I'm on the pill."

He paused, studying me for several seconds. "I've never been with a woman without wearing protection either. Are you sure about this?"

"I want to feel you. All of you."

It was the truth. I didn't want anything between us.

"What the fuck did I ever do to deserve you?"

He crawled over me, hovering just above me.

"All you have to do is exist, and you'll have me," I whispered.

He claimed my mouth and kissed me. It was different this time. It wasn't rushed or frantic. It was slow. Controlled.

Like we both knew this next chapter we were starting wasn't temporary. His hand gripped the side of my neck, tilting my head so he could take the kiss deeper.

We kissed for the longest time before he pulled back, and his lips moved down my neck and chest. He flicked my nipples with his tongue, and I gasped, so eager and ready.

"King, I want you right now." My breaths were coming hard and fast. "I need you right now."

"I know, baby. I need you, too." He moved back up, and before I even realized what was happening, he flipped us over, with him lying on his back. He settled me on top of him, one leg on each side, so I was straddling him. "I want you to set the pace. Take things as slow as you want or as fast as you want."

I nodded, still finding it hard to believe that we were here.

Together. No more worries. No more rules. But then I glanced down and saw his giant erection standing there waiting for me. Though it wasn't the first time I'd seen it, it was the first time we were going to have sex. And there was no freaking way it was going to fit.

"Baby, I'm going to come right here if you keep staring at it like that." His hand wrapped around his dick and stroked a couple of times.

"It's not going to fit," I whispered.

He chuckled. "It'll fit. We were made for each other. That's why I wanted to do it with you on top, so you can take me in inch by inch and set the pace. We'll take it slow."

I pushed up, positioning myself just above him; the tip of his dick teased my entrance. I started to slide down and gasped as my body tried to adjust to his size. "Okay, that's enough for right now," I said, my head falling back at the sensation coursing through my body, and he was barely even in.

"Look at you, taking me in like a fucking rock star. You're so fucking beautiful, Saylor. Seeing you like this." His hands were all over me, touching and exploring. He shifted forward and pulled my body toward him at the same time so his lips could cover my breast. His tongue flicked at my nipple, making me gasp as I moved down, taking in another inch of him. I was panting now, because I wanted this so badly. Wanted all of him. The feel of his lips and his tongue and his hands.

And the way he was filling me slowly.

It was a mix of both pleasure and pain as I moved down lower. His lips moved to my other breast, and my eyes fell closed at the sensation. I moved down further, feeling myself stretch around him.

He pulled back to look up at me with complete amazement. "You can take it, baby. Give me that sweet mouth."

I leaned down and kissed him, his tongue sliding in and out, as I pushed down further, moaning into his mouth. His fingers tangled in my hair as he brought his chest up to meet mine. I slid the rest of the way down and stopped moving completely, pulling back from our kiss as I adjusted to the intrusion. To the feel of him inside me.

"Fuck, baby. Nothing has ever felt better. I love you so fucking much," he whispered against my ear, his lips kissing along my neck.

My body was on fire, and my head fell back as I started to rock against him.

"Oh my God, King. It feels so good."

"It's all you, baby. Take your time. Show me what you want."

I pushed him back down to lie on his back, and I let my body take over. I rode him slowly at first before we found our rhythm. I looked between us, where we were joined, and watched as he slid in and out of me. It was the sexiest thing I'd ever seen.

His hands were on my hips, and he moved right along with me. His muscles flexed every time our bodies slammed together. We were both lost in the moment now.

Faster. Needier.

We were covered in a layer of sweat, our breaths and moans and gasps the only audible sounds in the room.

"King," I whispered. He knew exactly what I needed, and his hand moved between us, pressing little circles into my clit.

I couldn't hold on any longer.

My body started to shake, and I leaned back, my hands landing on the back of his thighs, as I rocked into him again and again.

"Good girl. That's it," his deep voice said in the darkened room. "Come for me, baby."

And I went right over the edge.

I cried out his name and fell forward as he captured my mouth with his.

He thrust into me again.

And again.

Before he followed me right over the edge.

With my name on his lips.

# 26

## Kingston

I had a ton of nervous energy, and there was no one better to spend the day with when I felt like this than Cutler. Nash wanted to go meet the guys over at the Halseys' ranch and get them started on building the addition off the back of the house. I'd offered to take the little dude to hit some balls to get ready for his playoff game coming up. He'd been getting better and better with each game, and most importantly, he loved it. He wanted to practice, and it was all he'd been talking about lately.

"Pops said you've always been good at every sport," Cutler said, as he swung at the slow balls that were coming at him. He hit every single one of them, and I was impressed. "That's how I want to be."

"I did all right. And you're already a rockstar, Beefcake. You've got nothing to worry about." I chuckled as I paused the ball machine and came over to help him adjust his hand placement on the bat. "Eye on the ball, and follow all the way through."

"Got it." He rubbed his foot in the dirt a couple of times, which made me laugh. He was sporting an orange and white tracksuit, but he'd taken the jacket off because the sun was out in full force today.

I turned the machine back on and watched as he hit the shit out of the next few balls. He definitely had his father's athletic ability, even though we'd wondered if he had an athletic bone in his body only a few weeks ago.

He paused and danced around in celebration when he hit the last ball so hard it slammed into the net. Nash had been working hard with him, and it showed.

He caught me off guard when he started wheezing, and I reached into my pocket for the inhaler Nash had given me for emergencies. We'd recently found out that Cutler had exercise-induced asthma, but I hadn't seen him react like this just from hitting balls and dancing around before now.

I bent down and shook the inhaler, and he breathed in two puffs like a pro. I walked him over to the bench and insisted he sit for a few minutes.

"You all right?"

"Yeah. I'm good, Uncle King."

I sent a quick text to Nash to let him know we used the inhaler. I knew he was concerned that it seemed to be happening more often, and he was keeping track of the number of times he used it.

"So, you want to head over to the bridal shower?"

"Demi said it's no boys allowed, except for you and me. 'Cause we're cool boys. Right, Uncle King?"

"The coolest. Of course, they bent the rules for us." He took a sip of his Gatorade after I unscrewed the top and handed it to him. "That's why I wore this tracksuit. Orange is my girl Demi's favorite color."

"How many girls you got now?" I asked, as I reached for his hand, and we walked toward my truck.

"Well, I've got Demi and Saylor and Ruby and Peyton. And now I've got my own girl at school. Her name is Eloise, and she's the smartest girl in the class."

I helped him into his booster seat and buckled him up before making my way around to the driver's side.

"It's always good to surround yourself with smart people. Those are some special ladies you got right there."

"Do you ever want to have just one girl, Uncle King?"

I chuckled and pulled down the road toward Demi's parents' ranch. "Yeah, I think if you find the right girl, that's when you decide you want to just settle down with one person."

*And I've found the right girl. She's always been the only girl for me.*

"I think Saylor should be your girl. You're always laughing with her, and she seems like she'd want to be your girl. And she's the best, you know? She's smart, and she reads lots of books, and she can ride horses, and she's real pretty and the nicest. That's how Eloise is."

"Beefcake, are you trying to matchmake me?" I barked out a laugh as I put the truck in park.

"Well, I think you like her."

*For fuck's sake. Does anyone not think I like her? We've clearly done a shit job of hiding it.*

"I think she's the best. But she's Uncle Hayes's sister, so we'll have to see how that goes."

His eyebrows pinched together, and he shrugged. "Uncle Hayes loves you, and he loves Saylor. He'd be real happy if you two were happy together."

If only life were that simple. But this kid sure did have it figured out.

"You know, brothers are protective of their little sisters. I understand that. So, Saylor and I are just friends for now, okay?" I didn't want to risk him running home and telling Nash I said differently. The first person I needed to talk to was Hayes. I'd already done things backward, and I should have gone to him from the start. I'd fucked up, and I'd eat crow and own it.

But he was the first person I needed to talk to moving forward, and he'd be home tomorrow. I'd planned to meet him at his house and pull this bandage off immediately.

Saylor agreed to let me talk to him first. I needed to have a man-to-man talk with him. Let him see my face and show him how serious I was about this.

"I don't know about that, Uncle King." I helped him out of the truck, and he pulled his jacket back on and asked me to grab his fedora out of the back. The dude had his own style, and he rocked it. I took his hand, and we made our way up the driveway.

"You don't know about what, buddy?"

"You know how you tell me not to worry about things that I shouldn't worry about?" he asked.

"Yeah."

"I think you're doing that."

How was this kid only six fucking years old and this wise?

"I'm good, Beefcake. I promise. Now, let's eat some fancy sandwiches and cupcakes."

"Yes!" He fist-pumped enthusiastically.

When we stepped inside, Demi's mom and grandmother started fawning all over us. My gaze immediately found Saylor's, and on instinct, it trailed up her body. She was wearing the white sundress that I'd helped her slip into after we'd gone at it like porn stars this morning, because now that we'd crossed the line, we couldn't seem to get enough.

I looked away because we'd made a deal not to tell anyone what was happening between us until I talked to Hayes. We may not have done everything right, but we could at least get this next part right.

One more day.

We could do this.

"Hey," Demi and Saylor said at the same time, as they came over and gave us both a hug.

"Beefcake, did you wear orange just for me?" Demi asked, bending down to get to his eye level.

"You know it. It's your special day. I wanted to wear your favorite color for you."

"You look amazing. And the hat just brings it all together," she said.

While they were busy chatting, I reached for Saylor's hand to give it a squeeze, pulling the dandelion from my shirt pocket and placing it there. "How's the party?"

"It's been so nice. Who knew the magic of a mimosa fountain?" She chuckled as she pulled her hand away and held the flower to her nose. "We're having a lot of fun."

She mouthed the words *thank you,* before tucking the flower behind her ear when Peyton called her over to take some pictures.

I spent the next thirty minutes working the room with Cutler, who was clearly in his happy place as all the women showered him with attention.

When the party was over, everyone said their goodbyes, and we made our way outside.

"Where are you off to, Saylor?" Cutler asked as he reached for her hand.

"I'm going to go see Pearl at Magnolia Haven." She held up a box that she told us was filled with pastries. Apparently, my grandmother wasn't feeling up to an outing today, so she hadn't been able to make it to the shower.

"Oh, man. I need to go see my grandma Pearl. Can we go, too, Uncle King?"

"Sure, buddy." I turned my attention to Saylor, knowing she'd walked there, but trying to play it cool in front of Ruby and Demi and the group of women standing nearby. "You want to hop in and ride with us?"

"Yes. That would be great. Thank you."

And just like that, I was spending the day with the people that I loved most.

* * *

We met at Romeo's gym for our usual meeting. We were all expecting Hayes to be back this morning, but that hadn't happened. They'd ended up needing him for another day, so my plan was completely fucked. I wanted to talk to him before the bachelor party. Before we were all together. But now it looked like he'd be coming late to the party tomorrow, and I'd have to talk to him the following day, because I sure as hell wasn't going to do it with an audience.

"At least he'll make it for the last half of the bachelor party," Nash said, wiping his mouth with his napkin after he set his sandwich down.

"Yeah. They sure stretched this out. He's given them weeks. And now he's going to drive straight to your house. Right, King?" Romeo asked.

"Yep. But he'll make it. We've got about twenty-five guys coming, and we've got two food trucks booked that'll be serving burgers and tacos outside. And then Lionel has two bartenders that will come and bartend for us, so it'll be a good time. I've got some poker tables rented, and I think it's going to be exactly what you wanted it to be."

Saylor and Ruby had helped me get this all organized for Romeo, as I'd offered to have it at my house. Romeo didn't want to have it at a bar. He wanted it to be casual, and we'd make it a good time for sure.

"Thanks, brother. You didn't need to do all that. A couple of six-packs and some pizzas would have been fine." He laughed.

"Fuck no. You're the first one to get married in the group, and we're doing this right," River said.

"Sounds good. Beefcake is pissed to all hell that he can't come. He's going to spend the night at JT's house with Jay and Susannah, so I won't need to worry about getting home at a certain time." Nash reached for his sandwich.

"Yeah, he talked to me about it the other day. Little dude hates missing out." I couldn't hide my smile. "Did you talk to Doc Dolby about the asthma?"

"Yeah. He said to just stay on the inhaler and keep an eye on it. But his teacher said he's been having some breathing issues during recess. It fucking kills me, man, because he's a kid, and he should be out there running around, you know?"

"Dude, he's going to be fine. You trust Doc, right? I know he's getting older. If things get worse, maybe you should consider getting a second opinion or seeing a specialist," River said, and we all nodded in agreement.

"That's not a bad idea. Doc didn't seem too concerned. He said for me to just keep that inhaler nearby. But I will keep an eye on it and ask at his next appointment if he can refer me to a specialist."

"And you know I'll go with you if you need me," I said.

"Thanks, brother. But one of us needs to keep an eye on our guys at work at all times. They'd love if we both took a day off." He chuckled.

"Fair point." I crumbled up my wrapper and air-balled it into the trash can on the first try. "Damn. I'm on my game today."

"When are you not?" Nash teased.

"Romeo, the countdown is on. How do you feel about the wedding being in just a few days?" I asked.

"I feel fine. I just want to marry my girl. The rest is just extra, you know? But Demi seems relaxed about it, so I'll just follow her lead."

"Atta boy. Happy wife, happy life." River reached for his soda and took a sip.

"And then I give River two weeks before he runs off to Vegas and ties the knot with Ruby." Nash chuckled, and we all nodded in agreement. "And then, who will be next?"

"I'm guessing King won't be all that far behind, once he figures his shit out." Romeo shrugged, and my eyes widened.

“Not sure what we’re talking about, but I’ll try to figure my shit out,” I said. My voice was light and filled with humor, but I was anything but relaxed. I knew what he was insinuating.

“Not going to talk about it, but Romeo’s right. You better get this shit straight and quickly, brother. Or it’s going to blow up in your face.” River’s gaze was hard.

“Agreed. Without saying it, we see it. We support you, King, but you’ve got to make this right.” Nash shrugged.

Damn. Guilt flooded, and I nodded. I wasn’t going to argue. We’d always been able to communicate without saying much, and it was clear they knew.

Everyone fucking knew.

Except for the one person who should know.

# 27

## Saylor

"So your brother is coming home today, huh?" my mother asked, as we sat at a back table at Magnolia Beans, sipping our drinks and munching on blueberry muffins.

"Yep. He'll make it to the bachelor party for Romeo a little late, but he'll get there. And he'll be here for the wedding this weekend, and that's the most important thing."

"I was happy to get an invitation, but I wanted to talk to you about something."

"You can't bring Barry, Mom. You just can't. There's too much water under the bridge," I said, shaking my head because we'd had this conversation too many times. "Hayes would lose it, and no one would be comfortable if he were there."

"That's what I wanted to talk to you about. We split up," she said with a shrug. "It's different this time."

"Did he touch you?" I asked, my heart racing.

"No. I've been honest with you about that. I think the anger management classes actually helped him. But it just hasn't been the same in a long time, if I'm being honest. He got a job promotion, and he's moving across the country. The position is in New York City."

My eyes widened. "What? Really?"

"Yep. And I think it's a good thing. He wanted me to go with him, but I had no desire to go. I actually felt complete relief when he said he'd be moving. I think I have wanted to end it for a while and just didn't know how." She sipped her coffee and then looked up at me. "I know it's too little, too late, but I want to rebuild my relationship with my children."

"It's never too late to make things better, Mom. I'm really happy that you're going to stay, and I don't know what it is, but you seem . . . lighter already."

"Well, according to my therapist, releasing yourself from a toxic relationship can do wonders." She chuckled. "I've filed for divorce. Barry moved out a couple of weeks ago. That's why I guess he showed up that day at your bookstore. He was angry, and I just didn't want to say anything to you or Hayes, because I know I've said it before, so why should you believe me now? But with him moving, I thought I should let you know."

"So why did he come by the bookstore all pissed off?"

"He was mad about me asking him to move out. It was different this time. There wasn't even a fight. I think I'm just tired of it. I was done, and I told him that I wasn't happy."

"I think you're going to feel a big weight lift off your shoulders with each passing day."

"It's going to be nice to not feel the need to defend him to everyone in my life. Probably would have been a lot easier to just have listened and walked away a long time ago."

"Life is all about learning, right?" I felt hopeful where my mother was concerned for the first time in a very long time. She was a good woman who just never had the confidence to do the right thing for herself or for her children. But beneath it all was a big heart. At least I believed so.

"My children are just a lot smarter than me." She shrugged. "And I don't mind that. My hope for you, Saylor, is that you make wise choices for yourself. You can lose a lot of time being with the wrong person. It can cost you a whole lot. So be picky, and don't settle."

I nodded. I was being picky. I'd found myself the best man out there. A man who made me feel like I could do anything I set my mind to.

A man who made me feel smart and wanted and special.

"I definitely think I know what I'm looking for, and I promise you I won't settle for less than I deserve. I hope you can do the same moving forward."

"Me, too. I'm really ready for a fresh start. That might mean being alone for a while, which I'm okay with. I'd like to focus on you and Hayes and making things right—or at least making things better."

"I think that sounds like a great plan."

"Do you think your brother will be receptive?" she asked.

"That's the thing about Hayes. He's all broody and protective, but beneath all that, he's got the biggest heart of anyone I know. I think if you are genuine, and your actions are consistent with your words . . . he'll soften over time."

"I feel really bad, Saylor," she said, and her voice broke. "He really lost out on his childhood, didn't he? I want to blame your father for that, but I hold a lot of responsibility for what happened, too. It just took me a long time to see that."

"Hayes didn't have it easy, Mom. I can't sugarcoat that for you. He made a lot of choices based on what he thought would be best for both you and me. And he has every right to be angry about the things that went down back then. So, maybe instead of arguing and getting defensive with him, you just own it. You say what you're saying to me. You apologize and tell him that you're sorry, and you want to do better."

"I will. And I'm going to prove it to you this time."

"I'm looking forward to that," I said, reaching across the table and squeezing her hand.

I didn't have a large family, and if I could repair this one relationship, it would mean something to me.

"I'd like to start volunteering at the bookstore. You know, so that you can have a break," she said, catching me off guard.

"That would be amazing. But with the way things are going, you don't have to volunteer. I think I can afford to bring on an employee next month."

"Nope. This one is on the house. Time is a gift that I can give to you now. So please let me do this."

I nodded. "Okay. I'd like that."

I felt like things were turning around. Like coming back to Magnolia Falls was the best decision I'd ever made.

Maybe my mom and brother could repair some of the damage that had been done.

I was going to do whatever I could to help that happen.

Hayes deserved to have family in his corner.

And he deserved an apology from my mother.

It was a start.

But that wasn't what was weighing on me at the moment.

It was my own relationship with my brother.

King's relationship with my brother.

I needed him to be okay with King and me being together. Because I loved my brother fiercely.

But I knew that King was the love of my life, and my brother was going to have to get on board with it.

The rest of the day went by in a blur. I'd felt good about the progress my mom and I were making, and I couldn't wait to tell Hayes about Barry, so I'd called him right away.

He sounded relieved and happy—in that certain Hayes way that was never too enthusiastic, but you knew he was smiling on the other end of the phone.

Peyton, Ruby, and I had spent the last few hours decorating Whiskey Falls. We'd rented the place out for the night. This was a perk of Ruby's dad owning the bar and letting us have the place to ourselves.

It was also a small town, so most of the women in town were coming, so there was that, too. It wasn't like we were closing down a nightclub in a big city. But we were thrilled to have the whole afternoon to decorate. Peyton was very excited about setting this place up.

"I mean, after Demi's mother's *Bridgerton*-themed bridal shower suited for an eighty-year-old queen, we need to make this a little sexy and fun for our girl. It's a bachelorette party, for God's sake." Peyton swung the two large rubber penises around in her hands.

"Girl, I have never seen so many dicks in one place," Ruby said over her laughter. She and I had just hung several banners around the bar that read: *The Last Hoedown, Demi's Last Rodeo, Let's Go Girls, She Said Yee-Haw, and Save a Horse, Ride The Cowboy.*

We'd convinced Peyton to let us do a theme because we knew that Demi would love that. And since she loved to ride, we thought we could tie in her love for horses with her bachelorette party. Peyton had agreed, but she'd taken the theme up a notch and had a cake made that said: *I'd rather ride my man than your horse any day.*

Ruby and I had fallen over laughing, and I knew Demi would do the same. I wasn't quite sure how her mom would respond, as she'd be coming with all her girlfriends tonight.

The biggest surprise was the mechanical bull that we'd rented for the party, because we were going to make this lots of fun. We had pink cowboy hats for everyone that were stacked on a table by the entrance.

Penis cookies, penis straws, and penis sunglasses accompanied the pink balloon arch with giant cowboy boots. It was a cornucopia of cute and ridiculously inappropriate.

The bar was stocked, and we were serving Pornstar Martinis and Ride 'Em Cowboy Coladas for the drinks tonight.

Midge was catering all the food for the party as Ruby couldn't bring herself to ask Calvin, the short-order cook, to make the items that Peyton had chosen.

*After-Sex Antipasto, Romeo Pork Sausages, Slide In Me Beef Sliders, Forbidden Fruit, My Husband's Stuffed Meatballs, Better-than-Sex Chocolate-Covered Bananas, and lastly, Sex on the Brownie.*

She'd worked hard coming up with her raunchy foods, so we were embracing it.

"So, I don't want you guys to be mad, but I do have one little surprise planned." Peyton chewed on her thumbnail.

"What?" Ruby whipped around. "She was pretty clear about what she wanted and didn't want."

"Listen, she's marrying her dream man. Her wedding and her bridal shower can be tame. But tonight, we're going to make sure our girl has some fun." Peyton raised a brow.

"The mechanical bull and the Blow Me bubble gum station aren't enough?" I asked.

"No. We're a bunch of horny women. We deserve a good old-fashioned cowboy striptease." She waggled her brows.

"Okayyyy. I see we're just taking the bull by the horns. Literally and figuratively," Ruby said over a fit of laughter.

"Wow. Okay. Strippers it is." I chuckled.

"I asked for the hottest guys they had. It'll be short and sweet." Peyton raised a brow. "Well, the timeline will be. I asked for a man who was hung like a racehorse. You know, to keep with the theme."

"Well, as long as we stay on theme." Ruby shook her head, and we glanced around the place. It looked freaking amazing.

We all went to the back room to change into our attire, which was basically jean skirts, crop tops, and cowboy boots.

Unless you were Ruby, and then it was black jeans, a crop top, and Dr. Martens.

When we came back out to the bar, the country music was booming, and the door pulled open as Romeo walked toward us with Demi, who was laughing hysterically.

"You brought your boyfriend to your bachelorette party?" Peyton shrieked, and Romeo laughed.

"No. He's on his way to his party, so he walked me over." Demi's gaze moved around the room, and she had a big smile on her face. "This looks amazing. Is that a mechanical bull?"

"Baby, that's what you noticed? There are dicks on the cookies and on all the tables. This is going to be a lot wilder than my bachelor party." He kissed her hard. "Have fun. I love you. Call me when you get back to Saylor and Ruby's tonight." We were all sleeping at our house after the party.

"Maybe she's going to pull an all-nighter," Peyton said, with her hands on her hips.

"Okay, you need a Ride 'Em Cowboy Colada and to bring it down a hundred or so notches." Ruby grabbed Peyton's hand and led her to the bar.

The next few hours were the most entertaining of my life. Demi's mom, Rose, and two of her close friends were ripping shots and dancing their asses off. Midge Longhorn had to be physically removed from the mechanical bull because the damn thing couldn't seem to buck her off. Apparently, Midge used to be in the rodeo. Who knew?

Demi, Peyton, Ruby, and I had laughed endlessly, danced to all our favorite songs, and had way too much to drink. The food choices were a real hit, and everyone was having a good time.

"I need everyone to take their seats!" Peyton shouted into the microphone. "That means you, too, Midge. Get your ass off that bull and sit in your seat. Get ready to enjoy the show."

Everyone was hooting and hollering when Peyton

disappeared and then returned with her eyes wide open and a big smile on her face.

"Please say she didn't do this," Demi whisper-shouted, but she couldn't wipe the smile from her face.

Sexy music started to play, and Peyton returned to take her seat beside us. "Relax, bestie, I told them no lap dances unless someone requests one."

And then she pulled a handful of singles out of her purse and handed them out.

The two guys were undressed in no time, and if I didn't have a well-endowed man of my own to compare them to, I'd say they definitely gave Peyton what she was looking for.

"My God. Those undies are so tiny they barely cover those giant bananas," Demi's mom said as she came to sit beside us.

Our heads all fell back in laughter at once, and Demi wrapped an arm around her mother. "Yep. Those are definitely some big bananas, Mom."

More laughter.

It was a perfect way to celebrate.

I glanced down and saw the text that had come through from Kingston.

KING

I heard there were a lot of penises at your party. 🍆

Your penis is the only one that interests me.

KING

Well, he only likes you, baby.

How's it going? Did my brother make it there?

KING

Yeah. He's here. He seems tired but otherwise okay. I told him I was going to bring him breakfast in the morning, so I'll call you after and let you know how it goes. You've got the girls spending the night with you tonight, right?

Yep. We're having a sleepover with the four of us.

KING

I don't like it when you aren't in my bed.

The feeling is mutual, handsome.

KING

Love you, Dandelion.

Love you more, Forbidden King.

# 28

## Kingston

The party had been great. The food, the booze, the poker games, and the music had all been a hit. It was dwindling down, and Nash and River were collecting beer bottles that were littered all over the yard as I walked Coach, Bobby, and Slade to the door.

"Thanks for a great night," Slade said, dabbing me up and clapping his hand in mine.

"Yeah, thanks for coming. Being sober at these is never easy," I said, surprised that he'd stayed as long as he had.

"Romeo's been really good to me. I can handle a night of nonalcoholic beers for that dude any time. And he's marrying my sister, so he's family now."

Slade Crawford had impressed the hell out of me. He'd been speaking at the high school about his struggles with addiction, and he was doing one hell of a job working at the gym. I knew it wasn't easy, and he took things one day at a time, but from where I was sitting, he was off to a damn good start.

Bobby clapped me on the back and thanked me after I pulled the door open.

And then there was Coach.

He held out a hand, and I did the same. "Thanks for having me. This was a lot of fun. And I'm glad that my mere presence doesn't seem to annoy you anymore."

He was a little drunk, but he was also pretty spot on, and I felt like an asshole, seeing as he'd clearly noticed that I didn't care for him.

"I'm sorry about getting off on the wrong foot."

"Don't give it a thought, mate. I think we both know why you had a problem with me. But I think it all turned out as it was supposed to. I'm happy for you. For both of you." He winked before walking out the door, and I realized everyone in town seemed to know what was going on.

Tomorrow morning couldn't come soon enough.

I'd made a conscious effort not to drink much tonight, because I feared I'd slip or say something before I got the chance to talk to Hayes.

I closed the door and made my way back to the family room, where Romeo, River, and Nash were sitting, staring up at Hayes, and I didn't miss the look of discomfort on their faces.

I cleared my throat. "What's going on?"

Hayes looked at me, and I knew in that moment that he knew.

*He fucking knew.*

It was the look in his eyes—pure rage and anger.

The disappointment.

"I went to use your bathroom because the other two were full at the time. And I wanted a magazine to read while I was in there, so I went to your nightstand. And I'm just asking the guys why the fuck my sister's evil eye necklace is on your nightstand. I know she's stayed here before, but she stayed in the guest room. And she's been back at home for a while now. So, I'm going to ask you once, King. Why the fuck is Saylor's necklace on your nightstand? In your fucking bedroom."

"Listen, I told you I wanted to talk to you tomorrow. I've got some stuff I need to say to you."

"You've got some stuff that you need to say to me? Because you don't talk to me every fucking day? You need a formal appointment for this?"

"Hayes, take a seat. You need to hear him out," Nash said, and that was not the right thing to say, because Hayes flew off the handle with that request.

"I need to take a seat? I need to hear him out? My best friends all seem to know something is going on, and no one has had the decency to tell me? So, I'm looking you in the fucking eyes, King." He moved closer to me, and I knew I was fucked. This hadn't gone down the way I'd hoped. "You tell me right now . . . did you fuck my sister?"

I gripped his shoulders and shoved him back. "Don't fucking talk about my woman like that."

Everything was a blur after that. He dove on top of me, and I didn't fight him. I had it coming. I'd fucked up, and I'd take the hits that came.

He punched me in the side of my face first and then gripped my shirt and shook me as I lay on the floor beneath him. "Your fucking woman? For how long, King? Until you get bored with her and throw her away? How the fuck could you do this to her?"

Romeo, River, and Nash were on their feet, pulling him off of me.

"It's not what you think," I said, pushing to sit up and wiping the blood from my lip. "Let me explain it to you."

He was clearly intoxicated because he stumbled back, shaking them off, as he turned to look at each of them. "You all knew? And no one told me?"

"Dude, we didn't know shit. We were suspicious," Romeo said.

"This isn't on them. This is on me. Let me walk you home, and we can talk about it."

A sarcastic laugh left his lips. "We can talk about it? You've had months to talk to me about it. And you didn't give a fuck about anyone but yourself."

I pushed to my feet. "That's not how it is, Hayes. You're my brother. I love you, man."

"Nah. You know she's all I have. She's been through so much, and you cared that little. You just wanted to get your dick wet."

Now it was my turn to throw a punch and hit him square in the jaw. "I warned you not to talk about her like that."

He stumbled back and then spit on my wood floor. His hands were up as he backed away and walked toward the door while still facing me.

He just stared with disbelief, like I'd betrayed him in the worst way.

And I had, hadn't I?

The look in his eyes nearly broke me.

Betrayed and angry and hurt.

"Ride or die. Right, King? *Ride or fucking die.*" His voice cracked on the last word, and a deep pain settled in my chest.

And he turned and walked out the door.

"I've got this," Romeo said, as he held up a hand and jogged out the door.

"I'll go with you. I think he's going to be raging for a while." Nash hurried out behind Romeo.

They both gave me a look that said it all.

*I'd fucked up really badly this time.*

I dropped onto the couch, and I ran a hand down my face. That had gone about as badly as it possibly could have.

I'd hurt someone that was a fucking brother to me.

River came to sit beside me after he'd stepped into the kitchen. He handed me a frozen bag of peas to hold on my face. "This is bad, King. And you're going to need to fix this."

"I know. I planned to talk to him tomorrow morning so we wouldn't have a fucking audience."

"Well, how'd that plan work out for you?" He raised a brow. "How about you own it with me right now? Is this thing between you two serious?"

"Do you think I would have punched him if it wasn't?"

"Yeah, that was a surprising move, but I need to hear you say it, brother. Because if this isn't the real deal, you might have just fucked up a lifelong friendship forever."

"I love her, River. I think I have for a very long time. Long before anything ever happened. We have a history from way back when she lived with us," I said, holding up my hands when he looked like he was going to explode on me. "Nothing ever happened. I swear on everything I know. Never. But the feelings, they've been there for a long time. I can't stay away from her. I've tried. I've tried so fucking hard." I buried my face in my hands and tried to keep it together.

"Why didn't you fucking talk to me? Talk to Hayes?"

"And say what? That I was attracted to her? Because that's what I thought it was at first. But then we started spending so much time together, and it's so much more than that. These feelings . . . they aren't going away, River. They just get stronger every day. I love her in a way that I know I can't exist in a world that she isn't in. So, I'll take my fucking lumps from Hayes until he'll talk to me, because this isn't some fucking fling. This girl—she makes me want to be the kind of man that deserves her."

"Wow. You really are fucked." River barked out a laugh. "You've got it bad, little brother. Does she feel the same?"

"She does. We've been keeping it a secret until we could talk to Hayes." I shrugged, knowing it was a lame defense now.

"Well, that sure blew up in your face. But you've got a few days to fix this before Romeo's wedding. We can't have you two brawling on his wedding day, so you better find a way to make this right, King."

"And how do you suggest I do that? He probably won't even fucking talk to me now." I fell back against the couch.

"You just keep trying until he does. And you tell him exactly what you told me." He leaned back beside me and turned to look at me. "You tell him you love his sister, and you should have come to him, but you fucked up. Because you're ridiculously in love. And you just keep saying it until you get through to him."

"All right. That's what I'll do." I let out a long breath. I couldn't believe we'd come to blows. He was my best friend, and I'd hurt him in a way that I didn't know if he'd ever forgive me. "I just hope he'll listen to me."

"Yeah, me too, brother. This might be the worst fight any of us have ever had."

"I broke the pact. Ride or die. I fucked it all up."

River clapped me on the shoulder. "You fell in love. That's not breaking the pact. The way you went about it wasn't great, but you'll explain that to him when he's sober and has calmed down."

My phone beeped at the same time River's did.

ROMEO

Hey, it's just the four of us on this thread. He's really pissed, and he's also really drunk, and he hasn't slept much since he's been gone, so I think he's also exhausted. He's going to crash at my place so I can make sure he's all right.

NASH

You need to make this right, King. He's really angry. I hope like hell that this is the real deal because he won't get over it if it's anything less than that.

RIVER

I'm sitting here with this whipped motherfucker who just told me he's in love. They both are.

ROMEO

I figured it was serious when he threw a punch at Hayes.

I wanted to take whatever hits he wanted to land on my face. But I couldn't hear him talking about her like she didn't matter to me. I love her. I love her so fucking much that I just fucked up my relationship with my best friend over it.

ROMEO

Let him sober up and get some sleep, and then you two can talk.

NASH

If anyone can talk themselves out of a shitstorm, it's you, brother. So get your head straight and then make this right.

I'll do whatever it takes.

My phone rang, and I looked down to see Saylor was calling.

"Hey," I said, as I pushed to my feet and walked out of the room, leaving River, who was sitting on the couch with his eyes closed now.

"You sound upset. Are you okay?" she asked, and she didn't hide her concern.

"He knows." I dropped onto my bed and ran a hand down my face.

"Hayes knows? You told him?"

"He found your necklace on my nightstand, and he lost his shit. It got physical, and there was just no explaining anything to him at that point. I fucked up, Saylor. I should have gone to him."

"No, King. This is on me. I asked you not to talk to him. I'm sorry. I can't believe I left my necklace there. I messed it all up, and I'm so sorry." Her voice broke on the last word.

"This is on me. I should have handled it like a man. If I could have seen into the future, to know with confidence that this was the real deal, I would have done that. But I really fucked up by not talking to him. He feels betrayed, and I'd feel the same fucking way if this were reversed."

"No one can see into the future. It wasn't about him, but I do think I should have realized how bad this would look if he found out the way that he did. Do you want me to come over?"

"Fuck, Dandelion, the last thing we need is him showing back up here and finding you here. I've got to fix this first, all right? It might take a few days, but I need to get this right before I do anything else."

She sniffled a few times. "Okay. I'm so sorry, King. I know I put you in a bad position, and I feel sick about it. I wasn't trying to be deceitful; I was just trying to give us a fighting chance. And at the end of the day, we were able to figure out that we loved each other, so I'd do it all again if I had to. But I don't want this to come between your friendship with Hayes. I promise you we will fix this."

"None of this is your fault. My relationship with Hayes is based on trust, and I broke that. It's between me and him. I could have insisted on telling him at any time, and I went right along with the plan to keep it a secret. I was a selfish asshole, and now I need to own up to it."

"Just promise me that this won't come between us." Her voice shook.

"Dandelion, there is not anything in the world that can come between us. I love you, and that will never change. But you've got to give me some time to fix this and make it right. Because I'm not okay with where things stand with your brother right now."

"Okay," she whispered. "Whatever you need me to do, I'll do it."

"All right. Let's just stay away from one another until I talk to Hayes. I love you."

"Love you. Goodnight, King."

I ended the call and fell back onto the bed.

I had my work cut out for me. But I wouldn't stop until I made this right.

# 29

## Saylor

I filled the girls in on what happened, and they all just stared at me, each with different reactions.

"Shit. I warned King that he needed to talk to Hayes," Ruby said, shaking her head.

"Wait. You knew?" Demi, Peyton, and I all said at the same time.

"I suspected, and I talked in code to him. But I thought I made it clear that he needed to have that talk with your brother."

"He was going to talk to him tomorrow. Hayes was supposed to come home yesterday, but he was delayed and showed up in the middle of the bachelor party. King didn't want to have this conversation in front of everyone. But Hayes found my necklace on King's nightstand and figured it out, and you know the rest." I chewed my thumbnail, feeling overwhelmed with the hurt I'd caused my brother, and also nervous about what this meant for me and King. He sounded devastated on the phone, and I wondered if he'd blame me for this whole mess.

*I'm the one who insisted we keep it a secret.*

He'd respected my wishes, and now his best friend wouldn't speak to him.

"I was suspicious, too, if I'm being honest, but I never imagined it coming out like this. But at the end of the day, you're in love. Hayes will get over it because all he really wants is for you both to be happy." Demi wrapped an arm around my shoulder.

"Wait. I wasn't suspicious at all. So you're telling me that all this time, you've been riding King Pierce like a wild stallion?" Peyton said, and Demi and Ruby burst out in hysterical laughter.

I chuckled, but I wasn't much in the mood to laugh at the moment. I'd managed to make a tough situation even tougher.

"Not really. That part is a recent turn of events. We've just been spending so much time together and exploring—things." I shrugged. "There was no sex until just a few days ago."

"Damn. Did he live up to the expectations?" Peyton whistled. "Because, my God, they were high."

"He did," I said, as a tear ran down my cheek.

Ruby leaned forward and gripped my shoulders. "Don't you dare cry. This is all going to be fine. You fell in love. You followed your heart. You just need to make Hayes understand that this is what you want. What both of you want."

"I'm sorry. This is supposed to be your bachelorette party, and I've just brought a big dark cloud with me." I wiped my cheeks.

"This is what slumber parties are all about," Peyton said. "Eating too much and swapping sex stories. And if it ends with a few tears—it's a win."

Demi laughed. "I agree with her on this one. This night couldn't have been any better. And I'm also glad that we're here for you right now. We love you, Saylor. This is what friends do."

"She's right. And I was dirty-cowboy'd out for the night. I was ready for some real-life events. After that freakishly oily stripper tried to give me a lap dance that I did not ask for, I was ready to go." Ruby smirked.

"I think when you pulled out your pepper spray and gave him a warning, that did the trick," Peyton said.

"Well, he sure as hell didn't try again, did he?" Ruby raised a brow.

"Please. That guy was one oily, well-hung stud muffin. Having him shake his ass and his unusually large, er, banana, as Demi's mother put it—well, it was a nice escape for an evening."

"You know you're ridiculous, right?" Demi said over her laughter as she hugged me tighter.

We all jumped when someone knocked on the door.

"Do you think it's Guapo?"

"Who the hell is Guapo?"

"The oily stripper."

"If that guy knows where we live, he is definitely getting pepper sprayed." Ruby moved to her feet. "Let me see who it is."

"It could be a murderer. It's one o'clock in the morning," Demi whisper-shouted as she ran to the kitchen. "I'm getting a knife."

We were all on our feet and huddled together as we looked down to see a butter knife in Demi's hand.

"Are you going to stab him or offer him some toast?" Ruby said over her laughter and peeked through the little hole in the door. "It's freaking Romeo and Hayes."

My stomach dropped at the mention of my brother.

"Awww . . . I'm so happy I don't have to murder anyone." Demi pulled the door open and lunged in Romeo's arms.

"Is it bad that I'm kind of disappointed? I was ready to go all girl-gang crazy on the guy. And death by butter knife seems very empathetic." Peyton shrugged.

My gaze locked with Hayes, and I could tell he was still intoxicated.

"So, this guy is refusing to go to sleep. I'm guessing you know why he's here?" Romeo asked, as they stepped inside.

"Yes. I know why he's here." I hugged my brother before pulling away. "Come on. Let's get some coffee in you, and we can talk."

"How about you come home with me now, baby?" Romeo said.

"Yeah. I think that's a good idea," Demi said.

They said their goodbyes, and she thanked us multiple times for the best night ever.

"Come on, Peyt. You can sleep with me. Let's give them some space to talk." Ruby led Peyton down the hall, and they closed the door.

I put on a pot of coffee, grabbed the pain reliever, and gave Hayes a glass of water to drink while he waited for his coffee.

"Take these," I said, and he took the two little pills from my hand. He hadn't spoken yet.

I poured us each a glass of coffee because, obviously, there wasn't going to be a lot of sleep going on tonight. I took the seat across from him at the kitchen table.

"I heard you had quite a night," I said, surprised to see that he had a little cut on his lip. So they'd clearly both thrown punches.

"Did you hear that from your boyfriend?" he said, sarcasm oozing from his body as he reached for the coffee.

"I did, actually. He's pretty devastated by the whole thing."

"Well, I think he's got good reason to be devastated."

"You realize how ridiculous this whole thing is, right?" I asked.

"Anyone else, Say. Any-fucking-one-else. He's my best friend. These four guys, they're my family, you know?"

"I know. They're pretty amazing guys. And I just happened to be in love with one of them."

He closed his eyes and groaned. "Love? You fucking love him? He's not that guy, Saylor."

"Look at me," I hissed, waiting for him to open his eyes. "We're in love, Hayes. We have been for a while."

He narrowed his gaze. "He told you that he loves you?"

"Many times."

"Walk me through this. Make me understand why I had to find out this way. Why you've both lied to me for God knows how long."

"I'd be happy to," I said, refilling both of our coffees. I took Hayes back to the months that I lived with the Pierce family. How he slept with me every single night, held my hand, listened to me talk about my day—and never touched me. Not once.

I told him about our connection. About the dandelions. I explained how it all started and paused because I knew this next part wouldn't be the most pleasant for him.

"He fought it hard, Hayes. He brought you up every day. Worried endlessly about crossing the line." I reached for my mug, remembering how hard he'd tried to stay away from me. "He stopped going out months ago, if you hadn't noticed. He was—suffering with discomfort."

He let out a long breath. "I do remember that. He thought he was dying from a bad case of blue balls. But I don't need the details on how you fixed that situation."

"The first time he kissed me, he was riddled with guilt, Hayes. He tried to walk away several times."

"But yet he never came to me. My best fucking friend. My brother," he said, shaking his head.

"You're not going to like this next part." I cleared my throat, and I looked him right in the eyes. "I am the one who didn't want to tell you. He insisted he go to you. It was my line in the sand, Hayes. I didn't want you or anyone else involved. I was adamant about it."

"What? Why would you do that?"

"Because I'm a grown woman, Hayes. And I know you

see me as a child, and I can't even be mad at you for it. But I wanted to see where it went without you threatening him and putting pressure on the situation."

"He's never been in a serious relationship, Saylor."

"Well, I hate to break it to you, but he's sort of been in one for the last few months. Even before anything happened—he and I were always together. It was a friendship at first, and then we couldn't fight it. I've never felt anything like this. And he tried hard not to feel it. He even put that dandelion tattoo beside the *Ride or Die* tattoo all those years ago as a reminder of a line he couldn't cross."

"Fuck. Why didn't he just come talk to me?" He scrubbed a hand down his face. His voice was not slurring anymore, but he sounded exhausted.

"Hmmm . . ." I said, not making any attempt to hide the sarcasm in my voice. "Maybe because you've threatened him about this for years."

"I didn't know it was this deep." His eyes locked with mine, and I saw the understanding there as his hand scrubbed over his peppered jaw.

"It caught us both by surprise. And he's really, really good to me." My hand found my chest, covering my heart, as a tear ran down my cheek. "He wanted to talk to you so badly, but I begged him not to, and he put my needs first. And next to you, no one has ever done that before."

"King's one of the best people I know, I'm not arguing that. I just didn't want him fucking around with you. Obviously, this is different."

"Obviously." I rolled my eyes. "If you'd just have trusted me and him, it might not have gone to blows."

"It's hard for me sometimes to let go where you're concerned," he said, and his voice was strained. "When Dad left, I remember hearing you cry in your room for hours. You wouldn't eat much, and you just laid in your bed, and I worried you'd wither away. Mom had checked out, and she wasn't taking care of either of us. And I made this pact that I'd be there for you, and you'd know you were taken care of. And I tried, Saylor. I tried to give you the life that you deserved."

The tears were falling so fast that it was hard to see through my blurry vision. "That wasn't your job, Hayes, but you stepped up for me, and I'm so grateful." I tried to speak over my sobs. "I wrestle with it, you know?"

"With what?" He leaned forward and patted me on the arm, in a total Hayes sort of way. Not overly emotional, but he wanted me to know he was there.

"With being grateful for you being the best brother a girl could ask for, but also being brave enough to make decisions for myself without feeling guilty. I think I've probably loved King longer than I even realized. But keeping this a secret, to see where it went, was not something I did to hurt you. It was something that I did for myself. And for him. I knew he doubted himself, and if he went to you and you lost your shit on him, he'd run. Running is easier, Hayes. And don't forget that King lost his parents at a young age, and he has his own baggage and hang-ups about loving someone enough to be vulnerable."

"And you're certain he's all in?"

"One hundred percent. He was planning to talk to you yesterday, and then you didn't come home. So, he had a plan to meet you in the morning and tell you man to man. But then you lost your shit, right?" I raised a brow.

The corners of his lips turned up, and he pointed at his mouth. "He got a damn good shot in, too."

"I didn't think he'd fight back. I thought he'd take whatever you gave him."

"Well, he didn't get to explain much before I hit him the first time. But then I ran my mouth the way you'd expect me to." He winced. "And he shouted something about not talking about his woman that way."

I chuckled, and so did he. "He's a good man, Hayes. You know he is."

"It was never about that. It was about making sure he didn't hurt you. And I'm not going to lie, the not telling me what was going on—it stings. These guys are my family, Say. And we've never kept secrets. So my mind went to the worst place, that he was taking advantage of you and all that shit, and that's why he'd kept it a secret."

"He would never do that."

"I know. But in the heat of the moment, I wasn't thinking clearly." He yawned.

"Come on. Let's move to the couch. I want to fill you in on our new siblings," I said with a laugh.

"King told me it was the craziest shit he'd ever seen." Hayes carried both our coffee cups into the living room.

We settled onto the couch, and we talked until the sun came up. About the disappointment regarding our father, and the fact that he'd never made an effort to introduce us to his new family. And the hope that maybe our mother might be trying to make things better for herself. We talked about that night that we'd avoided for such a long time. The night that had changed both of our lives in different ways. He'd grown more protective of me, and I'd formed a bond with the love of my life.

And we were both going to be okay, because we always had one another.

And we'd found a family of our own that we may not have been born into, but they were ours just the same.

These friends that were more like family.

We talked until our eyes couldn't stay open any longer, and we each took an end of the L-shaped couch and finally gave into sleep.

# 30

## Kingston

I'd been lying on the swing on his front porch since the sun came up. I'd barely slept. I'd texted him a dozen times this morning, before my phone died, because I'd never taken the time to charge it last night.

None of that fucking mattered.

I'd texted him that I was here on his front porch.

I'd assumed he'd come home this morning. The light was on inside, so I knew he was in there.

I'd banged on his door a few dozen times over the last few hours, and he'd continued to ignore me.

I pushed to my feet and pounded on the door again. "I'm not going anywhere until you talk to me. You can ignore me all you want, but I'm going to live on this fucking porch until you talk to me."

"That's a commitment right there." His voice came from behind me.

I turned around to see Hayes walking up the steps to his porch. "You haven't been here this whole time?"

"No. I'm not a complete dick. I would have answered the

door to give you a tablespoon of water." He raised a brow. "How long have you been out here?"

"Since around five-thirty this morning?" I shrugged.

"Jesus. You've been here for seven hours?"

"And it's bee season. So, I've risked my life just to talk to you."

He put his key in the door and pushed it open before raising a brow at me. "You coming in?"

"Are there any weapons or sharp objects nearby?" I asked, as I followed him inside.

"Dude, you threw a damn good punch too."

"Sorry about that. I planned to let you kick my ass, but then you pissed me off." I took a seat at his kitchen table, and he put a pot of coffee on.

He leaned against the kitchen cabinets, crossing his feet at the ankles. "I stayed up all night talking to Saylor."

"Oh, yeah? How'd that go?"

"Well, she told me how she'd been in love with you for a while. How you tried to stay away, blah, blah, blah." He smirked. "I begged her to skip the gory details because I can't hear that shit. But, the bottom line is, she's the reason you didn't talk to me about it. And she explained why she didn't want me to know anything, and as much as this is going to pain me to say—" He looked away for a moment.

"I can't wait to hear it."

"She was right. It's none of my fucking business, King," he said, setting one mug of hot coffee in front of me and another in front of himself, before he dropped to sit across from me. "I need you to know something."

"That you're going to tie me up in a white van, hire a clown to drive me around town, and then set me free in a swarm of bees?"

He barked out a laugh. "Last night, I might have considered it. But I was drunk and exhausted, and let's face it—I can be a real hot-headed asshole when I want to be."

"No? You? Seriously?" I said over my laughter. "Listen, Hayes, I wouldn't ever do anything to hurt Saylor. I think I've loved her since I was a teenager." I held up my hands in defense. "I never acted on anything back then. Not a single thing ever happened."

"Relax. She told me." He scratched the back of his neck. "I need you to know something."

"What is it?"

"This was never about me thinking you're not a good guy. King, you're my best friend. You're one of the best people I've ever known. It was never about that. My fear was that you'd just fuck around with her, not realizing the impact that would have on her. She's special, you know?"

"Dude, you're preaching to the choir. She's always been special. I would kill someone who hurt her, and I mean that."

"I figured that out when you knocked me in the face, which, by the way, still hurts like a bitch."

"Yeah, mine, too. And we better make sure there's no bruising for Romeo's wedding pictures, or Demi's mom will have our asses." I laughed. I felt the weight of the world lift off my shoulders as we sat here talking, and I knew everything would be okay with us.

"I know there are no guarantees in life, King. And I can't ask you for that kind of promise. But I need to know that you love my sister, and you will try like hell not to hurt her."

"Dude. There are a few things in life that I can guarantee. I will love my grandmother until I take my last breath. I will love my Ride or Die brothers until I take my last breath. And I will love Saylor with everything I have until I take my last breath. Hand on my heart, I give you my word." Our eyes were locked, and he studied me. "It's not a hardship, Hayes. Your sister . . . she makes me want things I never thought I'd want."

His eyes were wet with emotion, and then he smirked. "A white van?"

"Never going to happen." I barked out a laugh. "But in all seriousness, I'd propose to her today if I thought she'd say yes. I'd even have a dozen babies with her if she were willing."

"For fuck's sake. Know your audience, you dickhole. I do not want to hear about you putting babies in my sister." He tried to act offended, but I heard the humor in his voice.

"Little baby Kings could be running around, looking for Uncle Hayes," I said, and I jumped to my feet when he lunged at me, and we both bellowed out in laughter.

"How about you wait until she's ready, and you start with a proper proposal when the time comes?" He raised a brow.

"Should I come to you for permission?" I asked, my voice teasing.

"Well, you kind of fucked that one up the first time when you kept your relationship a secret. So, yeah, you better ask my fucking permission if it gets to that. And I'm going to be a real asshole. Make you mow my lawn and polish my shoes. Really put you through it."

"Really? Those shoes?" I asked, quirking a brow as I looked down at his dusty cowboy boots.

"These bad boys could use a shine."

"You know I'll do it, if it means I get your blessing." There was no humor in my voice because it was the truth. It meant everything to me.

"King," he said, his voice hard.

"Yeah."

"There is no one I would trust my sister with more than you, knowing what I know now. You are my brother in every way, and hearing you say that you love Saylor—that's all I needed, man. Had you come to me and told me that, I would have given you a hug. Instead, you made me punch you first." He chuckled. "But as much as it pissed me off, I kind of like that you did what she asked you to do by keeping it a secret."

"Why?"

"Because it shows me that you're her little bitch, and I think I'm going to enjoy this."

Laughter filled his kitchen, and he pushed to his feet and pulled me into a hug.

"I love you, brother."

"I love you, too." I cleared my throat and stepped back. "I just love your sister a little more than I love you."

More laughter.

His phone vibrated on the table, and he held it up for me to see.

ROMEO

What's happening, boys? I'm getting married in two days. Have we buried this shit yet?

"How about we have a little fun with them before we tell them we're good?" Hayes said.

"They don't call me Good Time Pierce for nothing."

"Nobody calls you that. Do you just make this shit up as you go?" He chuckled.

"Damn straight."

I pulled my chair over beside him and watched as he typed.

HAYES

Buried this shit? Sure. I just dug King's grave. I'll be burying him in my backyard so I can take a piss on him every morning.

"Dude. That's harsh." I shivered dramatically. "Relax. This is going to be fun."

NASH

You need to talk to him. It's not what you think.

RIVER

In all seriousness, I've tried his phone a dozen times. He's not answering, and he's been gone since before I woke up. You didn't kill him already, did you?

ROMEO

Can you wait until after the wedding? I'd be short a groomsman.

NASH

I can walk two ladies down the aisle if necessary.

"Give me that fucking phone right now."

HAYES

This is King, you dickfucks. No one is getting murdered, but thank you for the concern. We're good over here, assholes. 🖕

Hayes was laughing hysterically now.

ROMEO

Ahhh . . . good to know.

NASH

Damn. I was kind of looking forward to Hayes throwing King into the cake or something dramatic.

RIVER

King would enjoy that too much.

HAYES

He did just ask me if that was an option.

ROMEO

Yeah, Demi's mom would love that. 🙄

NASH

Glad all is okay. So what's the deal? Are you and Saylor dating? Hayes, you're good with this?

HAYES

The asshole just told me he wants to propose and put a baby in her. I told him to slow his roll, but yeah, I'm good with it. I'll still kick his ass if he does anything to fuck it up.

RIVER

Who had the better punch, Romeo?

ROMEO

Well, Hayes was giving rage vibes, while King was giving protective boyfriend vibes. Both fierce. Both left a mark. Neither should take up professional boxing, though. 😂

A slew of emojis came through, and Hayes and I talked for another hour before I took off.

I made my way to Saylor's house, because I needed her to know that everything was okay.

I parked in the driveway and walked to the door, just as it flung open before I could knock.

"Where have you been? I've called and texted," she said, and I saw the concern as she took in my fat lip.

"Baby, I'm fine. My phone died. I was with your brother."

I stepped inside and pushed the door closed before pulling her into my arms. She had my shirt bunched in her hands like she wanted to hold onto me.

"Hey, everything's okay." I pulled back, and she looked up at me.

"Yeah? He and I talked all night. He said he'd talk to you today, but then when I didn't hear from you, I just got worried."

"No more worrying, Dandelion. He knows everything. He knows how I feel about you. He knows this is the real deal, and he's good with it."

She let out a long breath. "I'm sorry that I caused a lot of this. You were right. We should have told him from the beginning."

"Nope. As much as I hate that we hurt him, I think this is how it was meant to play out. And the truth is, we needed that time. Just you and me."

"And now?" she asked.

"Now it's you and me, and we don't need to hide it. I can dance with my girl on country music night and kiss you at The Golden Goose and hold your hand when we're out in public."

"I like the sound of that." She sank her teeth into her juicy bottom lip. "Anything else you want to do?"

"I want to bury myself deep inside you without any worries that I'm betraying anyone. And then I want to go get Beefcake and take him to lunch and tell him that you're my girl. Because little dude has been pushing for it."

"He's always been an old soul. Wise for his years. So, how about you have your way with me, and then we'll go pick up our boy and take him to lunch." She smiled up at me before I reached around and grabbed her ass, lifting her into my arms. Her legs came around my waist, and I walked her down the hallway.

I dropped her onto the bed and hovered above her. "I remembered something today when I was talking to Hayes."

"Tell me."

"It was all those years ago when you were staying at our house." I cleared my throat. "You were telling me about a wish you made on a dandelion that day."

"I made a lot of wishes back then." She chuckled as her hand came up and stroked the side of my face. "What did I wish for?"

"You told me that you hated the instability of your home. You said that you'd had this dream the night before that you were standing in a field of dandelions, wearing a white sundress, and you described everything so vividly. The way your hair was styled and the way the sun was shining down on you."

She smiled. "Wait. I remember this, I think."

"You said that a man was walking toward you and that you realized you were getting married there in that field. But the man's face was blurred out, so you didn't know who he was. But you knew that he would protect you and love you to the ends of the earth, and you made a wish the following day that you'd find that someday."

She covered her face with her hands. "Oh my gosh. Yes. I still can't believe I admitted that to you back then. I wanted that, you know? Someone who would love me as fiercely as I loved them."

I pulled her hands away. "I think that's the moment I fell in love with you. I didn't know what it meant back then, because I was a dumb kid at the time. But I remember thinking how cool it was to know what you wanted. To not be afraid to say it and find it and live it, you know?"

"You ready to live it, King?"

"I already am." I pinned her hands above her head. "I want to be that man for you today, tomorrow, and forever."

A tear slipped down her cheek. "You already are."

I leaned down and kissed her.

Because forever started right fucking now.

# 31

## Saylor

"You look gorgeous," I said, as I watched Demi's hairdresser, Ariel, attach the crown-style veil to the top of her head.

"I can't get over this dress," Brinkley said, as she snapped a few pictures of Demi on her phone.

"Damn, girl. You are the most beautiful bride." Peyton swiped at the tear running down her face.

"Thank you. And you all look so amazing." Demi turned to look at each of us.

"I think it's so cool that you let us pick our dresses out ourselves," Tia said. Romeo's sister was stunning, and she was home from college for summer break.

"I really appreciate it, because if you would have forced me to wear some frilly monstrosity, I would not have enjoyed that." Ruby walked toward us, wearing a strapless peach sheath dress.

We were each given the freedom to choose our dress, as long as it was floor length and the color peach. I'd chosen a sleeveless satin gown with a high slit, showing off a little leg. Brinkley was wearing an off-the-shoulder tulle gown, while Tia wore a high-necked dress with a full skirt. Liz, Demi's college roommate, was wearing a peach high-necked princess-style dress. Peyton had, of course, taken it up a notch and was wearing a skintight peach sequined gown. Somehow, we all looked like we meshed well when we stood together and looked in the full-length mirror.

"You girls look stunning," Demi's mom said, in a taupe floral gown with a jacket that was giving Jackie O. vibes. "And, Demi, there are no words for how beautiful you are."

Demi pushed to her feet and hugged her mom before fanning her face to keep the tears back. "No crying. It's too early, and I'm going to try to keep it together today."

There was a knock on the door, and Ruby went to open it and see who it was.

"I came to check on my girls," Cutler said, and we all gasped when he stepped inside. His dark hair was slicked back with gel, he wore a black tuxedo with a peach bowtie, and he had a peach floral pocket scarf tucked into the front of his jacket. My favorite part was the black velvet dress shoes on his feet that had his initials embroidered in gold on the tops. Nash had been complaining for days that Cutler had begged him for these shoes that they'd seen when they'd gone to get his tuxedo fitted.

"You look so handsome," I said, pushing to my feet and bending down to straighten his bowtie.

"Thank you, Saylor." He winked. "You look real pretty today. All of you do."

"You are going to make some woman very happy someday, Beefcake," Tia said, and everyone chuckled.

"I plan to." He waggled his brows. "I'm supposed to tell you all that it's time, and, Demi, your dad is on his way in here right now. You'll come out last."

Demi pushed to her feet and smiled down at him. "Okay. Let's do this. Thanks for taking care of those rings for us."

"Pops is holding my pillow out there, and I've got the real rings right here in my pocket." He patted his chest.

More laughter. We all got emotional giving Demi hugs, as we made our way out the door.

When I stepped out into the gorgeous foyer at Demi's family home, the first eyes I saw were King's. Dark and sexy as they scanned down my body from head to toe.

"You look gorgeous." He pulled me close, his fingers intertwining with mine at my side as he whispered in my ear.

"So, this is how it's going to be, huh?" Hayes feigned annoyance as I pulled back and chuckled.

"Yeah, this is how it's going to be." King kissed the tip of my nose and then turned to look at my brother.

"What do you think of these two, Beefcake?" Hayes asked.

"I think Saylor's always been Uncle King's girl, and I think you like it, Uncle Hayes," Cutler said.

"I think my boy is onto something. I think he likes it, too." Nash winked at his son.

"Whatever. It's fine. If they're happy, I'm happy." Hayes smirked.

"Okay, take your positions," Gina, Demi and Romeo's wedding planner, said as she clapped her hands together.

We lined up with our partners, and Romeo was already standing at the other end of the aisle, where he'd stayed after he'd walked his mom and grandmother to their seats. The ceremony was taking place outside on the ranch, with the water off in the distance. It was a perfect setting for a wedding.

We got into our positions, with Nash and Liz leading the way. Next were Hayes and Tia, then Brinkley and Slade, followed by me and King and River and Ruby. Lincoln and Peyton were the last to make their way down the aisle. There were peach and white flowers draped along the chairs of the aisle, all leading to a giant arch covered in more flowers than I'd ever seen. Janelle had truly outdone herself with the florals.

King leaned down and whispered in my ear. "Someday, you'll be walking down the aisle toward me."

"Don't threaten me with a good time, Forbidden King." I waggled my brows as he kissed my cheek, and we took our places on opposite sides. Everyone gasped as Cutler escorted the flower girl down the aisle. Little Lacey was only three years old, and she was one of Demi's cousins' daughters. She took her time dropping one petal at a time, and Cutler did not look happy about it. He kept looking over his shoulder, and I could see Gina waving her hands for him to hurry up.

Cutler patted Lacey on the back before taking the basket from her and dumping the entire bunch of flower petals on the ground, and then he handed her the basket back. Laughter filled the air around us, and I looked up to see Nash shake his head with a big smile on his face.

Romeo didn't even seem to notice. His gaze was focused down the aisle, waiting for his bride to make her way toward him. The music started, and everyone turned and pushed to their feet.

Demi made her way down the aisle looking like a real, live princess. Her white satin gown had a fitted bodice with spaghetti straps on the shoulders. A full tulle skirt started at the waist and ran to the floor, swooshing around her legs when she walked. A crown sat on her head, holding the veil, and all the stones sparkled in the sun that was shining down.

She was breathtaking.

Romeo had made his way forward a few steps, and I felt a lump form in my throat when I noticed that his eyes were wet with emotion. He just stared down the aisle, like his whole world was at the other end.

I felt a pull calling to me and looked up to see King watching me, and he had the same look in his eyes.

I smiled because the feeling was mutual.

All my life I'd had terrible examples of what love was. My parents' marriage was an epic failure, and my stepfather was abusive and had been a terrible husband to my mother.

Our home hadn't been filled with love or laughter.

My brother had done his best to provide that for me. And in a lot of ways, I had him to thank for finding my happily ever after.

As challenging as he had made things, he'd been the force in my life that had urged me to believe that there was a better life out there than what we'd experienced. He'd been the one to remind me every day that I deserved better.

More.

And I'd found it in this beautiful man who set my world on fire. King made me believe that the men in the pages of my romance books actually existed.

He was both an alpha and a cinnamon roll.

The perfect mix of strong and kind.

My attention turned back down the aisle as Demi and her father stood before Romeo.

Romeo shook her father's hand and then turned to her and did the sweetest thing I'd ever seen. He rubbed his hands down her arms as he shook his head and then placed a hand on each side of her face. "You take my breath away. Thanks for marrying me today, baby."

There wasn't a dry eye in sight. And everyone in town was here to celebrate these two. You could feel the love all around.

Pastor Cliff cleared his throat, and Romeo chuckled as he led Demi to stand in front of him.

They'd each written their own vows, and I cried through the entire ceremony. Ruby had handed me some tissue, and by the end, everyone was reaching for a Kleenex.

"And by the power vested in me, you may now kiss your bride," Pastor Cliff said.

Romeo didn't hesitate. He dipped her back and kissed her hard as everyone cheered. When he pulled back, Romeo reached for her hand. She paused and glanced over at us and smiled before kicking up her heel and showing off her white cowboy booties.

They led us back down the aisle, and we spent the next hour taking photos, while the rest of the guests were taken to the large tented area for appetizers and cocktails. We made our way over to the tent and lined up to be called in, as music boomed from inside the reception. I wrapped my hand around King's arm, and he led me in, laughing as we made our way onto the dance floor. We all made a line, and then Romeo and Demi Knight were announced, and I don't think my feet ever hit the ground as we jumped and cheered.

My breath caught as I watched Romeo spin her around as she beamed up at him.

And before I knew what was happening, King pulled me into his arms, and we swayed back and forth to the music.

We weren't hiding anymore, and no one seemed surprised to see us together.

"Is this weird for you?" I asked.

"What? Dancing with you?"

"No. Being with just me. I'm sure all the single ladies here are disappointed that you aren't out there pulling them onto the dance floor," I teased.

His large hand wrapped around the side of my neck, and his thumb strummed along my jawline. "There is no one I want, no one I see—aside from you. It's been this way for a while, Dandelion. Long before we got together. So, no. There is nothing weird about it. For the first time in my life, I feel like I know what I want. What I need. And she's right here in my arms."

"I feel the same way," I whispered.

"But you've got to do me a big favor," he said, his voice lighter now.

"Of course. Name it."

"You're rubbing up against me in that sexy-as-hell dress of yours, and my dick is not handling it well."

My head fell back in laughter. "Is that so?"

"It really is," he said against my ear.

"Come on. Let's go to our table and get a drink. They're serving dinner soon."

We made our way to the table, and everyone was there, with drinks in hand. River handed me and King each a beer, and he wrapped an arm around my shoulder.

"I'm glad everything worked out, Say," he said.

"Thank you. Me, too."

He moved his chair closer, as King was talking to Ruby and Peyton now. He kept his voice low so only I could hear him. "He's different with you, you know?"

"Really? How so?"

"I don't know what it is. Maybe it's just this contentment that I see in him now. He's happy. Really, really happy. I noticed it before this all came out, and I suspected something was going on. I wanted to warn him to back off, but I liked seeing this side of King. He's not just having a good time, going through the motions—he's living. He's in it. And I fucking love it."

I felt a lump form in my throat, and I nodded. "I think we both found that with each other. Being with King feels like I'm finally home."

His eyes were wet with emotion, and he nodded. "I get that. More than you even know. And it's the best feeling."

"It is. And I know you and Ruby are planning to sneak off to Vegas and tie the knot, but you better have a party so that we can celebrate you guys, too."

He barked out a laugh. "We're talking about it. I think she'd like to have a party, but keep it casual."

"I'm happy for you guys."

"This looks intense," Kingston said, as he pulled his chair closer. "What are we talking about?"

"I was just telling him that if he and Ruby run off to Vegas and get married, they need to have a party so we can celebrate them after."

"Hell yeah, they do. You can have it at our place. You know I've got a great yard for it."

"Our place?" River and I said at the same time.

"Oh. Did I put the cart before the horse?" Kingston chuckled. "Ruby's lease is up, and clearly, she's going to move in with River, seeing as they're getting hitched and all. And I just thought it would be perfect timing for you to move in with me, Dandelion. We're together every night anyway."

"What am I missing over here?" Hayes asked, as he leaned in.

"I'm just watching King mess up the biggest moment of his life. He's asking Saylor to move in with him, but he actually forgot to ask her first." River chuckled.

My heart was racing because I loved that he wanted to live together. But I tried to remain calm now that we had an audience.

"You underestimate me, brother. I asked; she just didn't see it yet." He winked at me before his gaze moved to the plate in front of me.

There on the plate was a fluffball dandelion with a key tied to the end of it.

"For fuck's sake," Hayes said over his laughter. "Look at this romantic fucker. A key tied to a flower. Shit. He's so whipped he can't see straight."

"What's going on over here?" Ruby asked, coming over beside me and bending down.

"King just asked her to move in with him," River said, pulling her onto his lap.

"Oh, that's some romance book-worthy stuff right there. The key and the flower. Impressive."

"So, what do you say?" he asked, turning his attention to me.

"You had me at dandelion." I smiled up at him, and he tugged me into his arms.

I didn't know how we got here, but I wasn't questioning it.

Because all my wishes had already come true.

# 32

## Kingston

It had been one month since Saylor had moved in with me, and I'd never been happier. We'd moved her stuff over here a few weeks before her lease was up, and Ruby had officially moved in with River, because once you find your forever, you just want to start living it.

My brother had tied the knot shortly after Romeo and Demi's wedding, just as they'd told us they were going to do. They'd snuck off to Las Vegas, just the two of them, and were married by an Elvis Presley lookalike. And today, we were throwing them a reception at our place.

Lionel had insisted on having the party catered and providing the food and drinks. He hadn't pushed when they'd told him they were eloping, as long as they'd agreed to let him throw a big party for them. Ruby was his only child, and he wanted to invite everyone in town to celebrate.

Saylor, Demi, and Peyton had been working on getting this ready for the last two weeks.

"Are you ready, baby?" I called down the hallway, just as Saylor came walking out of our bedroom. Long blonde hair falling all around her shoulders. Turquoise blue eyes that always brought a peace over me that I couldn't explain. My gaze traveled down her body, taking in the lavender dress that fell off her shoulders and hugged her sweet body as it ran down to the floor.

"I'm ready." She smiled. "I like you in all black. You've got that bad-boy cowboy thing going on." I was wearing black jeans and a black button-up shirt that she'd purchased for me.

That's how we rolled now. My girl loved to take care of me, and I loved to take care of her.

"And I love you in this dress."

"Let's go take a look out back. Katie just texted me and asked us to come outside so she can take a few practice shots and test out the lighting." Katie worked for Saylor at the bookstore and was also a photographer on the side.

I reached for her hand and led her outside. The DJ was already playing some Frank Sinatra, which my brother was a big fan of. Lionel was bossing around his bartenders, and Katie waved us over.

"Sit on this large rock, Saylor. And, King, you can kind of hover over her and let me take a few shots. I think this spot in the yard has the best lighting."

Saylor sat on the rock, and my hand moved to the side of her neck. "Hovering over you is my favorite thing to do, Dandelion."

My nose rubbed against hers, and she smiled up at me.

"Damn. You two are so freaking hot. I think this photo right here belongs on a book cover." Katie walked over and showed us the photo.

"Oh, yeah? What would our book be called?" I teased.

Saylor didn't even have to think about it. "*Forbidden King*, of course."

Katie chuckled, and I pulled Saylor to her feet, just as everyone started arriving.

We both were pulled in different directions, but every once in a while, my eyes would find hers. It was just our thing.

Lionel had hired a few guys to come cook ribs and corn on the cob, and we'd rented tables that were spread across the yard, overlooking the water. We'd had too much food, plenty of drinks, and we'd danced our asses off.

"Happy for you, brother," I said, holding up my beer bottle to River, as all the guys and I settled around the firepit.

"Thanks for this. You went all out."

"Lionel did all the hard work," I said. "Grammie seems to be having a great time, huh?" I nodded to where the girls were chatting, and Grammie was right in there with them, wheelchair and all.

"Yeah. Thanks for getting her here," I said, turning my attention to Nash. He'd picked her up and would take her home, as well.

"Happy to do it. Cutler talked her ear off the whole car ride over," Nash said over his laughter.

"We've got the championship game in a few days," Romeo said.

"Yeah, he's looking forward to it. I can't believe how far he's come this year. The breathing thing still worries me, as he's had a few attacks, but they've been fairly mild. So I'm hoping this is as bad as it gets."

"You're doing all you can to stay on top of it," Hayes said. "And he's aware of it, because when I took him to the park last week, he kept making sure I had the inhaler in my pocket."

"I fucking hate that he has to even think about that shit." Nash shook his head. "But tonight's a celebration. Let's focus on that. Happy for you, River."

"Thanks, brother. Never thought I'd be sitting here, celebrating my marriage, but I'm here to say that it's the best thing I've ever done."

"Cheers to that," Romeo said, clinking his beer bottle to River's.

"I'm guessing King will be next," Nash said, looking between me and Hayes as he laughed.

"Seeing what a sappy fucker he's turned into, I'd be fine with it." Hayes shrugged.

"Appreciate that, brother." I held up my bottle in cheers, and he did the same.

"You never know. Hayes could surprise us all and be next. It happens that quickly," Romeo said.

"Hells to the no. Although it would help my career because that dickweed Lenny Davis is having his wife, Kimber, host a Fourth of July firehouse party now. He's doing all of this to show Cap that he'd be the best fit for the job once he retires. It's such bullshit."

"I hate that fucker. But he definitely knows how to play the game." River shook his head in disgust.

"Hey, maybe we can rent you a wife," I said over my laughter.

"I'd consider that long before I'd ever consider marriage again." He took a long pull from his beer. He'd been blindsided by his ex-fiancée and her betrayal, and I didn't know if he'd ever trust anyone again. "And maybe Nash will surprise us all and find a woman to help him raise Cutler."

"I have all of you, ladies," Nash said over his laughter. "I did things kind of backward, you know? Had the kid without having the solid relationship, so I just don't think it's in the cards for me. I got Cutler out of the deal, so I'm not complaining. But damn, you fuckers are lucky to have a woman to keep your bed warm every night."

"I can send you over a heating pad, if that would help." River barked out a laugh, and Nash flipped him the bird.

"I've got my hands full with Cutler. I don't need to complicate that. And look how attached he is to your better halves. I couldn't bring a woman into his life if I wasn't sure that it was the real deal. I need to focus on my boy. End of story."

"You know, I'm reading a single-dad romance right now," I said, and they all gaped at me. "What? It's a hot trope. They even call the single dads 'daddy' in the book. And if he's a businessman, they'll call him 'business daddy', or there's 'alpha daddy'. I think Nash would be 'contractor daddy'. It's a real thing, boys."

"If you ever call me 'contractor daddy', I will literally shave off both your eyebrows and draw a vagina on your forehead with permanent marker." Nash raised a brow.

Laughter bellowed around us, and I loved every damn second of it.

This is what life was about: spending time with the people you loved. But it also didn't mean I couldn't wait for everyone to leave so I could be alone with my girl.

As if they'd read my mind, everyone started pushing to their feet and saying their goodbyes. I scooped Cutler up and spun him around in my arms.

"Are you going to ride with us tomorrow, Uncle King?" he asked me. That boy loved horses, and the girls all rode with him on the weekends.

"Yeah. Wouldn't miss it, Beefcake."

He fist-pumped the sky after I set him on his feet.

The caterers had cleaned everything up, and Lionel had just finished packing up all the booze and breaking down the bar.

When River and Ruby left, I pushed the door closed, and Saylor smiled at me. It was this knowing look she always had on her face, which I fucking loved.

"What are you thinking, Dandelion?"

"Great party, but I'm happy it's just you and me again."

"Me, too. Thanks for making that so special for them." I tugged her close and tipped her head up to look at me.

"Of course. I loved doing it."

"Yeah? You look pretty tired. You want to go to bed?"

She shook her head, and her teeth sank into that juicy bottom lip of hers. "I've got something else in mind."

"Tell me. Your wish is my command," I said, as she took my hand and led me to the kitchen.

"Really? Anything I want? I don't see a fluffball around to wish on."

I pressed my hand to my heart. "It's right here, baby. You tell me what you want, and I'll make it happen."

"Oh, I see. You're my own personal fluffball?"

She paused in front of the kitchen island, and I wrapped my hands around her waist and lifted her to sit on the island. I moved close and smirked. "I'd prefer something more masculine. Like, Captain Wishmaker or Sexy Alpha Wishmaker."

Her head fell back in laughter. "Got it."

"So, tell me, Saylor," I said, my voice all tease. "What can I do for you?"

"Well, Sexy Alpha Captain of all wishes . . . I was thinking we share a piece of cake and a glass of wine in the bathtub. And then we can see where things go from there."

"Cake, wine, and your naked body. Is this your wish or mine?" I pushed up and kissed her hard before moving back and walking toward the refrigerator. I pulled the cake out and placed an unusually large slice onto a paper plate before pouring a large glass of wine for us to share. "Stay right here."

I took the cake and the wine into our bathroom and set it on the edge of the tub before turning on the water and pouring in the bubbles that Saylor loved.

I made my way back to where she was leaning back on her elbows, eyes closed. She'd worked her ass off for this party, and I knew she was exhausted. I tugged her dress up before scooping her up, her legs coming around my waist and her arms coming around my neck.

"Come on, baby. Let's go eat cake in the tub."

"Said the sexiest man on the planet," she purred. "Thanks for doing this."

I set her feet on the floor and turned her around and unzipped her dress. It fell into a heap on the floor, and then I turned her back around and dropped to my knees, pulling her lacy panties down her thighs so she was standing there completely bare. She tied her hair into a messy knot on top of her head as I pushed to my feet.

I had zero patience, and I fumbled with the buttons on my dress shirt before just ripping it apart. She stood there laughing as the buttons bounced off the tile floor. I pushed my jeans and briefs down my legs and walked her to the tub. Once I slipped into the hot water, I held my hand out for her to join me. When I'd built this house, I didn't give two shits about the tub, but I'd found a deal on an oversized Jacuzzi at the time, and I'd decided it would be good for the value of the home.

Fuck that.

It was one of the best decisions I'd ever made. We'd spent a lot of time in this tub together. My girl was a horse-riding, romance-reading mermaid, and she loved to end our days right here.

She sat facing me, one leg on each side, her ass settled on my thighs. I reached for the cake and forked off a bite for her and fed it to her. She closed her eyes and groaned as she chewed. I gave myself a bite, but I wasn't groaning because of the cake. I was groaning because her sweet pussy was rubbing up against my erection.

She reached for the wine, holding it to my lips first as I took a sip, and she did the same.

We talked about the party, and we laughed and ate some

more cake and drank some more wine until the water started to cool off.

"Do you want me to top it off with more hot water?" I asked, because sometimes we did that.

She shook her head, a wicked grin spread across her beautiful face. "Nope."

"No?"

"I want to get out of the tub and ride my cowboy for a while."

That was all I needed to hear. I moved her back enough so I could climb out quickly, and I grabbed a towel, wrapping it around my waist, before helping her out of the tub and drying her off.

She was laughing as I scooped her up and carried her to the bedroom.

I dropped her onto the bed and opened her towel, taking her in.

"How did I get so fucking lucky?" I traced her bottom lip with the pad of my thumb.

"I was just thinking the same thing."

"Yeah? Any more wishes you can think of?"

She shook her head. "Nope. They already came true."

And she was right.

There wasn't a single thing I wanted.

Because everything I wanted, everything I needed—it was right here.

I leaned down and claimed her mouth.

Just like I planned to do every day for the rest of my life.

# Epilogue

## Saylor

We sat on the bleachers, cheering for our favorite little guy, as he took to the plate. The Magnolia Falls Ducks had made it to the championships, and it was a tie game, final inning, and Cutler was the final player up to bat.

Their last shot to win this game.

It was a long shot, because no one was on base, so it would probably end as a tie game. They didn't do extra innings at this level.

Nash was standing behind home plate, talking to Cutler, who was listening intently.

"Why am I so nervous?" Demi whisper-shouted.

"I am, too," Romeo said, and I looked around, noting that everyone was chewing their nails or their legs were bouncing.

We were all nervous.

We'd been to every game this season, and we'd watched Cutler fall in love with the sport. So we knew how much this meant to him, which meant that we all wanted him to at least get on base for his last time up to bat.

King was on his feet, pacing in front of us, as he shoved his hands into his pockets. I loved how much he cared for the people that he loved. He felt so deeply, and it was one of the things that I loved most about him.

"You've got this, Beefcake!" King shouted, before he came back over to sit beside me.

"He's got this," I whispered, and he took my hand and pulled me closer.

He nodded. "He does. And he's scored two of the four runs they've gotten already."

Ruby chuckled as she sat on the other side of him. "Spoken like a proud uncle."

Cutler looked over at us, gave us a nod, and scraped his feet against the dirt two times like he did every time he was up to bat.

The first pitch was a little high, and he didn't swing. The next pitch had him swinging hard, and he missed. I noted the way his eyebrows pinched together, which told me he was concentrating hard on hitting that ball.

We all clapped and told him to brush it off.

And then the next pitch was moving toward him. His bat swung back, and he made contact. The crack was loud, and we all jumped to our feet. The ball sailed out into the outfield. We'd never seen a hit like this from anyone on the team.

He dropped the bat and took off running, with his teammates standing on the sidelines, going crazy.

He pumped his arms as he rounded first base and then cleared second. Nash was shouting for him to keep going as his arms swung around. Cutler tapped third base so quickly we were all stunned. He came down the final stretch as the other team threw the ball and raced him to home plate. He slid the way he'd been trained numerous times but never had to do before.

The umpire shouted the word, "Safe!"

You'd think the Ducks won the World Series with the way everyone was shouting and cheering.

"Beefcake pulled out a home fucking run!" Kingston yelled to our group, and we all high-fived one another as we jumped up and down.

"What's happening over there?" I asked, as I watched Nash drop down to the ground with Cutler, who looked like he was gasping for air.

His teammates stopped cheering and ran over, and before I could comprehend what was happening, King, River, Romeo, and Hayes were all jumping the fence and sprinting toward them.

I took off with Ruby, Demi, and Peyton right behind me, as we ran around the fence toward the dugout.

When we got onto the field, the assistant coach was backing the kids up and guiding them toward the dugout to give Nash some space.

Cutler was still gasping, even while Nash was giving him a puff from his inhaler. "Breathe, Cutler," Nash said, his voice remaining even and calm.

Cutler sucked in and then blinked up at his dad. "I did it, Pops."

His words were barely audible over his wheezing, and I saw Nash shoot a look to Hayes, who was trained in CPR as a firefighter. He just nodded, as if he understood what he was saying. I noted the way Cutler's nose was flaring, and his stomach was sucking in and out with every breath he struggled to take.

Hayes dialed the phone and spoke into it, and I knew right away that he was calling 9-1-1.

He'd stepped away because keeping Cutler calm was important.

"Don't talk right now, buddy," Nash said, and I heard the way his voice cracked on the last word.

"I'm calling Doc Dolby now, too," River said to us, as he dialed the phone and stepped away.

King was crouched down beside Cutler. "Just breathe, Beefcake. It's going to be okay."

I heard the sirens in the distance as Romeo ran out toward the road, obviously to guide them in as quickly as possible.

"I don't," Cutler wheezed, "feel good, Pops."

"I know." Nash pulled Cutler between his legs just as the paramedics came hurrying toward us.

We stepped back to make room for them, and they assessed him quickly and had him on a gurney with oxygen over his little face within seconds. Everyone stood there stunned, and as they wheeled him off the field, he held his little arm in the air with a thumb up.

And for whatever reason, that's what made me lose it. I covered my face as the first sob escaped my mouth.

Ruby wrapped an arm around me, and then Demi and Peyton did the same. The four of us hugged and cried in a huddle.

"Come on. We need to get to the hospital," Hayes said, and we all started moving.

"Hold up, I'll be right there." Kingston started running toward the dugout, and I came to a stop. I saw him talking to the assistant coach before he came jogging toward us with the gigantic trophy in his hands.

I smiled as the tears continued to fall. He reached for my free hand, and we both started running toward the parking lot. We piled into two cars, River's and Romeo's, as the rest of us had walked here.

River punched the dashboard of his car as we all got buckled.

"That's not going to help anything, River. He's going to be okay. Let's get to the hospital," Ruby said, her voice as calm as Nash's had been.

She had been in situations that were stressful before in her line of work, and she'd always told us that when you faced trauma, it was most important to remain calm.

"I know. But he just had this big moment and now he can't fucking breathe?" River hissed as he pulled out of the parking lot and followed Romeo, Demi, Hayes, and Peyton in the car in front of us.

"This was a bad one," King said, squeezing my hand. "I've never seen him like that."

"Did you see how calm Nash and Hayes were?" Ruby asked. "If you guys get upset, Cutler will panic. You need to not let him see that fear, okay?"

We all nodded as we pulled into the emergency room and watched as Cutler was wheeled out of the ambulance with Nash right behind him.

As soon as we parked, we were all running toward the hospital. Once we got inside, we waited in the waiting room, and Nash disappeared behind the double doors.

Doc Dolby came walking in shortly after, and River waved him over.

"It was bad, huh?" he asked, and he didn't hide his concern. "They seem to be getting worse."

"Yeah. He couldn't speak. His nostrils were flaring," Hayes said. "Ribs sucking in and out, and his color was off."

"You did the right thing calling 9-1-1. I'm sorry I couldn't get to the field quicker," Doc said. I was actually shocked he'd gotten here as quickly as he had. The man was really old, and it shocked me that he was still working full-time.

"Glad you're here now. Can you go back there and see what's happening?"

"Yep. Let me see what I can find out." He clapped River on the shoulder and made his way down the hallway.

"The oxygen will make a big difference," Hayes said as he pushed to his feet and started pacing alongside King.

"Yeah. He's going to be okay," Demi said. "He has to be. Should someone call Nash's father?"

Romeo nodded and stepped away to make the call.

"Did you see that fucking hit?" King said, turning to look at us as we sat in the chairs. "Beefcake is a rockstar."

"That hit, man. It was unbelievable." River shook his head.

"He wanted that win so fucking bad." Hayes dropped to sit in the chair and scrubbed a hand down his face.

The doors opened, and Nash came striding toward us just as Romeo walked back over. We all pushed to our feet.

"He's all right," he said, clapping his hands together. "They are giving him steroids now, and they've got his breathing under control. Doc is in there with him, talking with the ER doctors, and they might just keep him overnight as a safety precaution."

"Fuck, dude. I'm so sorry." Hayes pulled him in for a hug and clapped him on the back, hard.

"I'm guessing they won't let us all in there right now," King said, grabbing the trophy that he'd set on the table in the waiting room. "But you give this to him. He earned every inch of this thing."

Nash nodded and said he needed to get back in there after we each gave him a quick hug.

"We'll just hang out here for a while," Romeo said. "So text us with updates when you find out if he's staying overnight."

"Will do." He started to walk away and then turned around. "Thank you. Cutler is really lucky to have you as his family."

"I called your dad, and he had that meeting about an hour out of town. He's on his way back now, and he said he'll call you the minute he gets back."

"Thanks, brother."

Nash disappeared behind the double doors, and we all just sat there in silence, probably all still processing what had happened over the last thirty minutes.

Doc Dolby came walking out toward us. He'd literally been all of our pediatricians, as he had been the only children's doctor in Magnolia Falls since I was born. He had a few nurses who worked for him, but he was a one-man show.

"He's going to be all right, but his medication will need to be adjusted." He scrubbed a hand over the back of his neck. "I was waiting to talk to Nash this week, but I'm going to be stepping away. I just can't keep up with everything anymore, and Rose is ready for me to retire."

I wasn't shocked that he was retiring, as he was probably well past due. But what did this mean for Cutler? The timing couldn't be worse. He needed a doctor in town who could figure out what to do with his medication so that this didn't happen again.

"Are you already done? Who's going to take over?"

"No. I'll stick around for a few weeks, drop in for a couple of hours a day. My replacement is already here. She's young and a hell of a lot sharper than I am." His chuckle was raspy and slow. "She arrived in town last night and is getting settled. She'll be starting on Monday."

"She's not from Magnolia Falls?" River asked with concern.

"She doesn't have to be from here to be a good doctor." Ruby squeezed his hand.

"Exactly. We don't have any pediatricians living here at the moment. So we got really lucky that she relocated for the position. Having a doctor who did her residency in a big city and is willing to completely change course and come to a small town was lucky. She graduated top of her class, and the hospital where she did her residency had nothing but great things to say about her. They were trying to keep her themselves, but she decided she wanted something different."

"What's her name?" Romeo asked.

"Emerson Chadwick," Doc said before shaking his head. "I mean, Dr. Emerson Chadwick."

"Well, she better know her shit, because we need to get this figured out," Hayes grumped, and I shot him a warning look.

*That isn't helping anything.*

"I promise you, she's exactly what this town needs. I'm an old dog; I don't have any new tricks. She's trained at one of the best pediatric programs in the country, and she wants to come here. I suggest you all welcome her warmly. She doesn't know anyone and could probably use a friend."

"We don't need friends. We need a good damn doctor." River made no attempt to hide his frustration.

Doc Dolby softened his gaze as he took in all four men. "You're all exactly the same as you always were when you were little kids. But I wouldn't change a thing. I'd just appreciate you giving her a chance, okay?"

"We can do that," Romeo said first, and then they all nodded in agreement.

"Sorry, doc. Just worried about our little dude." River shrugged, and Hayes nodded in agreement.

"Listen, I know how much you love Cutler. And so do I. I've never met a little boy with more confidence, and that's because he's surrounded by love. From all of you. And he's a big part of the reason I've stuck around these last few years, but I just can't do it anymore. So, it would be a personal favor to me if you gave Emerson a chance."

"Of course, we will," Demi said. "She can have all the coffee she wants on the house."

He chuckled. "I appreciate your kindness, and I know she will, too. I need to get home, and you all should do the same. He's okay. They're just keeping him here to be safe and monitor his medication. I'll be back in the morning to check on him."

We said our goodbyes and went back to sit in our chairs. We weren't going anywhere right now.

Not until we heard from Nash again.

Kingston pulled me to my feet and told everyone we'd go grab some coffees and sandwiches from the hospital cafeteria.

"You okay?" I asked, as we walked hand in hand down the hallway.

"Yeah. I know he'll be just fine. It just makes you realize how lucky we are, you know?"

I nodded as we stepped into the cafeteria and started loading up two trays with food. When we got to the checkout, I looked down at my tray, and there was a dandelion resting beside the muffins I'd grabbed.

I smiled up at him, and he winked. "Love you, Dandelion."

"Love you, my forbidden King."

And I meant it.

Highs or lows, ups and downs, none of it mattered. We could weather anything together.

I knew I'd found my forever in this man.

And I didn't need any more dandelions from him, because all my wishes had already come true.

But I'd let him keep giving them to me, because he was my own personal book boyfriend, and this was his thing.

Our thing.

And I wouldn't have it any other way.

Acknowledgments

Greg, I am endlessly grateful that I get to call you mine! I love you!

Chase, thank you for letting me sprinkle you into this book and this character. #whitevans #scorpions #clowns, love you forever!

Hannah, when this book releases, you will officially be a doctor! I'm so proud of how hard you have worked! You inspire me every day! Love you to the moon and back!

Willow, I would be lost without you! Your friendship means the world to me. Thank you for the daily chats, encouraging words, laughter, and all the memories. Love you so much!

Catherine, so thankful for your friendship! T&T forever. I love being on this journey with you so much! Love you!

Kandi, there are so many days where your messages give me the push that I needed to get through a mile high task that feels impossible. I am so grateful for your friendship. Love you so much!

Elizabeth O'Roark, thank you for ALWAYS making me laugh, and for letting me pressure you into giving me all of your books early! I am so thankful for your friendship! Love you!

Pathi, I would not be doing what I love every single day if it wasn't for YOU! I am so thankful for your friendship, and for all the support and encouragement! I'd be lost without you! Thank you for believing in me! I love you so much!

Nat, I cannot begin to put into words how much I appreciate you! Thank you for letting me pass every single thing I can to you! LOL! You have created a monster! I'd truly be lost without you. So yes . . . you've got a stage five clinger on your hands. I'm SO GRATEFUL for you and I love you SO MUCH!

Nina, I'm just going to call you the DREAM MAKER from here on out. Thank you for believing in me and for making my wildest dreams come true. Your friendship means the world to me! I love you forever!

Kim Cermak, thank you for being YOU! There is just no other way to say it. You are one in a million. I am endlessly grateful to have you in my corner, but most importantly, to call you my friend. Love you!

Christine Miller, Kelley Beckham, Tiffany Bullard, Sarah Norris, Valentine Grinstead, Amy Dindia, Josette Ochoa, Kate Kelly and Ratula Roy, I am endlessly thankful for YOU!

Meagan Reynoso, thank you for reading all my words early, giving fabulous feedback, and working so hard creating the PR packages with me. I love you!

Logan Chisolm, I absolutely adore you and am so grateful for your support and encouragement! Love you!

Kayla Compton, I am so happy to be working with you and so thankful for YOU! Love you! Xo

Doo, Abi, Meagan, Diana, Annette, Jennifer, Pathi, Natalie, and Caroline, thank you for being the BEST beta readers EVER! Your feedback means the world to me. I am so thankful for you!

To all the talented, amazing people who turn my words into a polished final book, I am endlessly grateful for you! Sue Grimshaw (Edits by Sue), Hang Le Design, Sarah Sentz (Enchanted Romance Design), Emily Wittig Designs, Christine

Estevez, Ellie McLove (My Brother's Editor), Jaime Ryter (The Ryter's Proof), Julie Deaton (Deaton Author Services), Kim and Katie at Lyric Audio Books, and the amazingly talented Madison Maltby, thank you for being so encouraging and supportive!

Crystal Eacker, thank you for your audio beta listening/reading skills! I absolutely adore you!

Ashley Townsend and Erika Plum, I love the incredible swag that you create, and I am so thankful for you both!

Jennifer, thank you for being an endless support system. For running the Facebook group, posting, reviewing, and doing whatever is needed for each release. Your friendship means the world to me! Love you!

Paige, I love our chats, our laughs and all the magic that is YOU! So thankful of your friendship and to have you in my life! Xo

Rachel Parker, so incredibly thankful for you and so happy to be on this journey with you! Love you so much!

Megan Galt, thank you for always coming through with the most beautiful designs! I'm so grateful for YOU!

Willow, Kandi, Amy, Rebecca, Lauren, Corinne, Natasha & Jessica, I wouldn't have been able to finish this book without you! I am so thankful for your support and your friendship! Thanks for sprinting, for pushing me and supporting me on this journey. Love you!

Gianna Rose, Stephanie Hubenak, Rachel Baldwin, Kelly Yates, Sarah Sentz, Ashley Anastasio, Kayla Compton, Tiara Cobillas, Tori Ann Harris and Erin O'Donnell, thank you for your friendship and your support. It means the world to me!

Mom, thank you for being my biggest cheerleader and reading everything that I write! Love you!

Dad, you really are the reason that I keep chasing my dreams! Thank you for teaching me to never give up. Love you!

Sandy, thank you for reading and supporting me throughout this journey! Love you!

To the JKL WILLOWS . . . I am forever grateful to you for your support and encouragement, my sweet friends! Love you!

To all the bloggers, bookstagrammers and ARC readers who have posted, shared, and supported me – I can't begin to tell you how much it means to me. I love seeing the graphics that you make and the gorgeous posts that you share. I am forever grateful for your support!

To all the readers who take the time to pick up my books and take a chance on my words . . . THANK YOU for helping to make my dreams come true!

ONE PLACE. MANY STORIES

Bold, innovative and
empowering publishing.

FOLLOW US ON:

@HQStories